CHRISTINE

I saw a boy there. He seemed so different, not like any-body from around here. He had pitch black, curly hair. (I've always loved curly hair! Mine is poker straight and the kind of blond that doesn't look blond and doesn't look brown. I've always wished it were one or the other.) This boy was holding a little girl's hand, probably his sister's. He had on a funny shirt that made him look exotic and open-toed shoes that he must've made himself. The little girl stared at my bike like it was something special and not just my old green clunker that needed new tires.

ADAM

Mira's eyes fastened on a bicycle such as we had not seen for several years. Beside this bicycle was a very beautiful American girl. Her hair was a color I could not define. Surely the blond in it had talked to the sun while the brown had made long conversations with the earth. I did not notice the color of her eyes, only that they seemed to know nothing of hiding.

————

"Thought-provoking. . . . A timely story that probes the refugee issue with sensitivity and depth."

—*The Horn Book*

"A fine novel based, in part, on real-life incidents now more than 50 years passed, but still relevant today."

—*SLJ*

OTHER PUFFIN BOOKS YOU MAY ENJOY

Two Suns
IN THE *Sky*

MIRIAM BAT-AMI

PUFFIN BOOKS

PUFFIN BOOKS
Published by the Penguin Group
Penguin Putnam Books for Young Readers,
345 Hudson Street, New York, New York 10014, U.S.A.
Penguin Books Ltd, 27 Wrights Lane, London W8 5TZ, England
Penguin Books Australia Ltd, Ringwood, Victoria, Australia
Penguin Books Canada Ltd, 10 Alcorn Avenue, Toronto, Ontario, Canada M4V 3B2
Penguin Books (N.Z.) Ltd, 182-190 Wairau Road, Auckland 10, New Zealand

Penguin Books Ltd, Registered Offices: Harmondsworth, Middlesex, England

First published in the United States of America by Front Street/Cricket Books, 1999
Published by Puffin Books,
a division of Penguin Putnam Books for Young Readers, 2001

5 7 9 10 8 6 4

"No Love, No Nothin'," by Leo Robin and Harry Warren, © 1943 (Renewed)
WB Music Corp. All Rights Reserved. Used by Permission.
Warner Bros. Publishers U.S. Inc., Miami, FL 33014

LIBRARY OF CONGRESS CATALOGING-IN-PUBLICATION DATA
Bat-Ami, Miriam.
Two suns in the sky / Miriam Bat-Ami.
p. cm.
Summary: In 1944, an Upstate New York teenager named Christine meets and
falls in love with Adam, a Yugoslavian Jew living in a refugee camp, despite
their parents' conviction that they do not belong together.
Scott O'Dell Award, 2000
ALA Best Book for Young Adults, 2000
ISBN 0-14-230036-5
1. Refugees, Jewish—New York (State)—Oswego—Juvenile fiction. 2. Fort Ontario
Emergency Refugee Shelter—Juvenile fiction. 3. Jews—New York (State)—
Oswego—Juvenile fiction. 4. Holocaust survivors—United States—Juvenile fiction.
5. World War, 1939–1945—Jews—Rescue—Juvenile fiction. [1. Holocaust
survivors—Fiction. 2. Refugees—Fiction. 3. Prejudices—Fiction. 4. Fort Ontario
Emergency Refugee Shelter—Fiction. 5. Jews—United States—Fiction.] I. Title.
PZ7.B2939 Tw 2001 [Fic]—dc21 2001019594

Printed in the United States of America

*To the former residents
of the Emergency Refugee Shelter
and to all those within and outside Oswego
who aided them,
and to my son,
Daniel Rubens*

For stony limits cannot hold love out,
And what love can do, that dares love attempt.
Shakespeare,
Romeo and Juliet,
II, ii, 67-68

Part One

TWO SUNS IN THE SKY
June to November 1944

Chapter One
Selection

&

My Friends:
    *Yesterday on June 4, 1944, Rome fell to American
and Allied troops. The first of the Axis capitals is now in
our hands. One up and two to go!*
President Franklin Delano Roosevelt

CHRIS

It shouldn't have surprised me that Mrs. Dubchek was sitting on her porch. Ever since I can remember, Mrs. D. has always been there. Even when the wind was blowing so hard that it looked like only the sheer mass of her weight kept her from spinning into space, Mrs. D. still hung on, watching out for our block.

Maybe it was all that math computation that made me forget about her. One more week of school, then three months of freedom! That was nearly ninety days; ninety times twenty-four hours. Maybe I was thinking about how all that freedom didn't matter. Where was I going, anyway? If I were Dorothy, all I would've had to do was lie perfectly still, and a tornado'd pick me up and transport me to another place. It'd be somewhere I'd never seen before, where nobody knew me and everybody I met was somebody new. Where I lived, everybody knew everybody, and nobody was anybody I wanted to meet.

I wanted to do something. Anything! If only I were eighteen and not fourteen, then I'd have run off and joined the Wacs. In the Women's Army Corps, I could've done something important for the war effort instead of sitting around all the time listening to Mom and Dad talk about what they were doing.

That's why I didn't run past her house like I usually did, nodding her way and letting out a quick "Hi!" I shambled along, planning out the details of my escape—I'd make a phony birth certificate and lie about my age—while my eyes wandered over small items that were easy to identify. The iron fences. The Fourth-of-July flags twisting themselves around the poles. Mrs. Dubchek's porch with its wooden stairs you could jump all at once. Her scratchy brown porch rug that made your feet itch. Her flag, which wasn't behaving like Mrs. D.'s flag normally did, perched properly in its holder, tilting at the correct angle. It tilted forward.

Mrs. Dubchek fixed her eyes on me. Probably she'd begun the fixing way down the block—God has a whole world to keep His sight on, but Mrs. D. only had Second Street. "So they teach you something today?" she shouted, shifting her bulk forward.

"Uh-huh." My eyes fastened themselves on her toes. They looked like bits of puffy cookie dough you drop on a sheet. (Mrs. D. never wears real shoes. In the summer she goes barefoot. In the winter she wears huge white anklets under her black shower slippers.)

"You smarter than you was this morning?"

I almost told her that I'd become dumber. School was making me into a complete dumbbell. By the time I graduated, I'd have to start all over in kindergarten. That's why I had to escape to the Wacs.

"I guess so," I muttered.

"Good. Good." She rocked furiously. Perspiration dripped from her thin gray hair. Quivering, round drops lay in the crevices beneath her eyes. I stared at them the way you do rain on a windshield: waiting for the descent and wondering which drop would make it down first.

"Time flies," she said, like this was the first time anybody had made such a pronouncement.

Not from where I'm standing, it doesn't. The flag snapped once, then sagged, slanting. Her eyes followed mine.

"Benny put it up. Usually my boy does it, but you know, Christine, Joey's in Italy. Italy. He'll see the pope. Joey wouldn't miss the chance. He'll dress up in a fresh uniform—our Holy Father should know his mother taught him manners—then His Holiness will give my Joey a special blessing. He'll write me about it in a letter. Or he'll save the great news for when he comes home. They'll all come home soon." She wagged her finger at me.

I concentrated on the sidewalk cracks. That night, when everyone was asleep, I'd take my special Wac bag from under my bed and sneak out. It was all packed and ready to go: I didn't want to slow myself down by suddenly realizing that I had to do laundry. You could lose all momentum waiting for your underwear to get dry.

Mrs. D. heaved herself out of the chair and leaned on the porch railing. Her bosoms rose and fell like two tidal waves colliding in the center of a wide ocean. "So, Christine, when are you putting up your flag?"

"Soon, I guess." I wasn't going to tell her what Mom had said when I asked her the same question: "When I have time, and don't keep prodding me about how we're the only bare house on the block. It's not my fault our neighbor has everyone hanging out their Fourth-of-July flags in June."

Mrs. Dubchek mopped her wet forehead with a hankie she had balled up in her hand. "Never you mind. Your parents are doing important war work. How many tanks does your dad make? Only the other day he was telling me. Such an important job."

I didn't answer. With Mrs. Dubchek one question always led to another. If you didn't answer, she was liable to forget, which meant that much less time you had to spend trying to get away from her. Anyway, I was tired of the same old line Dad gave everyone: "We at Fitzgibbons Boiler Works make two tanks a week. Tanks for the army and boilers for the navy." Mom was no better. She loved to remind Dad of her sacrifices, particularly when he complained that supper wasn't ready.

"Now, Bill," she'd say, "we had to stay after at the plant tonight. Another shipment of special matches went out to our boys."

I could see it clearly. A soldier is on the battlefield. It's pouring like the dickens and dark as hell. Some Nazis are close by, but GI Joe doesn't see them—his flashlight is gone. He rummages through his pack, searching frantically. He finds a match. It's one that Mom made right here in Oswego at the Diamond Match Company. He strikes it, and the match doesn't go out, even with all that water, because it's one of those special water-resistant matches that Mom boxed. The soldier sees the enemy. He warns everybody.

You never know.

"My Joey and your family," said Mrs. D. "You have two over there, right, Christine?"

A layer of fog rolled across huge empty spaces until it sank into the corners of my cranium. "Yeah, my aunt Nell's sons. Are you gonna listen to the radio tonight?" Why was I asking her a question? The regression process must have speeded up. During the walk home, I'd slipped down to second grade. Soon I'd be napping on my kindergarten rug, sipping milk out of a carton and laughing to myself because I had finally figured out how to blow huge white bubbles.

"Of course I'm going to listen. When Mr. Roosevelt speaks, Mrs. Dubchek listens. Christine, what do you think of the flag? My grandson, Benny, made a special trip here to put it up. A little crooked, no?"

I cocked my head, pretending I was examining it. "It's fine." I nodded approvingly.

"No, it's crooked. Next time he comes, I'll get him to fix it. A flag needs to be right." She inched her way slowly back to the rocker. "They teach you something today?" *Plop.* She landed solidly in her seat.

I looked longingly at my house. Next-door never felt so far away.

• • •

Mom and Dad were in the living room when I made it home. Dad's chair was nearly on top of the radio. Mom was on the couch, knitting a Christmas present she was going to mail overseas early to my cousin Dick. (Another aunt was knitting one for my cousin Bob.) I collapsed into the corner chair and began thinking depressing thoughts, like how I had done on most of my tests and what kind of report card I was sure to get.

"How was school today?" asked Mom. Her pink needles slid back and forth, quietly clicking. They were telegraphing some secret message only Mom could understand. I've tried. I made a sweater for myself once. It turned into a scarf. I tried a baby sweater for one of my cousins. That turned into a scarf, too. Next, baby booties. Another scarf. Then Mom came up with one of her brilliant ideas. I was to concentrate just on scarfs, because if you do one thing over and over again, it's gotta be good. Mom, Dad, and I became proud possessors of strange and unusual scarfs that looked like striped snakes full of knots and holes.

"Did you have any tests today?" Mom's pink twins stopped chattering.

"When's Roosevelt talking?" I used the old derailment trick. Mom starts down one track; I bump onto another.

"How'd you do?" Mom bumped back.

My feet tapped out the chorus to an old radio hit, "Praise the Lord and Pass the Ammunition."

"Everything's fine, Mom."

Everything *was* fine if you didn't count math. I hated math, especially when it involved problems that had nothing to do with real life.

Ned travels 2 hours by train at 60 miles an hour. His brother

Ted rides his bike at 10 miles an hour and gets to the same place 5 hours later. How many miles is that? Ned and Ted should be traveling together. They're brothers, aren't they? And why doesn't Ned tell Ted to dump his dumb bike? And what dumb mother and father name their kids Ned and Ted? I bet their third son is Fred.

I tapped and hummed. Dad put his fingers to his lips. I shrugged and tucked my legs under me. They wanted to keep moving.

History was no better. "What is the other name for Bull Run?" Who'd ever ask me that question? I could see myself at a dance with some boy. "My dearest Chris," he'd say. He wouldn't call me Christy. That's too much like Sissy. And only teachers, my nosy neighbor, and my parents, when they're mad, call me Christine. Chris is strong and exact. It makes you think of someone who knows what she's doing. "Do you know the other name for Bull Run?" He'd gaze at me with passion in his eyes. They'd be the kind of eyes that couldn't make up their mind—sometimes blue and sometimes green—and he'd be the man of my dreams.

"Why it's . . . it's Manassas," I'd say, laughing breathlessly. Then we'd twirl around in absolute bliss because we both knew.

Why didn't I remember Manassas when it counted? At least Mr. Douglass would get a good laugh out of what I scribbled on my paper. Standing Bull.

Dad's hands were on his knees, ready to swing into action. Pass the ammunition. The drum rolls faded away. Static. Then the president's voice.

"Give us strength," said President Roosevelt.

"Give us strength," said Mom.

Strength wasn't going to do me any good when Mom and Dad saw my report card.

"Stop fidgeting," barked Dad.

"Give us strength!" I barked back.

Mom gave me one of those he-just-got-back-from-work-and-is-tired looks. I made my mouth into a clamp.

"Let our hearts be stout," said Roosevelt.

"Let our hearts be stout," repeated Mom. Dad and I joined in.

When Roosevelt said that some of our men would never return, Mom laid down her knitting, closed her eyes, and held the bridge of her nose with her fingertips. She was thinking about my cousins in the army. And how it'd be nice if I were a boy, too. Then she'd be able to say "our boys" and be talking about her son. Mom comes from a big family. She has five sisters and two brothers. Dad has three sisters and two brothers. They all have lots of kids. In our family there has always been only me.

Dad looked sad, too. Making tanks couldn't have been as good as being there in the action. Things were really heating up. Two days earlier our boys had taken Rome. In catechism we learned how everyone was getting together to liberate our Holy City, and Father Walters led us in a special prayer for our troops. And for the pope. And for the Vatican, too. Now Rome was free, which didn't mean that our prayers did anything special. Still, when you're doing nothing but thinking about a stupid guy who takes his bike when he should've been on the train with his brother, it feels good to pray.

I slid over to Mom and knelt on the floor beside her. We thought about our boys landing on the coast of France.

Let everyone come home, I prayed. Safe and sound.

ADAM

Who could believe what a party there was on the streets after Rome was liberated? Only a short while earlier I was doing what I had been doing ever since we escaped to Rome. In the morning I went off to the Catholic school. I spoke the best Italian so only the Vatican priests who agreed to hide my identity knew who I was. After school I escorted our buckets to the pump, where daily they congregated with the other waiting buckets. The pump was many blocks away. As usual the line was long.

"Oh," I muttered, "Mira is too young for this. If Villi were here, we would have more buckets. More muscles."

I laid a large stone inside each bucket and flexed my arms. When Villi returns, I thought, we will put our elbows on the table. My arm will not tremble, falling like some puny thing. In five seconds, *kaput*, his will go down.

I inched forward, engaging my energy in small arm curls that would not attract attention. Mama and Mira were at the market, buying whatever was possible without a ration card. The Italians had cards. We Jews had no such luxury. What could one buy without a card?

Turnips.

For three years this detestable food had been linked to the history of the Bornstein family. When we all first fled from Zagreb—all except Grandmama—it was there. Villi and I were wearing peasant clothes that Papa had somehow managed to get for us. Both of us thought it a good joke. We were sophisticated city people from the big, important Zagreb, with so many libraries and shops they could not all be remembered. How, then, could we be wearing white shirts made from hemp that some farmer woman on our Yugoslav plains spun into a coarse yarn and wove on her own hand loom? In Zagreb one must dress in the latest European fashion. We were glad, though. We were glad, too, for the crosses that Papa had placed around our necks. I shifted mine about vaguely, wondering who had worn it last. Perhaps some girl.

"Adam," said Papa, "don't play with the crucifix. Act as if it is something you wear every day."

I repositioned the poor thing on that foreign soil of my chest. One day I would find a good home for it, someplace where it would feel safe again.

We walked, hardly stopping while the rains continued falling. Our clothes remained damp, sticking to our clammy bodies.

Ahead of us was a chain of mountains appearing so rugged and forbidding my stomach sank. Further west was the border. *Italia.* The name itself sounded warm. We were tired and hungry, so much so that even Villi, who never admitted to being hungry or tired or cold, spoke of his little wants.

By some miracle, Papa found that food. We sat in a small circle, and he placed it in the center. "Look," he said as if he were a magician pulling a rabbit out of the thin air, "I have unearthed this . . . this TURNIP!"

I stared at the shriveled purple lump that had the nerve to pass itself off as a vegetable. For sure, it was blushing with excitement. To be reunited with the Bornstein family again! Above me the sky had become clear and blue, and I thought about the mystery of God and creation. When the great Almighty was exhausted from His six days of creating the universe, when, for once, He was not thinking about what it was He was doing, God made the turnip. It was a very big mistake!

But then there arose a most confounding question. How could one divide a turnip into five equal parts? One for Adam. One for Villi. One for Mira. And Mama. And Papa. It was a dilemma.

"Forget me," I said. "I detest the turnip." I consoled myself by imagining that Villi would remember my great sacrifice. With great sadness, he would concede that I was not the weaker brother.

Slowly, slowly Papa cut equally for us all.

Three days before liberation, when my buckets finished conversing with their relations, I returned to that place in Rome where we hid ourselves. There I saw that Mama and Mira had bought the wretched mistake that persisted in mixing itself up with the fate of our family. Twenty-four hours later, nothing was as it had been before. The Germans pulled out. Mama, Mira, and I watched from behind our drawn curtains. For hours we sat. When night made the watching impossible, still we sat. Mira, who had grown so big that Papa would not recognize her, fell asleep in Mama's lap with her clothes on. Mama and I kept company with the curtains while my mind commenced to make for itself the picture of a boy who is free. The face showed nothing. Hid everything.

Sunlight slid through small openings in the curtains. Below us a jeep moved down the Parioli. All alone it came.

Is this it? Such a small showing? How can the Allies win? Perhaps we are wrong, and the Allies have lost for good. I wanted to say all this to Mama, but fear swallowed my words and commenced to lap up the saliva in my mouth. Mama pressed my hand. We peered down, our eyes hugging the streets, and then such a procession we saw you would not believe. Jeeps. Troops. Military cars. Mama squeezed harder. She lifted Mira in her arms as if she were not seven years old but a baby again. We ran into the streets. Girls, very beautiful girls, kissed soldiers. I longed for such a kiss. Men threw the pins that they had worn high in the air. They were green, white, and red Fascist party pins that clattered to the ground. I picked one up and carefully placed it in my pocket. *"Siamo liberi!"* someone shouted. And the crowd swayed until everyone was shouting. Yes, we are free! Soldiers threw out chocolate and cigarettes. "Here! Here!" I waved my hands about.

That was the fourth day of June 1944. Rome was liberated, and I continued to ask myself what it would look like, this picture of a boy who was free.

● ● ●

Less than two weeks later, we sat at the one shaky table we had in that apartment. I was explaining to our uninformed mama the meaning of the Holy Ghost. With Mama, I had to start with basic catechism. Mira was taking her chances under the flimsy structure of the table, playing the quiet game that I had taught her the first week in Rome. She was a bear cub, safely hidden in her winter cave. Beside her was a huge bowl of pretend honey. (Even then, Mira believed that she was too old for the game, but it soothed her to think about those creatures in the world who sleep all winter long. When they awaken, spring has come. It soothed me, too.)

"Adam," said Mama, "today I heard from a friend that the Americans are bringing some of us to the States."

My mouth dropped. "Can we go?" In an instant I was Robin Hood, soaring through the air just as the great Errol Flynn flew, his legs sweeping over the table in the hall where the villainous Prince John dined with his men.

Mama drew circles on the table's splintered surface. One worn finger traced the outline of tulips as if Mama's beautiful tablecloth that Grandmama had given her was with us again. "They will only accept people who don't have children of military age," she said. "Villi is of military age."

"But he is not here."

That irritating finger retraced the same imaginary flower. "No, he is not, but he is somewhere. It is best to stay put and wait."

"We have not seen Villi for some time." I looked away from Mama so that I could pretend I had said this to myself. Mama was only overhearing.

"A little over a year. In a lifetime, that is not so long."

"What is the use to 'stay put' in Rome? Better in America, where we know we are safe." I leaned back.

"Don't tip the chair, Adam. It will break."

"In America we will have real freedom. Your son will have a chance to be somebody in the future. We will not wonder from day to day if there *is* a future."

"Adam, this is only for the duration of the war. That is what the announcement says: 'Upon termination of the war, they will be sent back to their homelands.'" She chewed on her words like a cow on its cud, deliberating with each bite. "That means we go back to Yugoslavia."

My elbows dug a space for themselves between the splintered wood. "And when we go back, we will find our family. After the war!"

Mira noisily lapped up honey. Mama was silent. I read her eyes.

We have not seen Villi because we allowed him to go back with Papa to try to find Grandmama. We watched them go and we said nothing.

I shielded my own eyes. Mama had only wanted Grandmama back again. I was jealous.

•   •   •

"She is my mother," Mama had said. "We have to go back and get her out."

"It is too dangerous," said Papa. "Aside from that, how do we know she is in her house or that it is still *her* house and not someone else's? She could be anywhere."

Mama frowned. Turning, she faced east back to Yugoslavia.

"I will go," said Villi. "Grandmama will come if I ask. She listens to me."

That is right, I thought. With Villi, Grandmama was a piece of taffy. Villi bent and twisted her any way his heart desired. With me she was steel.

"I will go, too," I announced.

"It is too dangerous," said Villi, echoing Papa. "You are young."

"I am fourteen. That is not young."

Papa's hands rested on my shoulders. He said nothing, but the hands spoke for him: Stay here. Your mother and sister need you. Be a man.

But I do not want to be a man. I want to be Adam, the finder and rescuer. Me, not Villi!

When all I could see of their backs were smudges of darkness, I studied the note Papa had handed me so I would not forget the place we were to find. We were to travel to a Madame Novara's in Rome. She would keep us in two tiny rooms behind her apartment. All had been arranged. Papa, Villi, and Grandmama would catch up. Two months. Three months at the latest. We would all be together once more. That was in 1942.

Mama had said a little over a year, but more than two years had passed. It had been almost three years since we had seen Grandmama.

Mira tapped on the table beneath us. "Spring is coming," she said. "Time to get Mama Bear up!"

I drew my face close to Mama's. "What harm will it do to see if we can go? If some miracle occurs and we are accepted, then we will write Papa and say exactly where we are."

"What a foolish thing. How . . . ?"

Mama did not say that she still wrote to him. At night she lay on a mattress full of straw and folded papers and scribbled out God only knows what message. To write, even without sending, was to hope.

"Also they want families." Mama searched through her thoughts as one does a suitcase one has fitfully packed.

"We *are* a family."

"And I think they look with favor on children who are—"

"Mama Bear," said Mira, knocking on the poor boards, "time to get up and find berries."

"Who are what?" I did not want Mama to end this conversation. That is the way it was with her: we are discussing a most important topic; Mira interrupts by asking for milk or to be read a story or to be kissed goodnight; Mama, who is not agreeing with me or Villi, says, "I must attend to Mira. Later, we will discuss." But there was never a later.

"Who are *what?*" I repeated. Mira growled.

"Who are missing a mother or a father." Mama's tortured finger ceased from its senseless circular journey.

"We will ask to go. We must ask."

The next day Mama went down to some office. She filled out papers. Two weeks later it was official. We had been selected by the United States government to come to America as guests. We were to stay somewhere in the north, where we would be taken care of until this terrible war was over.

But how could such a thing happen, and why did this happen

to us? When you are climbing a mountain pass that is almost three thousand meters high with a hundred and fifty other people who are fleeing from Yugoslavia, who has time to ask about these things? Instead you ask, "What can I use to keep this sole on my shoe? Aha, here is a piece of wire!" Who knew of America? Now, though, I was asking: *What does this mean?*

We just so happened to be in Italy. We just so happened to have heard news about America. We fit the requirements. Mama was unsure, but she wished her son and daughter to be safe, so she went to the office. She filled out an application and signed the statement. Yes, she understood that we were only "guests" of the United States. Yes, she understood that we would "live under the restrictions imposed by the American security officials," et cetera, et cetera. She agreed to all the conditions. Why not take the chance to be chosen?

But Villi's best friend, Nissim, had also been chosen. We learned what such a selection meant.

CHRIS

It seemed like we'd never get our Fourth-of-July flag hung. One evening, though, when Mom had to stay at work late, Dad and I went down to our basement and hunted it down. It was underneath some funny Halloween decorations that Mom insisted on taping to our windows every year. We didn't unfurl it downstairs. You need wind and sun. You need to hear the flag flapping and see all those stars slapping against each other. Outside, Dad stood on one of our porch chairs, stuck the pole inside an attachment we've got on one of our pillars, and let Old Glory loose.

Mrs. Dubchek was on her porch having one of her daily conversations with God and whoever else in the neighborhood would listen. "Fine night," she yelled over to Dad.

"Good evening, Mrs. Dubchek." (When Dad's with his brothers, he curses a blue streak, but he's Mr. Politeness himself when it comes to the neighbors.)

"My grandson, Benny, put up mine," she yelled back. "Joey's in Italy."

I chanted quietly to myself. One hippo-pota-mus. Two hippo-pota-mus. How many hippo-seconds was it going to take before she rattled off about how her Joey saw the pope when Rome was liberated and how handsome her son looked in his uniform? I didn't think I could take it. I was willing to bet that Mr. Richards, our neighbor across the street, had had enough, too. He sat tall and thin in his green metal porch chair, looking disgusted. Of course, Mr. R.'s face was in a perpetual state of disgust when it came to our block, and he never wasted his time on us, except when he heard us daring each other to race across his grass. Then he'd stand up, wave his two canes menacingly in our direction, and point to his various lawn signs, like the one in his bed of scraggly geraniums that had blue rusted flowers on it and said KEEP OFF or the one that said BEWARE OF DOG. Mr. Richards's dog was as thin and bony as he was, except the dog had more teeth.

"Do you think it's crooked, Mr. Cook?" Sniffing loudly, Mrs. D. cast a sideways glance at the other porch sitter and advanced toward her railing.

"Dad," I tugged at his shirt like I was some little kid, "let's get a soda. O.K.?"

"In a minute."

"Great!" I muttered under my breath.

Dad's muscles bulged while he fiddled with Mrs. Dubchek's flagpole and sang the tuneless, happy song that he sang whenever he was working on things. "There," he said. "Fixed."

Mr. R.'s dog wrinkled up his snout and snarled so I could check out his teeth. Still nice and sharp. "Too bad you're stuck on a rope." I shook my head, spreading my lips up. The dog got the full effect of my incisors. Mr. Richards stood up and leaned

25

on his two canes. I shut my mouth and faced Mrs. Dubchek's living room.

Below the open shades was the blue star she had put on the window when Joey had gone off to fight. Sunlight shone on its surface. Every once in a while, the flag's flapping shadow moved over it, breaking the brightness into bands of blue and gray.

Blue for our fighting boys. Silver for our wounded. Gold for the dead, because gold is the best. But what if something happened to my cousins, Bob and Dick? Or what about Mrs. D.'s son, Joey?

I walked up Mrs. Dubchek's porch stairs, jumping down hard. The soles of my feet stung. "Dad, do you mind if I go to Ann's?"

"Weren't you there all day?"

"We have a lot to talk about. We're best friends!"

"Don't stay out late. And don't ride your bike in the dark."

Don't stay out late. Wear your sweater. Don't catch cold. Watch for traffic. I swung my right leg over the ripped leather seat and straightened my skirt. At least he's letting you out of the house, I reminded myself. When he'd seen my final grades, I thought he was going to keep me stuck in my room all summer long. The 95 percent in French did nothing to impress him.

"Where will that get you?" Dad had asked after lecturing me on all the things I wasn't allowed to do that summer. That year. The rest of my life.

How about out of here?

"Next year I better see improvement," he'd added, "or it's not only me you'll hear from."

Something to look forward to. A whole new year of work with Dad smacking tables with newspapers just so I wouldn't forget what a threat sounded like. I pedaled fast. It'd take a half hour the way my green clunker was riding, but I couldn't ask for a new bike. All the factories that made them were being used for war production. Behind me Mrs. Dubchek's flag snapped. The front rim of my bike scraped against the thick tire. *Scrape.*

26

Scrape. Better do something about that, I thought, because tires are hard to come by, too. I didn't want to ask Dad. Let him fix Mom's old toaster and Mrs. Dubchek's flag.

A chill settled on my back somewhere between my shirt and my skirt. What was I going to do that summer? Would anything happen in my life?

Zagreb, 1941

ADAM

All during supper Villi was strangely silent while the food sat on his plate, getting cold.

"You shouldn't waste food," scolded Mama. "You need your strength."

My stomach grumbled: How much warmer such a lonely potato would feel in my mouth than on his plate.

Between his thumb and forefinger, Villi's fork twirled around and around. When Mama began clearing, he spoke. "They made us line up again," he said quietly to his supper.

Mama's hands lay on the stacked plates. Papa held his pipe in the way he was accustomed to, except nothing was in it: Papa could no longer buy tobacco. Still, there was pleasure in the holding. Mira was in the corner with her doll, Natasha.

"We stood in a perfect line, exactly as the first time," said Villi, his fork twirling faster. "We counted: One. Two. Three. Four. Five. Six. One. Two. Three. Four. Five. Six."

I leaned my back against the dining room wall, thinking about how my older brother got to be a worker and load horse-shoes onto trains from the warehouses while I did nothing.

"I was number three." Villi's voice shook. "Nissim was four."

Mira neatly dressed Natasha in a tiny fur cape that Grandmama had made especially for the doll. Papa sucked on his empty pipe. It made a terribly irritating sound. He tapped the bowl as if there were still ashes inside that had to be cleaned out.

"This time it was not number six," continued Villi. "It was number four. All the fours were taken out. That is the reason Nissim was chosen, not me. It just so happened that I was number three. Right next to Nissim but number three." Villi's voice cracked. Tears flowed from his eyes down his cheeks. He did not bother to sniff nor even to wipe his nose, which leaked in a pitiful, childish way.

My palms held the hard, white wall. Nothing would give there. I punched it once, twice . . .

If only he would stop. He had no right. He was the one who scolded me when I showed signs of weakness. "Stop your wailing, Adam," he would say when I fell from my bicycle and burst into tears. And when I had to get stitches, he said, "A man does not cry, Adam. You must laugh instead." I punched three . . . four times. My knuckles were sore and red. Still, he wept. The next day we found out what we all suspected: the fifteen boys who were number four had been shot.

Papa and Mama decided to get us false papers. We prepared ourselves for flight. Only Grandmama objected.

"It will get better," she said. "Just watch. Surely, it will get better."

CHRIS

We had the best holiday picnic on the lake. I love Lake Ontario. It stretches on so far you think you're looking into forever. One night I dreamed about swimming clear across the water. When my feet touched the shore, I was someplace no one had ever been before. The beach was clean, and the only footprints on it were mine. It was a beautiful dream, but it was also lonely.

Nearly all the relatives came. We said a short prayer for Dick and Bob, then we swam. I wore the bathing suit that I finally convinced Mom to buy me. I wasn't going to wear my one-piece with the accordion-pleated skirt one more time. I looked like a baby in it. "I'm not a baby," I told Mom. "I'm growing. Daily!" My new swimming apparel was what's called a "bare midriff" suit. It had a halter top and a short sarong skirt (NOT ACCORDION PLEATS), and there was nothing at all across my entire middle. The pattern made me think of a lily pond. If I stood still for too long, a frog would jump on me.

Later, we ate hot dogs and hamburgers and potato salad and watermelon and cherry pie, which is a tradition in the O'Hara family (Mom's side) because George Washington chopped down the cherry tree, and if you eat an O'Hara pie you never have to tell a lie. It's the best cherry pie you'll ever eat. The little kids threw snappers on the ground and got dizzy making circles with their sparklers. Us big kids waited until it was pitch black outside and the mosquitoes came out to join the celebration. We scratched bites that swelled on our arms and legs while we ran back and forth, lighting the bigger fireworks. All along the beach things popped and snapped and made it seem like it was raining bright golden drops that rose and fell so that my whole insides were shouting: *Happy Independence Day, America!*

INTERNEES & DISPLACED PERSONS SUBCOMMISSION
ALLIED CONTROL COMMISSION

Notice of Acceptance and Instructions

To: Bornstein, Manya Rut

This is to notify you that, subject to medical
and security examinations, you have been accepted
for movement to the United States of America and
maintenance there at the refugee shelter located
at Fort Ontario, Oswego, New York, as more fully
described in a notice and application dated June
20, 1944.

You will report at Transit Camp No 1 - Bari
on Saturday July 8, 1944 at 5 P.M.
Personal Baggage: Will be limited to 150 pounds
(68 kilos) per person. No bicycles, furniture or
similar articles will be carried.
Inoculations and Vaccinations: All persons shall
have in their possession inoculation and vacci-
nation certificates. It is important that this
certificate be retained by you at all times.
Passports and identity cards: Bring all papers
of this nature with you.
Registration forms: Registration forms giving
complete data about yourself and your family
must be completed as soon as possible.

for The Director
Date July 3, 1944
Leonard E. Ackerman, US War Ref. Bd.

THIS FORM SHOULD BE RETAINED BY YOU

One day I pushed Mama to get ready. The next she pushed me. She did not ask herself about things that could never be answered. Instead she ran. "Packing is what we must be doing," she said.

I folded what little I had and began on what I did not have any longer. The one suitcase we owned became full of nothing. It was Papa's suitcase and it was no longer in working order: the locks were broken; we used a rope instead.

Mama read the directions for our departure over and over. How official they sounded. Bornstein, Manya Rut. Is this my mama? I asked. Do not ask, I told myself. Someone somewhere had sat in front of a clattering machine and miraculously produced Mama's name.

Such a typist knows nothing of choosing.

Chapter Two
Two Suns in the Sky

&

We stayed in the hold where there were cots one on top of another. A thousand people in one big hold.
> Edith Klein, former resident of the
> Emergency Refugee Shelter

One night I looked into the sky and it appeared like two suns. I remembered an old legend: he who sees two suns in the sky will never be the same.
> Walter Greenberg,
> former resident of ERS

ADAM

For days we waited. First there was the trip to Aversa, where we were gathered together from all over Italy. From Aversa we were transported to Naples. Standing behind the letter of our surname, we waited some more. Finally, we boarded an army transport, the *Henry Gibbins*. We were stuck to the harbor like flies on flypaper. More waiting. When we had nearly used up the fingers on one hand counting the wait, we felt a shifting.

"We are moving!" I shouted, facing out to sea.

"The die is cast," said Mama, facing the disappearing harbor. "There is no turning back."

Mira's body wedged itself between us. Mama took one of Mira's small hands in hers. I held the other. We peered out onto the flatness of sea and sky.

Where was this back we would turn to, anyway?

• • •

Not once, but three times a day we lined ourselves up for meals! We stood with what the Americans told us was a mess kit in our hands. The line stretched along the length of the ship. In the mess hall, food was slapped onto our kits. More food was on the long tables. Goulash. Potatoes. Salmon salad. Onions. And not once, but three times, we ate, standing.

"Milk!" said Mama during one such breakfast meal. Her eyes were empty cereal bowls. "Fresh milk!"

The man in front of me scooped an egg out of a bowl filled with eggs. His other hand darted out, snatched two more, and hid them in a pocket. I stopped myself from doing the same. Instead I contemplated the mystery of the American food I had seen so far: hot dogs, which were long, thin frankfurters or a kind of bratwurst; soft white bread that refused to hold its shape in my mouth; and cereal that was cold and stiff instead of hot and soft, as ours was.

"Pah," said someone whose elbows made friends with mine at the breakfast table, "this cereal tastes like cardboard."

"Animal fodder," said another.

Then there was the food that allowed me to perform tricks right inside my mouth. Mira and I were introduced to it by an American sailor.

"Come, little girl," he said to Mira, "I have something for you."

Mira looked at me with her beseeching eyes.

"Go," I said. "It is all right."

Mira took small steps forward. She stood an arm's length away from the smiling man. He held out something wrapped in paper. "Go ahead," he said. Mira glanced back at me. I nodded. Quickly she unwrapped the item. The sailor pointed to his mouth. "It's chewing gum."

"Chew-ing gum," mimicked Mira. Politely she handed him the paper and popped the gum into her mouth.

"Don't swallow," warned the sailor.

Too late. Already the gum was making its way down to

Mira's stomach. She blushed. The sailor took out another piece and popped it in his mouth.

Before Mira had a chance to run off, he said, "Look."

Mira gasped. I stepped closer to see the spectacle. One rubber circle after another made its way out of his mouth, expanded, then burst apart.

"Try it," coaxed the American, holding out another piece for Mira. "Just chew until it softens. Make a ball. Stick your tongue inside. And blow. Like so." More bubbles formed and popped outside his mouth. I heard cracking inside his mouth, too.

"Take it," I said in Serbo-Croatian so the sailor could not understand, "and give me half."

Mira frowned. After I poked her a few times, she gingerly took the piece. She smiled broadly, tossed back her hair, and put the whole thing inside her mouth.

"Very generous," I said, still speaking our native language.

"Thank you," she answered in English.

The American handed me a piece. "You, too," he said. "Try some."

We all sat on the deck, Mira on the sailor's knee, me on the floorboards while the *Henry Gibbins* plowed through the waves. Except for the small wars we made inside our mouths—*Pop! Crack! Pop!*—we were quiet.

• • •

"What does *tutees* mean?" Mira asked me. We had been at sea for three days, and finally she spoke of Papa. She did not say his name at first.

"My dear one," I answered. "My very special dear one."

She sat silent. "Papa called me *tutees,*" she said. "He didn't call you *tutees,* Adam. Only me."

"That was his special name for you," I said. "Only you."

Shortly after that, we were attacked. Bells rang. We heard on the loudspeaker: "Enemy planes overhead. Remain in your bunks." Mira, Mama, and I put on our life jackets. We lay perfectly still, waiting.

All at once thick smoke entered our hold. Mira was frightened. "When we are in America," I told her, "I will get for you a doll. A new doll, even prettier than your old Natasha."

"Natasha must be lonely all by herself in Zagreb," said Mira, looking lonely herself. "I should not have left her behind."

"I am certain Grandmama found her. Besides, Natasha feels most at home in Yugoslavia. It is good that you forgot her."

"I did not forget her, Adam. I left her behind."

"Yes, that is so," I nodded, "because you knew how much she wished to stay."

"Tell me, Adam, what kind of doll will you get me?"

"An American doll."

"If she is an American, how will she understand me?"

"You will teach her, here and there, a Croat word. Soon, too, you will know English very well."

"Will my doll have her own comb, or will I need the big comb with the missing teeth that you and Mama and I use?"

"I will find a very small comb made especially for your doll."

"Can there be such a thing as a special doll comb?"

"In America there are even combs for dolls. They come in many colors."

"I will have a pink one, not black like our big toothless comb. But I only want it if Villi and Papa are in America, too. And Grandmama. Grandmama has to make my doll's clothes."

Everyone was coughing and choking from the smoke. In between coughs, I told Mira the story that Papa enjoyed telling us when we were tired of running. Mira knew the tale. But it was like *tutees:* she needed me to repeat the right version.

"Tell me, Adam, the story," she said.

"What story?"

"The story! You know! 'Once upon a time there was a man they called "the demented one," but really he was very smart.'"

I stroked Mira's hair while Mama put wet towels over our faces so we would not choke. "Once upon a time," I said, "there was a man they called 'the demented one,' but really he was very smart, so smart that he knew how to save himself."

Mira sighed contentedly. I held her elbow, because it was the one small and bony spot on my sister that seemed to need protection, and, as people all around us coughed, she listened.

"Adam," she asked as soon as I was done, "will Papa and Villi and Grandmama come to America?"

"Yes, they will come."

"How, when it is so far? How will they get on a ship?"

"They will find a way. Remember, Papa is a very smart man."

Mira's hand slipped inside of mine. "Adam, when Grandmama comes, she will bring Natasha with her, because Grandmama gave me Natasha. She made her clothes for me, and Grandmama knows that Natasha really does not want to be left behind."

"Natasha will love America," I said, attempting to sound brave and cheerful.

"Yes, but at first she will be afraid. Natasha can be that way. That is why it is a good thing she is not here now. She would cry. Natasha needs things to be safe, Adam."

My hands closed themselves gently around Mira's small hand.

"That is how it is with Natasha," said Mira. "She can be a very big baby."

A few days later we learned the smoke had been a screen to hide us. Someone, by accident, did not remember to shut the vents, and the smoke had the misfortune to get inside. More unfortunate yet was what happened to my new friend Ralph. He was caught in the toilet when the alarm went off. There he was, thinking, Am I going to die sitting on the toilet?

• • •

We were nearly a week at sea, and all of a sudden I made an amazing discovery: I had time to think. I had time to look and to think and to look again. It was very perplexing. In Rome I did not dare think or look or even imagine. I reminded myself to behave as one should behave if one is Italian Catholic and not a Jewish boy from Yugoslavia. Pretending you are someone you are not takes a good deal of energy, and I could not waste whatever was left over. I made sure to do well on my religion tests, better than those real Catholic boys who sat beside me. Then no one would question me. But I made sure not to stand out. You must appear smart but not too smart. Also my eyes had to behave properly. There were rules to follow, and if you did not keep them in mind, something could happen: If you see a German, do not look into his face; he may think you too bold and ask a question. Do not look away, either; he may think you have something to hide and ask you a question.

In Rome I had to act as if I had nothing to hide—which is to say always I had to act. But on the ship I could be free with my thoughts and my eyes. I could let myself imagine.

I lay on my cot. Above and below me men slept. The hold where we stayed was crowded and dimly lit. My hands rested on my chest. Who is this boy with the jungle on his body? Hair was growing in all the right places. I closed my eyes. I was in a hundred wonderful places, doing such things as I had never allowed myself to dream of. I opened my eyes. Why dream when they were all in front of me?

There were girls everywhere. I saw them all.

● ● ●

It did not take long before Mira began asking that infuriating question that Villi and I always asked on those long summer trips. She'd stand next to me on the deck, where we tried not to listen to all the seasick people who were leaning over the rails, and she'd ask, "Are we there yet?"

And later, "Adam, are we there *yet?*"

But before we got to this place called "there," we encountered yet another American food, surely the strangest of them all. We were standing at one of the long tables. In front of us was a big bowl of something that shook when you moved it.

"Do you think it is alive?" asked Ralph. He poked me and grinned. "Try some. Tell me if it bites."

I dipped my spoon into the large red mass. It pulled apart but just as quickly closed around the spoon. "It doesn't cut," I muttered.

"One of those animals that knows how to heal itself." Ralph winked at Mira. "Take a knife. Maybe you can cut it then."

Mira looked startled. "Don't hurt it, Adam," she said.

Mama frowned. She did not appreciate Ralph's jokes.

"It is not alive," I answered. "Ralph is teasing."

At the other end of the table, someone was spooning the substance with a soup ladle. I did the same. It slithered onto my plate, where it sat, shimmering.

"Defies all laws of chemistry," said Ralph, shaking my plate. "Not a solid or a liquid. Defies all laws of geometry, too. Not a square or a triangle or a circle. Go ahead. Try it, Adam."

"Go ahead," echoed Mira. "Try it, Adam."

Mama, too, seemed to wait for me.

My finger touched the top of the jiggling mass. It sank in. "Cold," I said, as if I were defining the surface of some newly discovered planet. "But not like ice."

"Not with the hands," said Mama.

I caught a bit on my spoon and swallowed. They watched intently. "Sweet," I said. "And good. Very good."

"It is called Jell-O," said Ralph. He had known all along.

I did not get angry. From the very beginning I liked Ralph. He reminded me of Villi.

• • •

We had been traveling almost two weeks; fourteen days; countless hours, waiting for our future to catch up with us. Are we there yet? I felt like Mira. To pass the time we spoke English—we all wanted to learn—or we sang our native songs. Some of the sailors tried to learn them. In exchange, they taught us American songs like "My Country 'Tis of Thee" and "I have a gal whose name is Sal, fifteen miles on the Erie Canal."

There were a few men on board who were not so kind, particularly one sailor who enjoyed jeering at Ralph and me. He did this for several evenings in a row while Ralph and I were dumping unused food into the water. (The Americans paid us boys to throw the extra food overboard. At first it filled me with disgust. America is a land of plenty, I told myself. That includes plenty of waste.)

Ralph and I decided to wait for the right wind and show this man what we were made of. Luck was with us. The wind turned. We dumped. Food splattered in his face.

That same night I stayed on deck long after Ralph left, and I witnessed the most beautiful sunset. On the water was the reflection of the setting sun. In the sky was the rising moon, which appeared orange because of the sun's reflection shining back on it. With the orange moon rising and the sun descending, there seemed to be two suns in the sky. Then I was reminded of a legend Papa once told Villi and me: A man who sees two suns in the sky is never the same.

I walked the ship. Where I was walking, I did not know. My feet, like my growing toes, followed their own destiny. I left the hold where we thousand were supposed to stay. Nobody stopped me. I came to that part where the wounded American men were. Staring at me was such a man. At first, my mind did not grasp what it saw. Why does his head seem so big? it asked in childlike wonder. Then it came to me. This man's head appears huge because he is only a head and a trunk squeezed into a basket. There are no arms or legs anywhere.

The man gazed at my legs. *He wants my legs!* My brain said this. My legs had their own understanding. They trembled as if they were feeling what his did before they were so cruelly torn away from his body.

This man most likely fought in Anzio, I thought. Most likely he fought to free Italy. That is how his arms and legs left him, not of their own will. He gave them up as a sacrifice. So now I am free. Still, I could not guess why this man had to give up his arms and legs. Who but he needed them? Who could make sense of such a selection?

I wondered if I would ever see Villi, Papa, and Grandmama again.

Why was Nissim chosen? Who chose me?

• • •

Morning. We huddled together on the deck trying to see through a blanket of fog. Such a dreary, overcast day. We will lose the chance, we all murmured. We will not see her after waiting so long only to catch a glimpse.

We jostled against each other, held hands, lifted our chins, sighed a communal sigh. I imagined those beasts selected by Noah—the ones chosen to live. They must have had to do a million things before they boarded the ark. Then to be squeezed together, one elephant's *tuches,* the hugeness of his rear end, smashed against some poor lion's face. Yet they persisted in waiting. To begin a new life in a new world.

"Are we there yet?" Mira pleaded, squeezing my hand so hard the bones cracked in complaint.

"Almost." My hand sought out Mama's. I did not look at her face. Without a look we could pretend that a boy my age had no need for such sentiment.

We swayed in unison. Were we beginning a prayer or ending one? Or beginning and ending at the same time?

"Will we see her?" asked Mira, squeezing tighter.

"Who knows!" answered several voices.

A prayer welled up inside of me. Dear God, please keep Villi and Papa and Grandmama safe. Please bring them here. Amen. And thank you for having brought Mama and Mira and me to America.

By some miracle, the sky cleared. In a rush we saw . . . green. Colors. Automobiles in different colors. So many colors. Sounds. Honking. Traffic. Buildings. Huge buildings.

"Is that her?" asked Mira. "Is that really her?"

My chin jerked up and down like a balloon tied to a child's finger. My mouth filled with water. I swallowed hard, while my fingers tightened between Mama's.

"Is that her?" she repeated. "Adam, is that her?"

My hand loosened its hold. "Yes," the lips said in disbeli
I waved. Mama waved. All around me hands lifted then
selves. Waving.

The Statue of Liberty waved back.

On the third day of August 1944, we arrived in America.

CHRIS

I was so bored I actually wanted school to begin again. Maybe
it was my summer job. The year before, I had loved getting
down on my knees and working on "the muck," which is what
we call the rich, black soil around Oswego that's used for growing onions. I loved topping onions and thinking about how
most people who go shopping don't know the whole history of
onion production. My brain must've been fried from overexpo-
sure to the sun and all the excitement I felt about starting high
school. Back then I thought everything would be different.
New. Exciting. I'd be different, too. I'd be smart, popular, and
interesting. I wasn't unpopular. Or dumb, either. I was just aver-
age in everything except maybe looks. One day I'd think yes.
The next it was no.

But by the middle of the next July, I didn't even bother about
figuring out how I felt about my looks. Who cares? I made up
my mind that summer that I was going to work with people
who, unlike onions, could talk. Listening to just myself talking
to myself was very boring! That's when I decided to have a
party—a real birthday party with music you could dance to and
friends who'd dance.

It was the best party. The whole day was wonderful. I woke
up at six so I'd be awake for the minute of my birth—July 25 at
6:10 A.M.—except this was fifteen years later, which is a good
thing: nobody wants to repeat 1929. Except for my birth, that
was a pretty dismal year in United States history. "You are fifteen years old," I said to my reflection as I dressed and got

.dy for work. The face in the mirror did not look at all bored.
seemed older, too—not like the face of someone who's four-
een.

When I got home, I rolled up the rug in the living room and
got out my favorite records. I also double-checked the portable
plug-in phonograph that I'd persuaded Dad to buy me for
Christmas. Then I waited for Mom to get back from the factory.
Together, we made ice cream and cookies. We didn't use real
cream, and the butter cookies were made with margarine—that
cost a lot less in ration stamps than butter—but everything tasted
great. Right before the party began, Mom gave me my presents:
one practical gift and one fun one. The fun gift was roller skates.
(I'll never be too old for those.) The practical gift was a new pair
of nylon stockings. I didn't expect silk hose, because they were
hard to come by. I promised Mom I'd keep them for church.

"You can only have one pair of stockings," said Mom,
"because we can't forget about—"

"—the war effort," I finished. (I didn't want to think that
some poor soldier wouldn't have a parachute because girls like
me were buying too many stockings. I promised myself to be
very careful about runs.)

In the beginning I was scared it'd be a horrible party.
Everybody stood around the food that Mom and I had put on
a table in the corner of the living room. The boys huddled
together on one side and the girls on the other. We made stupid comments about how good everything was, except you
could tell nobody was interested in food, even if it was good:
nobody was eating. The girls looked sideways at the boys, and
the boys looked everywhere except at the girls, while we all pretended we were listening to music. *When is this party going to
start?* I wished I were up in my room, talking to the reflection
of my bored face in the mirror.

Finally we ate, and when we couldn't hide behind our noisy
chewing any longer, we danced. At first the girls danced with
the girls—I danced with Ann—while the boys hung around the
food table, spinning platters and pretending they weren't watching the girls. Everybody was laughing. Then several boys walked

together over to what had become the girls' side of the room. I danced the jitterbug three times with Ned, which didn't count: he's my cousin. Then I put on "No Love, No Nothin'." Patti Dugan's voice sank inside of me. *No love, no nothin', Until my baby comes home.* I didn't know if I wanted to be off in Europe fighting or if I wanted to be home, waiting for my man. *I promised him, I'd wait for him Till even Hades froze. I'm lonesome heaven knows, But what I said still goes.* Hmm-hmm. Hmm-hmm. I closed my eyes, humming softly and doing nothing.

When my eyes pried themselves open, John Sanders was so close to me I nearly fainted. Hmm-hmm. Something kept singing inside of me. He must've been waiting to ask you the whole song, I thought. Now it's almost over. Put on another slow one, Chris, like "I've Got a Crush on You."

But I chickened out, and we danced fast to a big band record. Every once in a while, between all the twirling he was doing—John even twirled me backward—his body bumped mine. John made out like it was an accident. It was on purpose. All this time Dad had been working in the garage: Mom had gotten him to promise he wouldn't watch over us the entire evening. Suddenly, though, he appeared in the archway between the kitchen and the living room, his eyes stuck on me.

"Mo-om," I bleated. She came downstairs, grabbed Dad's hand, and pushed him toward the door. We raised the volume and danced fast dances back to back. Ned started a contest with the other boys to see who could get a cap off a Coke bottle with his teeth and squirt soda the farthest. The one who hit the ceiling first won. Ann and I exchanged "we should've known" looks.

Fifteen-year-old boys are so immature. I was going to find a boy who was at least sixteen. He wouldn't be like all the other boys I knew. When you looked at him, you'd wonder where he came from. It'd be someplace exotic that I'd never heard of before, and when he spoke, he'd sound different, too, so I'd feel different just hearing him. We'd go away together. Somewhere far away.

• • •

Fifteen years old. That's 15 times 365 days, not counting leap years. And in all that time I had not once been kissed. Not really kissed, like in the movies. Just imagine how much kissing Bette Davis must've done. And Lana Turner. She had to have been kissed a trillion times. I bet even the Andrews sisters, who acted in all those stupid singing army musicals that Dad loved watching, had their share of kisses. (They got to do something for the war and kiss at the same time.)

I'd been kissed during Spin the Bottle. That did not count.

A few times Ann and I played Post Office with her younger brother. Having a little squirty brother kiss you during Post Office did not count, either.

John bump-kissed me at my party. That was too fast to count. You should expect a kiss like a birthday present you know you're going to get, but you're not sure until it's in your hands.

I wanted to know when it was going to happen.

I wanted to be really kissed.

• • •

Eleven days after my birthday Oswego had its own great event: Waste Paper Salvage Day. Dad prepared us for the big day by sitting Mom and me down at the breakfast table and reading directions out of the newspaper. (Dad was being an absolute stickler for details. Mom let him go on. Working on the vibrating hopper with potential fire hazards spilling all around you must do more than shake up your insides.) "Now, this is what our mayor states in his proclamation to the citizens of Oswego," said Dad, clearing his throat.

I groaned inwardly. Here goes another word-by-word recitation, as if we can't read the *Palladium Times* ourselves.

"'WHEREAS, waste paper salvage days are being held in many communities of the state and nation at the present time, and WHEREAS . . .'"

Dad read at a snail's pace, emphasizing the whereases while I tore out a few strands of hair and poked them between my front teeth. I felt desperate. Pretty soon I'd bite my fingers and clean my teeth with the jagged pieces of nail. Maybe I could

44

excuse myself and check my Wac bag. I'd try on the bra and console myself because it was too tight. First, though, I'd make a general inventory review. One pair of pants, a skirt, one shirt, a bra (replacement necessary), a pair of warm socks, an extra pair of shoes, toothbrush, toothpaste, hairbrush, some chocolate, which Dad bought me before we had to use so many ration stamps (I love chocolate—Dad loves to buy it for me), some water-resistant matches (you never know), and a copy of *Johnny Tremain* (my favorite book).

One day soon I had to run off. I'd been waiting too long. I'd be a spy for the Wacs and sneak behind enemy lines. I wouldn't forget to write Mom and Dad, but each postcard would need decoding. Only "your loving daughter" would remain in normal English. I didn't want them to worry.

I sat at the table, daydreaming about my runaway bag and the perfect body from the chest up. Maybe I was becoming too big. You have to be big, but not too big. Girls who are too big jiggle. When they walk down school halls, boys stare at them. That's very embarrassing. I didn't want to be too small, either. My cousin Grace was as flat as a pancake before it's gotten a chance to rise. Too small is bad, too. Then girls stare at you, particularly when you're crowded together for the yearly health exam, and you're the only one wearing an undershirt with a little pink bow.

"Someone's not listening," said Dad, huffily. "Only fools read aloud to themselves."

"I'm listening," chirped Mom.

"I'm listening, too," I said. I wanted to say, "So don't read." I poked my tongue around a piece of hair that had gotten stuck and looked cheerful.

Dad raised his voice. "'THEREFORE, I proclaim Saturday, August 5, as Waste Paper Salvage Day, and call upon all Oswegonians to search attics, basements, and storerooms for waste paper, including newspapers, magazines, books, etc., make compact bundles and deposit at the curb for collection. I also urge that such men as have any spare time volunteer their services . . .'" He paused so we'd let "men" and "volunteer" sink in.

I was glad Dad would be away all day Saturday, volunteering his services. Then he wouldn't have his eyes glued on me. And I was glad that he was consumed with paper. Otherwise he'd have been talking about the refugees who were going to stay at the old army base outside Fort Ontario. He'd have told me for the hundredth time that I was not allowed to be anywhere near the fence where the refugees would be coming in.

"Just you wait and see," he'd say like he was predicting a major disaster. "They'll be scarfing up all our food. They'll scarf up *our* food and cigarettes and walk around *our* streets in their funny clothes as if they owned the town. Christine, I don't want to hear that you've been around any of them. You are not allowed to talk to any of those people! You are not even allowed to watch them come in!"

I *am too* going to watch, I later confided to my onion friends. (They'd never breathe a word.) Half the town plans on watching, because no other town in the whole United States is taking in nearly a thousand refugees from all over Europe. President Roosevelt chose our town and our fort. That is very exciting! I planned to hop on my bike and go down Ninth Street to the fence. I'd pick up my cousin Ned on the way. Maybe we'd both figure out how to get inside. I wouldn't talk—not directly to the refugees—so I wouldn't be entirely disobedient. I'd communicate with Ned, who'd relay my message. If they said something back, Ned could tell me.

What languages will they speak? I wondered. Would any of them go to Oswego High? Maybe there'd be an older boy. We'd meet. I'd love to hear about strange places. But what would I tell him? Who'd want to hear about my working on the muck? Or wanting to be kissed? Or wanting to do something, *anything* to help the war?

Chapter Three
The Fence

⚘

I came with a winter coat that I had made when we first came to Italy. I was fourteen then, and now I was twenty.

Steffi Steinberg Winters,
former resident of ERS

CHRIS

Nearly everyone in town went down to the fence to watch the refugees get off the train. Some people stood on the roof of the Fitzgibbons factory where Dad helped make his tanks. Ninth Street was jam packed. There were all the families who lived right across from the fence plus everybody from both the east and west sides of town. The refugees looked so poor. Many of the children didn't have shoes on, or they wore sandals that were falling off. They stood watching us, too. Everyone tried to say something. And there were guards with guns.

I saw a boy there. He seemed so different, not like anybody from around here. He had pitch black, curly hair. (I've always loved curly hair! Mine is poker straight and the kind of blond that doesn't look blond and doesn't look brown. I've always wished it were one or the other.) This boy was holding a little

47

girl's hand, probably his sister's. He had on a funny shirt that made him look exotic and open-toed shoes that he must've made himself. The leather on top was cut, and his toes poked through. The little girl stared at my bike like it was something special and not just my old green clunker that needed new tires.

I made Ned and a friend form a pyramid. I climbed on their shoulders, and they held my ankles. Someone else gave me the bike. I lifted it over the fence, then jumped back down. What if they take the bike and don't return it? I thought. What would I tell Dad? I wasn't supposed to be anywhere near the fort. I could've made up a story about its being stolen, but nobody ever stole anything in Oswego. It was a safe place. Boring, but safe. What do I know about these people? I asked myself. How come I'm giving a strange girl the bike? She seemed so happy, though, like she hadn't ridden in a long time. I pointed to my watch to indicate when they should return it, but I was worried that they didn't understand what I meant. I should've used my French. The one time I needed it, and I was tongue-tied. Of course, I don't think many of them came from France. They came from someplace that I'd never heard of before. Besides, I wasn't supposed to talk to any of them.

I was worrying about all these things when, all at once, newspapermen surrounded me. One reporter asked me dumb questions. "Why did you pass your bike over the fence?" and "Are you glad these people are going to stay in Oswego?" and "Do you think you'll want to make friends with someone inside the camp who's your age?"

How silly! I passed the bike because the girl wanted to ride. And of course I'm glad. And I'd like to make friends. I nodded and smiled, saying "yes" a few times, and that seemed to satisfy the reporter. I was glad he didn't interview Dad, although I'm not sure if Dad would've repeated the things he said at home.

"They should stay where they belong," Dad liked to repeat. "We have enough poverty right here in our own backyard. We don't need to bring in someone else's dirt." He'd look at me

when he said that. He was always looking, but he was never seeing. And he thought he was Christian.

A photographer wanted to take my picture, which was
tempting. I'd never had my picture in the paper. I'd never even
had my name mentioned. If I'd made the High School Honor
Roll, I'd at least have had my name there, but that hadn't
happened yet. I thought it never would.

I turned my back just in time. If Dad had seen my picture,
he'd have probably stopped speaking to me. He'd have also
looked at me like I'd caught some dread disease and needed to
be put under quarantine. I wouldn't be able to leave the house.
Not for months. Not for years. Forever.

That night I couldn't sleep. I'd come home from my secret
adventure and eaten too much chocolate. Dad had gotten it for
me on his way back from doing his civic duty. He made a special side trip to the Long chocolate factory and bought me a bar
with his extra stamps. "Here," he said, slapping it in front of my
plate like it was no big deal.

"Thanks, Dad," I said. I almost told him where I'd been,
but I didn't. I brought my nose to the wrapper and smelled.
Dad was pleased. I could tell.

I didn't want him to be pleased. But I didn't want to say
anything, either, because even if I loved my dad, and he loved
me, I did not always like him.

My dad believes that he's the only one who knows the right
answers, but he's not always right. He also has this attitude
about being American that I could never understand, since once
upon a time the Cooks and the O'Haras immigrated to
America. For Dad, Ireland is not Europe. It's a special place,
and the United States should feel very fortunate that there was
a potato famine there. All these wonderful people immigrated
and made America what it is today. Outside of all his people,
Dad hates all immigrants. He hates anything that doesn't come
directly from America. My mother's different. She has always
been different.

More waiting. But this time it did not matter. We were in America. In the New York harbor. In front of us was a skyline with so many lights they seemed like stars. I could not count them all. We were told we were to stay on the ship overnight.

"The moon," said Mira, "looks like canned peaches. It is a big, bright globe." (Mira had fallen in love with anything that lived in a can, including evaporated milk. She drank that directly from the can.) My eyes made themselves into moths longing for those lights.

Early the following morning we were hurried off to a hut, men and women separately. We had to remove our clothes, which were taken to machines. Some men began whispering among themselves, "Here in America, they will gas us. We will die." Others yelled, "What are we? Cattle?" We moved in front of soldiers who sprayed a horrible substance over our bodies. "To delouse and disinfect," someone said. "To kill us," someone else said. Amidst all this, there was such a confusion. Somehow the disinfecting machines ruined many things. Ralph's shirt was reduced to a sleeve.

"Let us have an English lesson," he said, waving the sleeve as one does a white flag. "What do you call a shirt without sleeves?"

"A sleeveless shirt," I answered, shivering. Are they doing this to Mama and Mira? I wondered. Will Mira try to hide? In the abandoned asylum in Aversa there were holes in the doors where knobs and locks had once been, and Mira refused to undress.

"And what is this sleeve that has so sadly left its shirt behind?"

I shrugged, too involved with thoughts to answer.

"A shirtless sleeve."

Another man frantically waved two sections of leather in front of our faces. "My belt!" he screamed. "Look what the American idiots have done. See the many holes I made. All the time I was growing thinner, I kept my belt. Now I will have to wear string around my pants. It is a humiliation to walk on American soil with string around the pants."

After all of this, we took a ferry to a place called Hoboken. Around the buttons of our shirts was a string that was attached to a cardboard tag. "U.S. Army Casual Baggage," it read. Were we the baggage? And what did "casual" mean? We were put onto trains. It was night again. We drew closer and closer to our destination. Fort Ontario. Oswego, New York. What would this camp be like? I sank inside an ocean of silence. Beside me Ralph continued to talk.

"Did I ever tell you my restaurant story?" he asked.

Why do the Americans again separate us? I thought. Why do they put the women and girls into one train, and the men and boys into another? What if I got off and I did not see my family? What if they had disappeared as Villi and Papa did? Here one day, gone the next. My head felt waterlogged. I envied Ralph. He knew where his papa was—directly across from us.

"One morning," said Ralph, "our guards were gone. They vanished from the Ferramonti concentration camp just like that. We did not leave. Where would we go? The Allies took over, and we waited some more. One day some other boys and I decided to walk to the closest city. We had a bit of money and we saw a restaurant. We went in. They had meat on the menu. Of course we all ordered it. In five minutes we slung down the meat. It was the best meal we had had in a long time. A week later, still at Ferramonti, we decided to go back to the same place. Unfortunately, it was closed. Do you know why?"

"Why?" It was no use to drown myself in silence.

"The sign on the door told us: 'The Allied government has closed this restaurant for having served human meat.'"

Ralph laughed. So did I. It was the kind of laughter one makes when one wants to believe that everything one has said is only a story. Finally, it was morning again. We arrived at our destination.

How often I had wished to be left alone. I was almost a

man, and a man cannot always be with his mother and sister. But I nearly cried when I stepped down and saw Mama still holding fast to Papa's suitcase with the rope around it. The Italian rope and the Yugoslav suitcase all together. Mira held Mama's hand tight. Then we saw it.

I felt for Ralph's shoulder. He felt for mine. "Chicken wire," he said quietly. "A few strands of barbed wire on top of chicken wire. Six feet maybe." He scrutinized the barrier.

"It may be we are staying outside of it," I said hopefully.

Ralph shook his head.

"It may be we can come and go at will," I persisted.

"It might as well be Ferramonti," he replied, mocking all my maybes.

"We are all safe," said Mama. "Who cares whether we are safe inside a fence or outside?"

"A fence is an offense," spoke up the man who wore that string around his pants.

Guards stood at the entrance. People were all around, watching as we got off the trains. Some stood atop high buildings. Others sat on the steps of funny square houses made of wood instead of brick or stone. The only thing dividing us from this crowd of people was the street. So it seemed at first. People looked at me. I stared back. Behind the fence I felt like a monkey at the zoo.

I tried to see with their eyes, but it felt strange. I had forgotten that there were so many colors in the world—that clothing came in many colors and that there are clothes made especially to keep your feet safe, your hands warm, your chest protected. Shoes. Gloves. Sweaters. Once upon a time I wore these things, when I was a different person, someone who freely wrote his name: Adam Bornstein.

Do not think about this "once," I told myself. You are living now.

Inside the gate, at a long table, the Americans checked us in. Everywhere there were uniforms. In Yugoslavia every uniform appeared frightening. Even the mailman's. Here it had to be different.

Men with cameras ran among us. The Americans took many shots of us. I was certain that one girl would become famous. She was eating a hot dog and remarked that this was the first time she had done so. Bulbs went off. I imagined the caption. "Girl eats first American hot dog!" No one asked her about cold dogs or soup from boiled tree bark.

We found the places where we would stay, got towels and sheets, and had our first breakfast on American soil. People still stood, leaning against the fence. Some of them must have gone to their homes and come back again. They pointed to here a boy and there a girl and threw shoes and dresses over the fence. A few jammed cigarettes through the barbed wire so that I felt, with all these gifts, that it was like Hanukkah. Mira stood next to me. Her hand was in one of its usual places: inside my hand.

"Adam, Adam," she cried. Her hand flew to her mouth.

"It is all right," I said. "You do not have to be quiet here!"

Mira's eyes fastened on a bicycle such as we had not seen for several years. Beside this bicycle was a very beautiful American girl. Her hair was a color I could not define. Surely the blond in it had talked to the sun while the brown had made long conversations with the earth. I did not notice the color of her eyes, only that they seemed to know nothing of hiding.

The girl smiled. She nodded. Mira smiled. The girl held up her finger to make us wait. She put two boys who looked to be my age in a line and climbed on top of their shoulders so that she nearly reached the top of the fence.

"Be careful!" I shouted instinctively.

She looked at me quizzically.

I grinned in a piteous fashion. How can she possibly understand Italian, Adam? You are not in Rome. Several men with cameras elbowed their way toward her. Someone gave her the bicycle. She lifted it over the fence. I reached for it, and she jumped down.

Mira grabbed the object of her desires. "I know how."

"How? The last time you rode, you were on a bicycle with three wheels. This has two."

"I know how!"

The American girl pointed to her watch. Yes, I nodded, we would return the bicycle by the time she indicated. The last I saw of her, she was surrounded by the men. Later Mama told me that this girl looked surprised when Mira came back with the bicycle. Did she think we would forget? Or that we would not return it? Why did she turn away when someone tried to take her picture?

I wanted to speak to her, but what could I say? Would she want to listen?

Chapter Four
Language Lessons

&

To me it was a miracle—six years after losing our home in Germany and then being uprooted again in Italy, I had lost hope of ever being a student again . . . and one fine day, we were allowed to walk out of the camp as students and trotted off to Oswego High School. I was in an American school, almost like an American every day from 8 A.M. till 3 P.M.

From "My Memories of the Fort Ontario Experience"
Steffi Steinberg Winters, former resident of ERS

ADAM

In our new home, I could sit in three rooms at one time: the kitchen, the living room, and my bedroom. There were two floors with several small apartments in our building, which was once an army barracks. Mama and Mira had the room with the door. I had this three-in-one room. My bed was an army cot. When I stretched my arms out, I touched only the air. Even a shaky table such as we had in Italy was missing from this place. There was no stove or refrigerator, since we ate in a big hall all together.

One night, when Mama and Mira were in the women's shower room, which was located on our floor (the men's was above), I sat cross-legged on my bed and felt the luxury of being alone. Underneath me was a clean American sheet—Mama liked to remind me of this so I should not forget to take off my shoes. Outside our window was a huge, beautiful lake called Lake

Ontario. I wanted to get swim trunks so I could enjoy the lake. I could not use my pants, because I had only two pairs. Maybe that is a good thing, I thought, since there is no closet in this apartment. Instead there was a rack built into the wall. My eyes stretched themselves across the lake. There seemed no end to the water that looked so cool and inviting. I would have to wait. Even if I had swim trunks, I could not swim. None of us could go outside the fence that surrounded us until the Americans were sure that we were not spreading any diseases. No visitors were allowed in, either, except those who worked in the shelter hospital or the mess halls. I decided that when the quarantine was over, Ralph and I would find a rowboat that did not leak. We would jump off the sides and see who could swim the farthest. Then we would catch some good fish.

"I am hungry." Our walls were so thin I could hear our neighbor practicing his English. He continued with the conjugation. "You are hungry. He are hungry."

"He *is* hungry," I said back.

The man tapped on the wall. "I am hungry. You are hungry. He is hungry. Am I hungry? Are you hungry? Are he . . . *Is* he hungry? How is that?"

"Excellent!" I tapped the wall twice.

Silence. He and I, we were thinking about hunger. I am not hungry, I thought, and neither is he. But Grandmama, Papa, and Villi, were they hungry?

CHRIS

I don't know when I stopped talking—or nearly stopped. I didn't want to use a whole lot of words because, if I spoke to Mom and Dad in full sentences, they'd be like Mrs. Dubchek: they'd keep going, and I'd have to use more words, and before I knew it, we'd be having long conversations that were just as boring as the ones I had with the face in my mirror. So I began to communicate with them through one-word answers. *How was work*

56

today? Fine. How are you doing? Fine. How's life in general? That's fine, too. Fine was my favorite word because it can never get you in trouble: it stops people dead in their tracks. Maybe that was why Mom thought something was wrong: I used to have long talks with her. But something was not wrong. We just had different feelings when it came to talking. She thought it was like plastering a wall that has cracks. But sometimes talking's like trying to plaster the sky.

I felt that way right after I saw the boy at the fence. Mom and I were seated in the living room. I was half listening to some stupid radio program and stretching out my legs. She was finishing Dick's sweater, which was red, white, and blue. I knew that Dick would never wear it. Who'd want to look like a walking American flag? Stars and stripes lay across Mom's lap.

Alabama. Arizona. Arkansas. I pointed and flexed my toes, singing to myself. *California. Colorado. Con-nec-ti-cut.* Funny about songs. You could memorize a lot through them, like the names of all the states and the periodic table of elements and how many days there are in each month.

Dad and I were both singing, except he was humming that happy tuneless I'm-working-on-mechanical-things song. He was in the kitchen, and by the sound of his voice, I knew what appliance he had managed to get his hands on.

"I betcha Dad's fooling around with the new toaster," I mentioned to Mom.

"Your father is fixing the dial. It fell off, remember?"

"He probably took it off so he'd have an excuse. He has the whole thing open by now and he's examining every single piece of machinery." I pictured him pulling apart all the toaster's mechanical guts, staring at every nut and bolt. Even the coils weren't safe from his scrutiny.

"Your father likes to see the way things are put together."

"Yeah, but to see the way things are put together, you first have to pull them apart. Dad likes that, too. Even better than putting things together."

"What's wrong, Chris?" The creases on Mom's forehead formed a wobbly triangle.

"Nothing's *wrong*. I'm just singing the states. *Delaware. Florida. Georgia. Idaho*. You finished stars all the way up to Indiana. Or maybe it's Illinois. I've lost my place, so I have to start over."

The humming in the kitchen stopped. There was silence. Then cursing.

"He broke something," I muttered. "Or he can't figure out how to get everything back. The toast will get stuck in there now. We'll have to use a fork to pry it out and we'll all be electrocuted."

"Oh, Chrissy, stop being so melodramatic. He'll figure it out. He always does." Mom wrapped up her knitting.

"He should look closer before he pulls things apart. He never looks close until it's too late. And why didn't he stick to the dial? Nothing else was wrong!"

"Something *is* wrong. With you."

"Something *is not* wrong! I just happen to think the toaster might want to be left alone. Things like being left alone." I stood up, then sat down again. The house felt small and closed up. If I stayed inside, I'd run out of air.

"Chris—" Mom started.

"Mom, it's O.K. I'm just going outside."

"Outside where?"

"SOMEwhere!" I stood up again, this time more purposefully, and walked out.

The following morning I made up my mind not to tell Mom or Dad that I went down to the fort. "That's my secret," I told my mirror face as I held my hair away from my ears and brushed the ends up so it'd look less straight. "And I won't tell them I'm planning to go back."

The face in the mirror looked back at me. *Fine.*

• • •

Mrs. Dubchek's son did see the pope. She read me his letter three times. I don't know if Joey dressed up, though, like Mrs. D. had said he would. She told me that she'd ask him in her next letter. When he answered, she'd let me know. I was certain she would—probably four times—but I didn't care. So much was

58

happening. First, I snuck into the Emergency Refugee Shelter, which, I found out, was the official name for the fort. Most people, though, said "camp." I wasn't sure why. It didn't seem like much of a camp, except lots of people were living together, and it was isolated. The fence made it feel that way. When you went inside, it was like being in the United States and not in at the same time. I can't explain it.

The refugees, who I also found out were mostly Jewish, were under quarantine, so we weren't allowed in yet. But I had to look around. The men wore their jackets over their shoulders—they didn't put their arms inside—and the women's clothes were old and not very attractive.

"Let's dress up like refugees and sneak in," I suggested to Ned.

We went up to Aunt Jenny's attic because Ned's mom is a regular pack rat. I dug out one of her old dresses from a pile of musty clothes, and Ned located a sweater that looked as if a few moths had beaten Ned to it.

The real adventure began one night after supper, not that I ate any. Dad yelled about how I was going to turn into a bean. He had no awareness of all the expansion that was going on—or if he did see things, he wouldn't admit it. That would mean I was growing up. He refused to see that!

"I'm going over to a friend's," I said. (Friend is like fine: it's a nice vague word that covers a lot of ground, including your cousin.) "I'll be back early. I won't ride my bike in the dark and I'm taking a sweater."

Dad opened his mouth and closed it again.

After we dressed up, Ned and I ran down to the bank near the lake. We knew the fort really well. When we were little, we'd go down near the railroad tracks and steal inside the old fort wall, where soldiers lived during the Civil War. Then we'd play we were shooting off guns.

"Ned," I said, "the refugees don't speak English, so when you get across, speak French." I taught Ned some essential French phrases like *Ou est la toilette?* and *oui* and *s'il vous plait.* I figured we'd pretend that somehow we had gotten outside, and we were moving back where we belonged. If a guard came up close, Ned could turn to me and say "yes" or "please" several times. We'd never be questioned.

The guards were stationed along the lake, but we managed to sneak in through a hole that we found under the fence. I don't know why the army didn't fill it, but I was glad. I met a girl named Tikvah, which means "hope" in Hebrew. (She was from Yugoslavia but had a Hebrew name.) Tikvah asked me for a cigarette—at least I think she did. She said something foreign and interesting that sounded like cigarette. I shook my head and stared, and she tried again in another language, then another, until I finally learned she could speak English. We visited her room, which she shared with her mother. It was small and plain, and there wasn't any furniture at all, unless you counted two army cots. (Tikvah said they'd probably get a table and two chairs. People were setting up a camp workshop to build them.) The mattresses were thin, too. And there were no pictures on the wall, other than the photographs the newspaper men had taken of the refugees.

"This man," said Tikvah, drawing me to the wall, "is Mr. Finestein. He is one of my mother's friends. Look here. He holds a magnifying glass and is signing the document we all signed."

"Where did you learn such good English?" I asked.

"Oh, from here and there." She waved her hand carelessly, as if it were nothing.

"Do you know other languages?"

"A few. Let me see. There is Italian, French, German, and, of course, my native Serbo-Croatian. That is fluently. English I speak, as you see. And Russian. A little Spanish. Perhaps a few more. I cannot recall."

"Where did you learn all those?" I felt very ignorant.

"From here and there. You pick up. And you?"

"I know a few languages, too." I smiled weakly. "I didn't learn them from here and there. I learned them at school." I moved closer to the pictures on the wall. If I asked questions about them, maybe she wouldn't pursue the language issue. (I only know French, and not much of that. And Pig Latin, if you count some secret language only American kids speak.)

"Why does Mr. Finestein have a magnifying glass?" I asked.

"His glasses were broken a long time ago. So he uses the magnifying glass from the stamp collection of his son. The reporter does not say that."

"Tikvah, did you actually fight in the resistance?" In front of me was the picture of a beautiful girl in a leather jacket. She was leaning against the camp fence and she stared straight ahead like she wasn't afraid of the camera. She wasn't afraid of anything. Underneath was a caption about how this girl fought with the Partisans.

Tikvah nodded, like fighting in the resistance was no different than those languages you just pick up. "My mother insists to put my picture on the wall. I much prefer the old ones we had in our home. Our walls had many pictures not from magazines."

"What were they of?" I felt full of questions.

"Family." Tikvah held her chin in her hand and stared past me. I didn't say anything. "So," she said, breaking the silence, "the girl in the picture is not bad looking, is she?"

"She's very pretty," I murmured. "Tikvah, are you Jewish?" I don't know why I asked.

"Yes, are you?"

"No." That was all I said. I didn't mention what I am. I don't know why not. "I have to go," I said. I thought of Dad. Of what he said. "Can I come back and visit you again?"

"Certainly." Tikvah smiled. "Then you will tell me what languages you know." The smile stretched itself across her face. "Americans know many languages, and they don't pick up from here and there. They learn at school!"

"You can learn a lot at school," I said defensively. *Did I say that?*

She touched my blouse. "Pretty," she said. Her fingers felt the neckline.

"It's a Peter Pan collar." At least I knew something. Some stupid thing.

"I, too, would like to learn at school," she said wistfully. "I have not been to a school in three years. From here and there is not something I choose."

"I'm sorry." Sorry felt stupid, but I didn't know what else to say.

"It is nothing you should feel sorry for. Come to visit. I am pleased."

"Really?"

"Yes, really."

Do Jews get blessed or absolved? Do they have confession? I wanted to ask Tikvah all these questions because I didn't know anything about Jews, or hardly anything. They don't have Christmas. Their Sabbath is on Saturday and not Sunday. And the men wear little hats on their heads. I thought I had those three facts down, but I wasn't sure. A Jewish kid at school once told me that the hats were only for praying, and not too many men at camp had hats on. But there was one boy who wore something that looked knitted. I bet I could've knitted something like that myself—it wasn't any bigger than a doily. But probably that would've turned into a long snake, too.

I'd ask Tikvah to explain things. Maybe all Jews didn't have the same customs. But what if Tikvah thought I was stupid? When you know nothing, your questions are bound to be stupid. But when you know everything, you don't need to ask.

ADAM

A few days after we arrived, Ralph and I found an abandoned barracks near the main fort. "A place to be private," said Ralph. "Alone. Without family."

"It is good to find a place away from everyone," I answered. "I cannot remember the last time I am sitting somewhere and I am not hearing other people."

"Seeing, too. It is good to be in a place where no one sees you and no one hears you."

"That is true. One needs to hear one's own thoughts."

We sat together in this empty barracks, listening to each other's thoughts.

"Tikvah," said Ralph, unable to keep quiet for long, "that girl is very beautiful. What do you think she would say about such an empty place as this?"

"I would not show it to her just yet."

"You will not show it to her at all." Ralph grabbed my wrist, and we wrestled until he forced my arm down.

"I was not ready," I said, making a show of unconcern. I thought about the buckets filled with water that I used for arm exercises in Italy. There were no buckets here. No long lines, either. I'd have to squeeze under my cot and lift that instead.

"You are never ready, my friend," said Ralph. "Me, I am someone who seizes the opportunity."

"Someone who seizes *loses* the opportunity. I would not show it to her just yet," I repeated.

"All right. Not yet. But she, too, will find it a good place to be private. Alone. Without family. Everyone needs that."

"Yes, but if you show it to her, you will not be alone." I enjoyed teasing Ralph. Usually he was the one who teased me. But a boy in love is easily teased.

"Not entirely alone. Everyone does not want to be entirely alone."

"That is correct. Some people like to be with others. Like the two of us together."

"That is one way of not being alone." Ralph sighed.

I grabbed his wrist. "Come, let us wrestle. Now I am ready."

Ralph put his free hand around the wrist that held his. "And what about you, Adam? Do you also think of being with some girl?"

We listened to our thoughts and our breathing.

"I am glad to know of this place," I admitted. But I wasn't prepared yet to use it.

I needed to learn how one behaves with a girl. All the rules

63

I knew were for ways to act when you were surrounded by an enemy. A girl is not the enemy. Ralph did not know, either. He would put his fingers to his lips as the Italians do and kiss the air, but he did not fool me. He, too, knew only of how to survive. I decided I would ask an American boy. Someone who had the time not only to think and to look but to do. I had met a few American boys who lived across the street. Several of us had found a hole under the fence and introduced ourselves to the Americans. We did not talk about girls, though. Only baseball. When I played again, I would have to ask. But what if I appeared ignorant? When you do not know, you are appearing very ignorant. If only Villi were here, I thought. I would have asked him. No, I would not, because Villi would never have let me forget my foolish questions. I would have asked Papa. Of course, then *I* would never have been able to forget my foolish questions.

Perhaps it is best to only play baseball. Baseball is an easy language. You do not need to say a thing.

CHRIS

I began thinking about walking into a Jewish church. I'd do it just once and I'd wear my cross under my blouse—I didn't want God to get confused. I *was* Catholic. I wondered if Jews knelt at all. I knew Baptists didn't. I'd never been to a Baptist service. I wasn't allowed to go to any church that wasn't Catholic, but a Baptist kid once told me that knees didn't go down at her house of worship unless people were called to the altar. I'd have to find out what to do in a Jewish service.

I thought I'd like to visit all kinds of churches—just to see what they were like. My father has never stepped into a Jewish church. Or a Baptist church. Dad has to see a saint's name on the sign outside, like St. Mary's or St. Augustine's or St. Cecilia's, before he'd bring his feet into the vestibule. He hates things that are different and he always has to know what he's doing. Doing something different is confusing for Dad, and my dad doesn't like confusion. Confusion disturbs your ability to think.

I thought about visiting churches and about my dad. I could picture his world. It's like one of those fresh black walnuts—the kind that falls from the trees near our house every autumn. The outside layer is soft and green and stains your hands, but you keep peeling because you think you'll reach the meat inside. Instead, there's a hard shell underneath all that softness. No matter how much you try cracking the shell open with your shoes, it won't break. Dad likes to sit inside all that hardness. That way, everything stays solid. But my world has never been like that. It's a bubble whose shape keeps changing. I was inside all of that—inside and outside at the same time, especially when I dreamed about things like walking into a Jewish service.

I'd go to the one that the boy at camp went to and I'd look around. I'd do it so no one was aware I was looking. When I spotted him, I'd stroll over. Of course, there'd be an empty seat on his left side. I'd enter on the right. "Do you mind," I'd say breathlessly as I moved in front of his legs. He'd shake his head and pull his knees back. He'd be just a little late about it so I'd lose my balance. He'd have to steady me.

"Are you all right?" he'd ask.

"Yes, I'm fine," I'd answer. But it wouldn't sound like the fine I said to Mom and Dad. This fine would be like a door you open a crack at night because you need to see the hall light.

I'd sit. Next to him. We wouldn't look at each other. We'd look at our prayer books, but we'd be seeing each other in our minds.

• • •

Dad and I switched places. Just like that, one night, I became the official paper reader at the dinner table. When I saw the story, I knew I had to switch. I'd heard so many rumors, and the refugees had only been in Oswego a few weeks. One person said that they were doing the town good. Look how many shoes they needed. The government was giving them a small allowance so they could keep buying at our stores. That helped business. Another said that they should be allowed to work. They had to feel wanted and useful. The German prisoners of war were working, and they weren't behind barbed wire. What did the refugees do to be treated like prisoners? Still another said, "Make one camp, and you invite trouble. The entire USA will be a camp soon, filled with refugees." Another answered that remark by saying, "But this country was built by refugees!" It got so bad a Subcommittee on Rumors and Stories was created to address questions. The results were editorialized in our paper. I hoped it'd stop Dad and some of my relatives from making nasty remarks.

Right after dinner, I whipped out the paper. "This is what today's editorial says," I began.

"Fiction: (I read the fiction part in a stupid, silly voice, just in case Dad wasn't choosing to listen.) The refugees have all the cigarettes they want, while the Oswego people cannot buy.

"Fact: (said with authority) Only thirty-seven cartons have been donated by national relief agencies.

"Fiction: The ice cream supply is limited because of refugee demands.

"Fact: No ice cream is served in dining halls.

"Fiction: Turkey dinner was served.

"Fact: It was lamb stew."

Dad and Mom were absolutely silent. "Well, that clears things up," Dad finally said.

I snorted—quietly.

Dad has never ever doubted newsprint or what's written in books. He has never needed to see faces to know the truth about things. He didn't need to hear stories, either. I was different.

The Americans make the best lists. Not only that, but they love to spend their time constructing lists. Before they do something, they write a list, and the list gives them a sense of accomplishment. After I came to America, I began seeing this. How excellent! I thought. To feel as if you have done something even before you begin with the doing. I must learn the art of list-making. So I wrote my first list. It appeared like this:

I am Adam Bornstein. That is my given name.

I am a boy. A male. Son of Manya and Max Bornstein. I have a sister and a brother and a grandmother and many relatives besides my mother and father. These are my family. I do not know where everyone is.

I am a citizen of Yugoslavia, belonging to the region of Croatia. That is my nationality. I am also a guest of the United States.

I am Jewish. That is my religion.

I am a resident of Fort Ontario Emergency Refugee Shelter. That is my temporary address. I do not have a permanent address.

I am a refugee. One who seeks refuge or shelter. I do not like that new word. Refugee. I would like to be an American and have a permanent home with an address and a post box of its own. Not House #179, Building 17.

I looked at my list. This says who you are, not what you are about to do, I thought. It cannot be the excellent American list. Moreover, the Americans gain great satisfaction when they cross out from their list all the things that they have done. Just to draw a line across items that have been dealt with makes the American feel as if he is doing that thing a second time. In fact, if I made a count, the list-making Americans receive a pleasure three times for what is done once: first in the writing, then in the doing, then in the crossing out. I have this written list, I thought, continuing to stare at my poor specimen. Not only is it the wrong kind of list, but there can be no pleasure either from the doing or the crossing out, and the writing itself gives me no pleasure.

I tore up my list and threw it away. What did all that writing and doing and crossing out matter? It was how I lived that counted. I would have lived in a tent if I could have been free.

Chapter Five
Confessions

⁂

My father said, "I don't want you going anywhere near the Fort, because there's federal guards and they're under quarantine." I didn't usually disobey, I just had to go in.
Geraldine Rossiter, Oswegonian

CHRIS

I wasn't just doing things I hadn't done before in real life, like switching places with Dad at the table and reading the newspaper and going to the fort. At night in my dreams I was being different, too. I felt that way after the funny dream I had one night.

I was running, and men were chasing me. They had high boots and guns, like the men I'd seen in newsreels, and they were leading fierce-looking German shepherds with muzzles across their mouths.

I ran and ran until I was out of breath. Someone ran with me. He looked like the boy at the fence. But his shirt was torn, and there were scars all over his chest. My feet hurt from running—I didn't have shoes—and I was screaming. I heard myself, which is even stranger, because all my dreams are silent, or at least I don't remember talking.

"We have to get to America," I screamed. "We have to get to America."

I don't know how long I shouted like that. My throat felt terrible. Someone was holding me and throwing me inside a high fence. "Get in, Jew," he yelled. He took a stick and poked me in the arm where I was wearing a yellow star. I don't know how that got there, either.

"I'm not Jewish," I said. "I'm Catholic. My name's Christine Cook, except I don't like Christine. I like people to call me Chris."

"Christy Jew girl," said the soldier, jeering and poking. My arm hurt.

"Not Christy. Christy sounds like Sissy." (I was being very stupid in my dream. I'm always stupid in my dreams. I've tried to change it, but I can't.)

There were people all around me, sad-looking people with newspaper around their feet and rags that hung from their bodies like clothes on metal hangers. Everybody was so thin. They all spoke a strange language—at least at first it seemed strange, until I figured out they were speaking Pig Latin, which was even stranger. I didn't know where I was, except that across from the fence were houses that were exactly like the ones across from the fort.

"I ave-hay oo-tay et-gay oo-tay merica-Aay," I said, slowly and carefully. You could tell I hadn't spoken Pig Latin for a while. "I have to get to America!" I repeated (still in Pig Latin).

This black-haired boy who'd been running alongside me earlier said, "Everyone here is a refugee." (Finally somebody was talking in English. He spoke with a beautiful accent.) "We are all refugees. So we stay right here. Behind the fence."

"I'm not a refugee. I'm American. I'm Catholic, too. I don't belong behind a fence."

The boy held my face in his hands. He had strong, rough hands. "Nobody belongs behind a fence." His fingers tickled my cheek. And he kissed me. A long kiss, like in the movies. I was kissing back.

Then I woke up. I didn't want to wake up at that part. But I didn't want to be in such a crazy, mixed-up dream, either, and I thought that if I had come all the way from Europe, from some camp behind some fence, how would I feel behind a fence in America. This was supposed to be a free country.

"This is an army camp," Mom had said. "The fence belongs here for the army. It's always been here. They're not going to change that."

But it wasn't for the army now. It was to hold the refugees in.

• • •

Usually I'd go to Saturday confession. I'd say "Bless me, Father, for I have sinned." Then I'd trot out my offenses: "I had nasty thoughts about some girl," or "I talked back to Mom and Dad," or "I missed church last week," or "I took twenty cents that dropped out of Dad's pants pockets and I didn't give the money back because I pretended it was found money." Then at Sunday Mass I'd go to communion with Mom and Dad and feel good for the whole week. But the day after I had that funny dream, confession was all wrong. It went as I planned, like always, but it didn't feel right, not even from the very beginning.

My knees felt nice and comfortable and at home on the old, familiar kneeler. My eyes felt comfortable, too, staring at the screen the way they always did. My soul felt good. It got itself ready to be penitent, and my mind prepared itself to go blank. (I liked to make my mind blank when I was in confession. I didn't want to think of anything except the sins I was going to confess. Before, when I hadn't tried for blankness, I'd find my mind wandering off while I was waiting. Suddenly I'd be thinking all these new sinful thoughts: Does Father Walters always starve himself before Mass like we do? Or does he sometimes sneak in a Host or two?)

I stared at the screen while my mind went blank. My knees felt penitent—they began to suffer from the kneeling because the person before me was taking extra long. Then that funny nightmarish dream filled up the place in my mind that was supposed to stay blank. Me being thrown into the camp. That boy. His hair. His fingers touching my cheek. Him leaning into me. That long kiss.

I felt sick.

What if the person before me had some mortal sin to confess? Or maybe that person had fifteen brothers and sisters to talk about. That could account for a lot of minor sins. I'd be here forever imagining that boy and me. Our being together. His lips and mine.

I wanted to cry.

"Bless me, Father, for I have sinned." I mouthed the words silently. "I yelled at my mom four, no, five times." All those sins that were ready to be heard flew out of my soul so all I had left were thoughts of that kiss. Him kissing me. Me kissing back. But it was only a dream! Lots of girls I knew had their share of kisses in real life and not only in dreams. They didn't go confessing it. Maybe, though, they didn't kiss with their tongues. They held their closed mouths steady while they lifted their chins. In the dream I must've had my mouth open, because I felt a tongue, and it wasn't mine. There were two tongues involved, mixing together in a very disgusting way.

My soul felt disgusted with itself. It wasn't clean and pure and white. Somebody had stuck it in with the colored wash, and now my soul was a shade of gray. I hate white when it gets gray. It looks so dingy. You don't want to wear a dingy gray shirt that is supposed to be white.

I couldn't call up one small sin. Not even one. If I'd had brothers or sisters, I'd never have been at a loss. Ann always relied on the tons of fights she had with her brother and sisters. I had to depend on what I was doing at school or against my parents. And in the summer it got worse. A person can't go to confession in August and talk about a joke she played on some teacher or another way back in May. "Father Walters, this terrible sin has been festering in my soul. Three months ago I took part in a joke on our substitute teacher. At 1:30 me and Ann and a whole lot of other kids all dropped our history books on the floor. *Wham!* Then we all stood up and slapped them on our desks." Father Walters is not stupid. He knows nobody thinks of a school sin in August, unless they're going to summer school.

Father Walters slid back the little black door between us. He had his light on inside, and I saw his shadow behind the screen. "Bless me, Father, for I have sinned," I said in my usual way. "My last confession was last Saturday. And since then I have . . ."

My tongue wrapped itself in knots. A pile of words formed inside my mouth. I wanted to say that I'd gone to the refugee camp against my father's order. I saw this boy there, too, who is so handsome. He's not of our faith, Father. He's Jewish. But he's very handsome. And I had a dream, Father, about kissing him, which I shouldn't like, but I did. At least in the dream I did. And I was Jewish in my dream, Father. I've never been Jewish in my dreams, at least I don't think so. I've been a boy many times. One time I was my best friend Ann. I was going to get roasted on a fire. I never told Ann that dream. And once I was a chicken, flapping my wings around. I was going to have my head chopped off. And I've fallen and nearly gotten killed, and I've flown once. I flew above my house. It seemed so small from the air. But I've always been Catholic in my dreams. At least I think so. I never asked myself. I just figured that I was.

There was silence on the other end. A waiting silence. Ask him about the Host, a voice inside of me said. I coughed, clearing my throat. "I yelled at my mother five, no, six times this week," I said, squeaking. "And I disobeyed my father twice. Once I didn't pick up something he asked me to pick up." I stopped. "And the second time I didn't pick up something else." Moron, I thought. I am a moron!

"For your penance," said Father Walters, "you will say three Our Fathers and three Hail Marys." His voice sounded sad, like he knew there was something more, and I almost said it then. But I didn't.

Father Walters mumbled out his absolution while I tried to make myself contrite so I could say the Act of Contrition.

When I said it, though, I felt like I was singing some stupid radio ad I'd heard a hundred million times. None of the words made sense. Rushing over them didn't help.

OMyGod,IamheartilysorryforhavingoffendedThee(gasp), and IdetestallmysinsbecauseofThyjustpunishments,butmostofall (sigh) becausetheyoffendThee,myGod,whoartallgoodand deservingofallmylove (sigh). Ifirmlyresolve,withthehelpof Thygrace,tosinnomore (more gasping) antoavoidthenear occasionsofsin (more sighing).

But avoiding near occasions is so hard, I thought. When do you know when some near occasion is going to turn into an occasion?

I knew I was fooling myself. I stumbled home.

The next day at church, when I was kneeling behind the communion rail, I didn't look up at Father Walters. I opened my mouth to take the Host and stuck out my tongue. Then I closed my eyes and prepared myself for Christ's body. I know Our Lord can't be mad at me, I said to myself as the Host lay on my tongue, feeling light and airy. Only new souls are absolutely white. Like shirts that haven't been worn at all. Like white snow before it's walked on. It's so beautiful. But it's not fun! Fun is running on the new snow. Fun is taking a new white blouse out of its box and putting it on. It's . . . My lips shut over my tongue.

I wanted to kiss him. Just once.

ADAM

Even before the quarantine ended, Ralph, Tikvah, and I had made plans for what we would do when we could leave the shelter. We wanted to see the shops, the American supermarkets, and restaurants where you could sit down on soft chairs and choose your own food from a very long menu. We wanted to eat ice cream. Ralph said that there is an art to eating the American ice cream cone. I wished for someone to show me. Someone other than Ralph.

But most importantly, we all wanted to see an American school. We would stand in front of it and we would imagine ourselves walking through the door. We would be carrying books that we were allowed to read, and no one would stop us from learning.

And then, to my amazement, after the quarantine was lifted, we found out that we were permitted to attend school. A most wonderful gentleman who was the head of Oswego High School came to our fort and asked us questions. By how we answered, he placed us in classes. I should have been a third-year high school student, or as the Americans say, a junior, but my English was not good enough.

"What if they put us with young children?" I asked Ralph. Everyone at the fort was behind.

"So what!" he said. "I would sit with a baby to be in school again."

There was an added benefit to all of this. Because of our school attendance, we got to leave the fort. Each of us had a pass. In the morning we showed it to the guards, then walked up East Ninth Street to East Bridge. We walked along Bridge Street over the Oswego River until we reached West Bridge, where we walked many blocks to Hillside and up to Oswego Senior High School, which was on West First Street. Ralph and I memorized the route. In our minds we had walked all over the city. In my mind, that first walking day, I also saw Villi beside me. He was taking long steps so I had to run to catch up, and he complained very loudly since he had to accompany his younger brother to school. In my mind I wasn't listening. I held his hand and walked with my chin up and my shoulders back.

And right before I entered the school, I thought of the month and the day: 7 September. Soon it would be Villi's birthday. I always remembered his birthday. He always forgot mine.

When school started, I had to pinch myself to make sure I wasn't dreaming. In homeroom I was supposed to sit near him! If the first two letters of my last name had been Br instead of Co, I'd have actually sat right behind him, but instead Jack Bruener did. Bruener behind Bornstein. I found out that was his name, Adam Bornstein. I like the name Adam. It's direct and strong, like Chris. I wished he hadn't heard the teacher call me Christine. I didn't want him to call me that.

What if he doesn't call me anything? I wondered. What if he won't talk to me?

I began to panic. I considered dropping my pencil. He was right across from me and could pick it up. But what if he didn't? What if he knew I was playing a trick? It was such an old trick, and stupid, too. I didn't want him to think I was stupid.

If only it had been me behind him instead of Jack Bruener. Then he would've had to turn his head around to see me, and I'd have known that he was really trying to look at me. Sitting next to me, he could glance around and take in everything, including me, and still appear not to be looking. He did look at me once. I was sure of that.

I decided I was glad not to be behind him. If I'd been behind him, I wouldn't have seen anything except his neck. Next to him, I could see his whole face.

But he could see mine, too! I wanted to be behind him again. Way far behind him. I hated being looked at.

Then I thought, What if he doesn't look at me? What if he doesn't look this way all day long?

I needed to get back to work. I had one more problem to finish for fifth-period math. At least I thought math was fifth period. It was hard keeping track. My mind hadn't adjusted to school yet. Maybe it'd never adjust. On the first day I had walked into what I thought was math class. What an idiot I was. Everyone was saying, *"Je suis, tu es, il est, elle est,"* and I blurted out, "Is this Algebra II?" Everyone giggled. Sure, Chris, that's what they do in algebra. They conjugate the verb "to be."

I tried concentrating on the problem. It was the hardest one in the whole assignment. What is the efficiency of a machine if a force of 4 lbs. moves 3 ft. to raise a resistance of 5 lbs. 2 ft.? I multiplied 5 times 2 and divided that by 4 times 3, which gave me 83.33$1/3$%. But what exactly happened? I started to draw the problem out, then saw he was looking my way. I was sure he was looking! And he knew that I knew, because he was smiling. And then I wished my last name began with Z so I would've been in the very back of the room.

His hair was even blacker than I'd thought, and he had freckles, too. They were very cute. They didn't cover his whole face but were only on his nose and cheeks. I loved his hair! And his freckles! And his voice! I was not sure how I felt about his smile, especially when it was directed at me, but I loved his stories, too. Except they weren't stories; they were real things that happened to him.

Already he had told us what it was like when he came to America. It was so beautiful and sad, all at the same time. He made me see things that I hadn't seen or heard, like colors. When he saw the Statue of Liberty for the first time and all the activity around New York's harbor, he felt it was like a carnival of colors. Sounds were different, too.

"How different?" I asked. (We got to ask him questions.)

He looked straight at me. "They were peace sounds instead of war sounds," he said. "The cars that go *honk honk* and not the *boom boom* of bombs."

I looked back at him. We both smiled.

Someone else asked him about colors, and he talked about our Green's Five and Dime. I never thought of color in a variety store. Even toys can seem full of color. Even eyes. Inside his eyes was so much color. They were totally alive, green eyes with bits of gold scattered all around the irises.

I wondered if he remembered some girl passing a bike over

the fence. Maybe he thought I was stupid to climb up on a boy's shoulders. Maybe he'd seen under my dress—I was wearing a dress that day. Maybe he'd seen me in camp with Tikvah and knew her new boyfriend, Ralph. Did he have a girlfriend? And what did he dream about? I decided I'd never tell him about that dream I'd had.

Maybe, I thought, I should ask to change my seat so I'd be sitting right in front of him. Then he'd see my neck, and I wouldn't see him at all. But I couldn't stand the thought of him staring at my neck. And I wouldn't see his face.

I loved looking at his face.

ADAM

The first English assignment I wrote out—practice with prepositions—looked liked this:

September 28, 1944
Adam Bornstein
English 1
Oswego High School

(1) I shall go to school <u>in</u> Oswego five times a week.
(2) I put my handkerchief <u>into</u> my coat pocket.
(3) I put my pencil <u>into</u> my little box where my other school things are.
(4) Here <u>in</u> the lake Ontario are many big and little fish.
(5) My pen is <u>on</u> my desk.
(6) My lips are <u>on</u> her lips.

I erased number six. Still, it was nice to write. It was nice to look at the writing and imagine.

I made it a regular thing to visit the fort. I was learning so much about different countries and customs that I felt I was in a whole new world there. And I didn't need a boat to take me across. When I started getting mad at myself for all the sinful thoughts, I made a resolution. I would not feel guilty and I would not confess them to Father Walters, either.

I heard lots of sad stories that I wouldn't have believed if I'd only read about them. I mean, maybe I'd have believed them, but I wouldn't have *felt* them. When somebody sits right across from you and tells you something, you can't ignore it. You can't close the book and just walk away.

It was hard for me to understand how people could be so cruel. How could they treat another human being like he wasn't human? When I heard these stories, I wanted to cry and scream at the same time. All these horrible things were going on in the world, and hardly anybody knew about them. Even right here. There were people who lived a few blocks away, and they had no awareness of the camp. People can be ostriches. Real ostriches!

But maybe I was an ostrich, too. When Tikvah told me about how she was raped, I was so shocked. I couldn't imagine anything like that happening, but things like that do happen— all over the world. She said it like she was telling me what she ate for breakfast. Toast. Bacon. Eggs over easy. Or like it was some order she was reading off a menu. Or she was reciting some passage from a book that she had read a dozen times, so she knew the ending. It gave me the creeps.

We were in the Social Hall—Tikvah and I, a girl named Esther from Poland, and Ralph. Tikvah had a whole stack of letters with her. Every day she'd receive love letters from servicemen because of her picture in the magazine. I think she was also trying to make Ralph jealous. She and Esther and I were laughing. One guy wrote this very funny letter about how he'd take the next plane to her side if she'd marry him. He'd get immediate leave. He had sent Tikvah his picture.

"He's sort of cute," I said, "But his right eye shifts off to the left." That made us laugh even harder.

Then she told me in that flat reading voice of hers about how she was pinned down and raped. She looked at Ralph when she spoke. Ralph always joked around, but he didn't say a thing. It was like he'd heard the story, too, but he had to hear it again, and she had to tell it.

How can I be worried about underwear when some people are just trying to survive? How can I think about boys and the shape of the world and if I'm growing enough or too much? That is all very stupid, particularly when people are being raped and murdered and we stand around doing almost nothing!

"Hitler is going to burn in red hot flames," I told Tikvah. "His tortured spirit will cry out for mercy, but there won't be any. He'll burn for eternity, which is forever and ever."

"The afterlife does not concern me," she said. "What is happening this very minute is my concern."

"Oh," I said, looking down at the picture of the guy with his shifting eye. "Oh."

•　•　•

In late September Aunt Nell, Mom, and I made up Christmas presents for Bob and Dick. Mrs. Dubchek joined us. She rang the doorbell, and I answered.

"How are you, Christine?" she asked, panting.

"O.K., I guess." I was being my usual talkative self.

"Good. Good. Is your mother in?" Her tongue moved across her thick, cracked lips while she caught her breath.

"Do you want me to get her?" What a stupid question! Why else was she standing here? I stood behind the screen door, wondering if I should open it or not. Everything felt so strange. Mrs. D. had never stepped into our house. All her life, or at least all of mine, she had sat on her porch rocker and helped God watch out for our block. I'd never thought she could do it from anywhere else, or that she wanted to be anywhere else, unless it was *in* her house.

"Is she busy? I don't want to disturb her if she's busy."

"That's O.K. We're just wrapping Christmas presents. Aunt Nell's with us, but we're not really busy." I held the screen open. "Do you want to come in?"

"I shouldn't disturb you. Your mother's a busy woman."

We were going nowhere fast. "Mo-om!" I yelled. I opened our storm door wider.

"Nell is your mother's sister, isn't she, Christine? The one with two boys in the service." Perspiration beaded up on her forehead while she clung to the screen.

"Uh-huh." From the kitchen came the sound of Aunt Nell's horsey laughter. Mom's laugh slipped in between the whinnies. A Japanese beetle buzzed loudly, flying by us into the living room.

"Stupid beetles," said Mrs. Dubchek. "They're destroying my roses. They make huge holes. They are also very ugly."

"I hate them, too. So does Mom." We were definitely on our way to the most idiotic conversation of all time. "Mo-om, Mrs. Dubchek's here," I yelled even louder.

"I better go." Mrs. Dubchek shut the screen, but she still grasped the knob.

"Who is it?" asked Mom, yelling from the back room.

Finally. "It's Mrs. Dubchek."

There was a pause. Mom must've been as surprised as I was. "Tell her to come in, Chris. Don't make her stand at the door."

"I did, but she thinks you're busy." A fly followed the beetle. Soon we'd have a regular picnic right inside our living room.

"Are you busy, Joan?" yelled Mrs. D.

"Hello, Bea," said Mom, holding the older woman's arm. "Come in. I don't know where my daughter gets her manners."

"I told her—" Oh, why bother explaining.

"We're getting Christmas presents ready to mail off to the boys," said Mom. "Come on in."

"I have a present for Joey, too. He's . . ." Mrs. Dubchek's tongue licked her lips again. "I don't know where he is, Joan. I haven't heard from him. That's not like Joey. He's a good son. He always writes."

We bunched ourselves around the screen door while the flies set up shop in our living room.

"Christine," said Mom. "Go help our neighbor get her present and bring it back. We'll wrap together."

Slowly Mrs. Dubchek and I walked back to her porch. Midway there she grabbed my elbow. I didn't mind, as long as she didn't think I was Florence Nightingale. Besides, I wanted to see her house. I'd never been inside.

It smelled musty and old but not bad. Everything seemed to know its place and was comfortable there. There was an old clock on her mantel with pictures of Joey and his wife and son beside it. Some knitted pillow cases were on a wide sofa that looked like one you'd want to bury yourself in. The sofa and pillow cases were orange and brown. So was a lot of stuff, like a braided rug that was handmade. I could tell. Mrs. D. was like Mom. Her needles told her secrets, too.

"Sit, Christine," said Mrs. Dubchek.

I sat, listening to the radio while she retreated to the kitchen. I betcha she keeps it on all the time, I thought. The house smelled lonely.

"I'm ready," she said, cheerfully panting away. We were going on a grand adventure. Maybe coming to our house was a grand adventure for her.

We crossed the continent from her house to mine. When we were halfway there, she yelled, "Hello, Mr. Richards!" She nodded at the other porch sitter across the street, clutched my arm tighter, and held back her shoulders. Mr. Richards stared straight ahead. "He's jealous," whispered Mrs. Dubchek, smiling like she'd just won some great prize, and that was me.

We all sat in the living room near the window. Mrs. Dubchek, Mom, and my aunt Nell, busily wrapping Christmas presents. It felt weird and good at the same time. I had to remind myself it was only September.

"We wish you a merry Christmas," I hummed. The others

hummed along. Every once in a while one of us stopped to swat a fly. Mrs. Dubchek also swatted—and killed—the Japanese beetle. We laid the gifts down on the paper: Mom's sweater for Dick, Aunt Nell's sweater for Bob, my socks for them both, and Mrs. Dubchek's gloves for Joey plus some linen handkerchiefs, because maybe he'd be stuck in a foxhole with his nose running.

Later we walked to the post office. None of us said much. My oxfords made clumping sounds. *Clickety-click* went Aunt Nell's heels. Mrs. D.'s slippers were silent. A block away from the post office, a Western Union man got off his bike. He approached a house that had one blue star in the window. Blue for the boys still fighting. Silver for the wounded. Gold for the ones who died.

"Her only son," said Aunt Nell hoarsely. She pulled her coat tightly around her packages.

"She might have younger boys," said Mom, like that was really going to console Aunt Nell.

"She might have lots of girls, too," I added.

Aunt Nell ignored us both. "Now she's a Gold-Star Mother."

Mrs. Dubchek slipped her arm through Aunt Nell's. "God is looking out," she said, casting her eyes up to the sky.

I ran ahead. If I moved, I wouldn't think. Did God look out when some strange, horrible man held Tikvah down, and she had to take it or be killed? Or when that girl Esther's dad was taken away from her? I couldn't figure it out. And all day long I felt sad.

The newspaper didn't make me feel any better. "Christmas may find them in Berlin or Tokyo this year. Mail Packages Early. Santa Claus is boarding ship early to make sure your service man or woman overseas is not disappointed this year."

What if Bob was in Berlin and Dick was in Tokyo? What if by the time Christmas came, Bob was in Tokyo and Dick was in Berlin? And they got the wrong presents? What if they were both somewhere we didn't know about at all? And they never came home?

Before bedtime I walked up Bridge Street toward the normal school and the lake. The trees lining the center of the road were still green. Soon they'd be bright red and orange. I longed for change.

• • •

The next night I stayed at the camp past ten. Visitors weren't allowed to be there so late unless some concert or play was going on—the refugees had begun putting on all kinds of camp performances. They had so many talented musicians and actors and singers. They even had their own newspaper. No event was going on that evening, though, to excuse my lateness. I was just having so much fun talking to all my new friends that I lost track of time. Then, suddenly, I knew it was late. I ran from tree to tree until I got to the bank, but I couldn't find the hole. I crawled along until finally I found it. The drama wasn't over yet. Right before I got home, I realized that I had to figure out what to tell Mom and Dad. I slipped inside and hurried to the stairs. Maybe I could make it to my room, and I wouldn't have to say a thing.

"Where have you been?" asked Dad, catching me halfway up the steps. He was in the living room, glued to the radio—as usual.

"At Ann's." I was trying to think fast.

"Your mother called Ann's mother. You were not there."

"What time did Mom call?"

"Around nine, which is already long past the normal time for children to be home with their family."

I'm not a child, I almost answered, then thought better of it. "I left around eight-thirty," I said.

"Do you know what time it is now?"

"No." The wheels in my brain began turning.

"It's ten-thirty." Dad looked at me, waiting.

"Is it?" My voice sounded so small and quiet. I knew I had a foolish grin on my face. I stared at my hand on the bannister listening to the wheels that were turning so fast my head felt hot.

"Eight-thirty to ten-thirty is two hours, Christine."

"I know." My voice got even smaller and quieter. I breathed deeply. "I went to another friend's because we're having a test tomorrow. Then I just walked around because walking makes me remember everything I've learned." Any minute now the racing wheels would make a fire break out in my head.

"You walked alone in the dark at this time of night?" Dad looked at me strangely. "And since when are you so interested in schoolwork?"

"I want to do better this year." I coughed. I knew he didn't believe me, but for some reason he didn't ask any more questions.

"I hope your report card reflects all those good intentions. In the meantime get home early, and always let us know where you are. You hear?"

I nodded, racing up the stairs.

I hadn't wanted to lie. I hate lying. It was just . . . I really was learning—a lot.

Chapter Six
I Am Living Now

&

There was no future to look at. The past was gone. Maybe we had to go back. Maybe not. If a kid asked, "What are you going to do after school?" we couldn't answer. We just . . . we had a great time. All of a sudden you could open up and be a kid again.

David Hendell,
former resident of ERS

CHRIS

November 4, 1944. I will remember this date forever. We finally met—officially met—and everything was perfect. Like a romance. Like in the movies. Ann's mom set it up. She felt sorry because the kids at the camp were living in such bare houses that were not really homes. Everybody had a table and a few chairs that they had made in the camp workshop, but there wasn't much else except for the cots and hot plates people got so they didn't always have to walk outside and sit down with a lot of other families for their meals. All of that plus tacked-up magazine pictures and clothes lines strung between buildings doesn't make a place feel like home. Ann's mom wanted my friends to see another America.

Right after school, I went into the camp while Mrs. Baldwin waited in her car outside the fence. I showed my visitor's pass. I think the guards recognized me, because I hardly held it up and they were waving me in. I wondered if they'd seen me that time I stayed past ten.

"Do you know Adam?" asked Tikvah when I met her in her barracks.

"Yes," I said nonchalantly. "Why?"

"He wishes to come with Ralph and me. Your friend's mother will be angry?"

"No, she said I could invite whoever I wanted to."

"Is Adam someone you wish to invite?"

"He sounds fine." I couldn't believe how flippant I sounded.

"Good, because we are meeting him on the field."

Tikvah and I walked to the Parade Ground where the army used to do maneuvers. The wind blew under my coat and attacked all those places that weren't covered enough. At least I had a warm coat. Tikvah's hands were crammed in her pockets, and the top of her exposed wrists were red. Probably some charity had given her the coat. It was too small and babyish.

"Cold," said Tikvah, pressing her chin against the collar.

"Winter's are very cold here," I said, "especially near the lake."

"Yes, some are wearing their coats inside the mess halls. Their hats, too. I do not mind. I am used to such weather. But those who have been in Italy some years, their blood is thin."

Ralph and Adam walked over. I knew which one was Adam even from a distance. He walked on the balls of his feet, and his step was springy and light. Some boys walk like that—not at all deliberate, but as if life were full of bounce. I loved that walk. It made me want to laugh.

"Hello," said Adam. "Fine weather." Snowflakes fell on his hair. I thought of black licorice and vanilla ice cream and was suddenly hungry.

"Adam, this is Chris," said Tikvah. "She says that she knows you."

My face felt hot and cold at the same time. "I remembered you from class," I said, looking sideways at Adam. "You were with us in September."

"Yes, they moved me up a year. In the beginning they put me back because I am new. That is how I get to be with you. How is your class?" He sounded genuinely interested.

"O.K., I guess. It's better than being a freshman." I didn't say how much I missed seeing his face. In his place was some pimply kid who had a mole on his face. A long hair stuck right out of the mole. I kept wishing he would cut it off. "Do you like your teachers?" (I can't believe I asked that. Who cares?)

"Yes, but I was liking your class, also. You were beside me. I was thinking that is nice because . . ." He blushed, or maybe it was the cold. His skin seemed very fair. I wondered if it burned easily in the summer. Next summer we'd sit next to each other on the beach, and I'd watch his face. I wouldn't let it burn.

"Because why?" I asked, my voice barely audible. Was I really teasing him?

"Because . . ."

"Well, now," Tikvah pushed through our embarrassed silence, "since everyone knows everyone, let us go."

We ran away from the row of barracks. The snow wasn't deep enough yet to wear boots. We slid as if we were ice skating, making long trails behind us.

"We should be careful," I said, glancing over my shoulder. "The guards will see."

"If they will see, they will pretend not to," said Adam. "They do not care with us. Only the parents."

"Better not to test them," said Tikvah. "If they pretend not to see, then we pretend we are sneaking."

We found the hole and rolled under it. Outside was the car. We jumped in.

"Just a minute," I said, "I have to cover our tracks." I got out.

"I will cover, too." Adam stood next to me.

"This is how they do it in the movies." I moved backward from the car to the fence and spread snow over the tracks with my hands.

"I will make it look as if no one has walked here." Walking backward, too, Adam bent over and swirled the snow around.

We looked at each other. We both realized the same thing at

the same time: if we walked forward again, we'd have new tracks.

"This is what we do," demonstrated Adam. "We walk with our backs to the car. As we step backward, we brush the snow like so."

Together we moved in a funny backward way, brushing our footprints quickly. Adam moved much quicker than I did. I jumped back and nearly fell into him. I wish I had, but you can't plan things like that. Besides, I wasn't helpless. I'd only wanted to feel his arms.

Ann's mom drove us to a very fancy restaurant in Rochester, a place that didn't just sell coneys. There was a band playing. And a white tablecloth on our table. And two forks, one for the salad and one for the main meal.

Adam and I danced, and the band played.

Do you know the other name for Bull Run? something inside my mind said, then answered, Why, it's Manassas.

ADAM

"We are waiting for our life to begin," said Mama.

"What are we doing now then?" I asked. "Are we not living?"

Mama made her fingers into a comb that untangled the knots in my hair. Mama's fingers rejoiced in the untangling of knots. "We are waiting for our *new* life."

"How can the life I am living now not be a *new* life? It has never happened before."

"You have good friends here, don't you, Adam?" Mama's fingers rested on my neck.

I shook myself free from her touch, my mind commencing its list-making. Ralph. Tikvah. The American girl, Chris. *My lips are on her lips. My tongue is in* . . . I sighed.

"Be careful." Mama tapped my shoulder so as to remind me

89

of her presence. "You are a boy. You must take responsibility and be respectful. You are a handsome boy, also, which means the girls will like you."

Rain pelted the windows, which seemed defenseless under such a hard attack. They rattled fearfully. Mama held my shoulders, first grasping and then petting them as one would a cat or some small child, not someone as old as I was.

"Adam," she said softly, "your father should be here to talk to you. I do not know from boys, and you do not tell me."

"I tell you."

"You tell me! What are you telling me?"

"What you are needing to know."

"I see." Mama patted the shoulder more. "Adam, listen, do not get too attached. Especially not to a girl. When we leave here, you will both be unhappy, and we *will* leave, Adam. Even should we stay here in America, it will not be in this camp. This camp is for waiting. Somewhere else is for starting over again."

Soon I will be seventeen, I thought. And I have spent my life waiting to live. Life will begin when we come back to Zagreb. No, it will begin when we reach America. No, not yet. It will start when we are with Papa and Villi and Grandmama again. In America. When we are all American. When we have a real house in America. Life will begin when we have our own money. And always what we are doing is not the beginning yet. It is waiting.

Let Mama do the waiting, I told myself. I am living now!

• • •

So I did live. Every day was a new kind of living, but the camp had begun to feel like a prison, with the guards and the passes and the fence and House #179, where I slept in my three-in-one room without a door of its own. Besides all this, the weather had become progressively colder so, by early November, I almost wished for Italy again. I wanted to be warm—and not just by myself. One day we were dismissed from school early, and I did not have to get back to the prison, so I decided to take my chances. I met her at her locker. I knew where it was—I had known for some weeks.

"Will you take a walk with me?" I asked, standing in front of the open door. "I do not have to be in the camp for several hours." Her locker was so neat. I would have to clean out mine before she saw it. Also, I would have to find the apple that had managed to hide itself under a collection of old homework sheets and crumpled candy wrappers: it had begun to make its presence known.

"Sure," she said. She seemed surprised and pleased all at once.

We walked for a long time. At first this did not matter. Outside was free. As of yet, no one had dared to fence off the sky. Outside, with her, I was happy. But we had begun stopping at corners and looking around, and the wind had become like a good Swiss knife: it cut through everything with sharp precision.

"Where do you want to go?" she asked.

I made as if I hadn't heard her. To invite a girl for a walk and then not know where one is going was very foolish. "You must be cold, Chris." I said. I called her that since she seemed to prefer the short name. To me it sounded like a boy's name—not the name of one so beautiful.

"I'm fine." She moved away from me toward the street.

I moved in front of her and stood beside the curb. "A gentleman always walks on the outside." Suddenly I remembered my manners. "That is the customary thing to do."

"How come?"

"To protect you from the carriages and horses that splatter mud onto the sidewalks."

She laughed. "We'll have to watch out for a lot of carriages and horses here."

We walked more, stopping and looking until I realized that I was following her direction—we were moving faster. We are going to her house, I thought. We got to the corner of her block. "My house is down this street," she said, pointing.

"Yes, I know."

"How do you know?"

"Once I saw you walking home," I admitted. I did not say that I did not actually see her. Instead, I searched for her address in the phone book. There were many Cooks, but only three whose name began with William. I learned that was her father's name. One evening, I walked to her home. The curtains were drawn. It seemed as if no one was home, and I almost walked up the front steps. I imagined the porch belonged to my house. If I opened the front door, I would be inside the Bornstein residence. I must have been standing there for some time, but then I saw the woman who lived next-door to Chris. She was bundled up in a sweater and a blanket, watching me, so I bent down, pretending I had stopped to tie my shoe and commenced to walk again.

"I would like to invite you home," said Chris, interrupting my thoughts. "It's only . . ." Her voice was bitter and hard. That, too, felt like a knife, but it was not cutting at me.

She hurried forward. I strode long steps to keep up.

"Nobody's home. They're working. So I can't invite you today, but I will soon. I'd like you to meet my mom. You'll like her."

"And what about your father? Will I like him?"

"Let's go to the camp," she said hurriedly.

"What about your father?" I said once more.

"What about him?" she repeated.

Why did it seem as if I had offended her? "Let us go to the camp," I assented.

I did not want her in my small apartment. My mother was there. She would offer Chris some tea and ask her questions. Then she would leave us alone, but she would not be leaving us alone. She would be sitting in her back room with the door partly open and a chair near the door so I would have to walk over and shut it.

I wished to be alone with her, someplace that did not belong to parents. We could step inside and make it our own. I

92

will take her to the empty barracks, I thought. I felt bold. Later, I could tell Ralph, too. I would not speak of what we did there, only that we went.

We passed through the fence. I drew close to her. She did not move away. We walked toward the abandoned building.

"Are we going to your place?" she asked. "I've never been down this way."

"No, we are going somewhere else. There is an empty barracks that I know of."

"Nobody lives there?"

"Nobody."

Except for the wind, which persisted in moaning, it was very quiet.

"Is that all right with you?" I asked.

"I guess so. Is there any heat there?" She bent into herself.

"No, we will have to make our own heat. Is that all right?" I, too, leaned into myself. It was a lonely kind of leaning.

"As long as we don't stay too long."

My feet moved along. What would I say to her? What does one say to a girl when one is alone? How should one act? I was nervous and happy all at once. Such a mixture of feelings was new to me. I had always been afraid and nervous. Or happy and excited. Never nervous and happy.

We walked into emptiness. I wanted to put my arm around her, but the arm did not feel ready. No, it did, but it was unsure as to how to act upon such a readiness. Should a boy ask a girl if she wants? Or does he try first and then ask? Around us were the pieces of a radio that Ralph and I had begun constructing.

"What are you making?" she asked.

"A radio. Ralph and I have all the parts. As soon as we know what to do, we will put them together."

She sat in the corner away from our project. I sat next to her. Close but not too close. "Do you look closely before you build?" she asked.

"What do you mean?" It was a strange question.

93

"Like, do you see the whole thing in your mind?"

"Yes, first I am picturing the whole thing part by part. Then I build." I showed her the tubes and how they fit together. She seemed satisfied for some reason. In the middle of this, my stomach growled. Lately it was like that—never satisfied.

She laughed. "I'm hungry, too," she said. "I'd like a hot fudge sundae."

"What is a hot fudge sundae?"

"You've never had one?"

There was a look of astonishment on her face. I shook my head and thought of all the food I knew of that, I was sure, she had not tasted, but I said nothing. To bring some American girl to an abandoned barracks and then inform her of her ignorance was not a good idea.

"A hot fudge sundae is made from ice cream. You put it in a dish and you pour hot chocolate sauce all over it, and then you scoop up a little bit of ice cream and some hot fudge, and when you eat it, you taste cold and hot all at the same time."

She closed her eyes. I was very hungry, but it was not just for food, no matter where it came from.

"I would like an ice cream cone," I said. My eyes sat on her lips. "Except I do not know the proper way to eat one. Ralph tells me there is an art to eating the cone." I shivered. Why were we talking about ice cream? It was so cold, even in this barracks. If only I could sit closer to her.

Then we did such a funny thing. We made the pretense that we were eating ice cream. I ate the cone. She, the sundae. When it appeared as if I was doing it all wrong, she showed me. "You must tilt your head to the side," she said. She cocked her head and turned her chin up. She moved a pretend cone around in the air. Her tongue moved to catch at the pretend drops. "Like this," she said, catching them all.

I must have been staring at her tongue, too. Her lips and her mouth and her tongue. I felt cold and hot all at the same time. She looked at me with a shocked expression, and the mouth closed over the tongue. Her lips trembled. She turned the pretend cone upside down. We heard the ice cream falling.

"I'm not hungry anymore," she said.

"It is too cold for ice cream," I answered, slamming my hands into my pockets.

How does one look with girls? I wondered. I had to learn to appear interested but not too interested. She was so beautiful, though. It was hard not to touch her cheek or her lips.

"I'm cold," she said. "My feet feel numb."

She stood. I looked up at her. I did not want to stand just yet. She held out her hand. I took it.

Next time we would not discuss hot fudge sundaes. Instead, we would make our own heat.

CHRIS

I didn't want a boyfriend then. I wanted a friend who was a boy. I wanted . . . I don't know what I wanted. But I wasn't going to keep thinking about it. About him, either. I wondered if he liked me.

ADAM

I did not want to think about all that I did not do. I did not want to think about her. She liked me. I was sure of that. No, I was *almost* sure. She had to like me. I was a likable person. All right, I could be a fool. But she *did* like me. I was certain. Well, no one could be entirely certain about anything—certainly not—but I was *almost* certain that she did like me. She had to like me—at least a little. I have always been a likable person.

I must save myself from thinking, I thought. I decided to write a letter to Papa:

My dearest Papa,

I have met a girl. If Grandmama were here, she would not forgive me. "Be careful," she would say. "Marry a Jew. Then you will not wake up one morning and find out that the one who wakes beside you suddenly hates you. Or worse yet, that you're both in prison. You, for being the Jew. She, for being married to you. Then, what is even love surely turns to hate." But, Papa, this is not Poland or Germany or Yugoslavia. This is America. We are free here. Besides, we are not serious. We are very young. Only Grandmama thinks right away of marriage and children and her own great-grandchildren. We do not need to think about serious questions. I like her. That is all. I would like to know her better. That is all.

I have joined a Boy Scout troop here. Do you know what the Boy Scouts of America do, Papa? We do public service, such as bringing coal into the homes of the old people and collecting cans of food for people who are needing it. We also learn survival techniques. That does not mean crossing over mountains or hiding in woods or pretending you are something you are not. We learn many kinds of knots. When I see Villi again, I will tie him up. See if you can untie him.

Here are some requirements for Tenderfoot. I am hoping also to accomplish these things soon.

1—Know how and when to wear scout uniform
2—First aid
3—Know semaphore code, Morse code, Indian Sign
    Language, or Manual Alphabet for the Deaf
4—Track half-mile in 25 minutes
5—One mile in 12 minutes at Scout pace
6—Use properly knife and hatchet
7—Build fire in open, using only 2 matches

Your loving son,
Adam

I knew I could not mail this. Nothing got into enemy territory. Nothing got out, except bad news. But it felt good to write. As I was writing, I was thinking, Surely, Papa must be alive. Surely, someone must be hearing these words. As I was writing, Papa was alive in my mind. Alive and safe. So was Villi, who, in my mind, was now shorter than I was. Shorter and weaker. But Papa hadn't changed. In my mind Papa never changed.

Although I could not mail out my letter to Papa, I found that an altogether different letter had been mailed to me:

November 16, 1944
Adam Bornstein
Emergency Refugee Shelter
G.P.O. Box 20 (House No. 179)
Oswego, N.Y.
Dear Mr. Adam Bornstein:
My mother, my father, and I would like to invite you and your family to have Thanksgiving dinner with us next Thursday. If you do not have a previous engagement, please confirm by writing.
Sincerely,
Miss Christine Cook

And attached was a second note.

Dear Adam,
Along with this letter, you're getting a very formal letter in the mail because I'm practicing letter writing at school. In eighth grade we were preparing for ninth grade. In ninth grade we reviewed things we learned in eighth. I'm not sure what we're doing this year in English, but letter writing is part of it.
Can you come to our Thanksgiving dinner? We're having everybody from my family, and a huge turkey and lots of stuffing and gravy and mashed potatoes.
Chris

I quickly responded.

Dear Chris,
My family would be delighted to come and share this
American holiday with you.

Adam

CHRIS

I invited Adam for Thanksgiving, though at first Dad had said no. "Thanksgiving is just for our family!" he said. Dad loved to talk about *our* things, especially around holidays. There was *our* church, St. Mary's, and *our* heritage, Irish Catholic. There was *our* president, meaning Roosevelt, and *our* country, the United States of America. And *our* boys fought to keep our country free. When Dad talked about *our* things, I felt that there was a *your* which wasn't as good as *ours*.

Mom and I said that Thanksgiving meant we were thankful for having as much as we did, and that was why we should share all our things with people who weren't so fortunate. The people at Fort Ontario had so little. They'd lost so much. Wouldn't it be nice if they got a home-cooked meal outside the camp? I didn't tell Dad that I went there often. Nor that I really liked Adam, although Mom had guessed.

Finally Dad said yes, and I replaced one set of worries with another: What will I wear? What will I say? How will the family act?

Would Ned open Coke bottles with his teeth or talk about how we snuck under the fence? Dad would've killed me for sure if he'd heard that.

Would Aunt Mary stuff her face with turkey and eat with her hands?

Would Aunt Nell keep mentioning Dick and Bob? "Dick loves my stuffing. Remember how he'd always eat two servings of it? Of course, he can't stand the raisins. He has to take out every single one." Would she explain Dick's feelings about mushrooms and cooked celery in stuffing and exactly what part of the turkey he wanted? Maybe she'd even lay out a place setting for him. Then she'd start on her second son, Bob. "Now my Bob makes the best cranberry sauce. Remember how his always had just the right amount of tartness, and if my Bob were home right now, he'd know how to make the sauce despite our sugar rationing, but, of course, he's not at home because he's with all our other brave fighting boys." Sighing heavily, she'd lay out a place setting for Bob, too, so we'd have to stare at two plates full of Thanksgiving dinner that nobody'd want to touch. And we'd wonder, What kind of Thanksgiving are they having? Army turkey can't taste like real family turkey.

When we weren't staring at the empty chairs and the full plates, we'd be trying not to listen to Mom going on and on about the Diamond Match Company.

"What kind of work do you do, Mrs. Cook?" Adam would ask, and I'd groan inwardly.

"Well, as I said," she'd reply, her eyes glazing over with joy because she had found a new victim, "I work at the Diamond Match Company, which is a very large factory. Do you know what they make there?"

Adam would be too polite to say, "Diamonds?"

"Matches, that's what we make, but not the regular kinds." Mom would pause, expectantly waiting for somebody to ask her to describe all the different kinds of matches, but nobody'd ask, so she'd look disappointed for a split second, like her family had failed her, and then keep going. "In our factory we have all kinds of matches. We make strike-anywhere matches sold in several box sizes. We have double-dip kitchen matches, book matches, safety matches, and water-resistant matches, which, I'll have you know, the government asked us to make. These matches came right off the machines in our factory on the second anniversary of Pearl Harbor."

"That is very interesting," Adam would answer. (I'd be dying in my seat because once Mom got started on the water-resistant matches there was no stopping her.)

"Did you know that water-resistant matches will ignite even after four hours of complete submersion? That means these matches function in the wet jungles and in amphibious operations." Mom would breathe deeply, coming up for air and look triumphantly around the table.

We'd all be nodding our heads vigorously so they wouldn't drop onto our plates from boredom, but Mom would think that meant we were enthusiastic because we were a part of her family, so she'd smile at all the O'Haras and the Cook in-laws. Beaming, she would pick up a platter and stand beside Adam or Mira or their mom or all three of them. "You must still be hungry," she'd say, spearing pieces of meat that she'd slap on their plates. "Have some more turkey."

That would be just the opening my cousin Beth was looking for. She'd jump right in and ask about the food at the camp. Everybody asked about food, as if that was the most important thing going on at the Emergency Refugee Shelter.

My cousin Grace would chime in with the second most asked question: "So tell me, Adam, how does Yugoslavia differ from the United States?" Why did I have so many cousins? All my relatives should've had families like mine!

Then all the Cook men would take their beers to the chairs that had been set up near the radio. They'd raise the volume up so nobody could hear anybody, and all of us women would have to shout to each other as we cleared the table.

Why did I invite him? I'd be just as stupid as everybody else!

To escape from my worries, I went upstairs to my room and did my chest-building exercises. If I was going to be big on top, which seemed to be the way things were going, I was determined that I'd be firm.

CHEST LIFTING AND FIRMING EXERCISE

Stand up straight.

Put your arms out. Elbows extended in wing position.

Fingers of left hand should be pointed to fingers of
right hand.

Push elbows out and extend chest.

Repeat exercise fifty times every evening for full and
firm breasts.

• • •

Thanksgiving came and went, and it did not go as I'd imagined it would. I couldn't figure out whether it went better or worse. Sometimes I thought it was a beautiful day. Sometimes I thought it was dreadful. At first everything seemed to be going perfectly. There was so much wonderful food. Mom's turkey. Aunt Nell's stuffing. Aunt Mary's gravy and her apple pie. Aunt Mary didn't eat with her hands like she usually does. Aunt Nell didn't fill plates for Bob and Dick, although we did pray for their safety. Uncle Harry didn't tell nasty jokes about some priests, or some ministers and priests, or some priests, ministers, and rabbis.

I'm not sure how it all got started. Probably it was Dad's fault. He was trying to be nice, but what a stupid thing to say to Adam. "I bet you must be anxious to get back to Yugoslavia."

Adam's mom frowned and pushed back her plate.

"I am not anxious," said Adam, looking at his mom as if he were continuing a conversation they'd had. "I enjoy living now in America at your American table." He smiled at me. I fixed my eyes on the leftover piece of turkey on my plate.

Dad stood with his beer in one hand near my seat. The other hand lay on my back rest. My dad's noticing me, I thought. He's noticing all the changing.

I leaned forward and crossed my arms over my chest. Adam's fork made ridges up and down a mound of potatoes still on his plate. Butter drained into the cracks. "Do you want some more mashed potatoes?" I asked, squeezing my fingers together.

"Yours must be cold." I talked into the special white tablecloth Mom had put on our dining room table.

"I don't think your friend is hungry," said Dad. (I hated the way he used *your* and *my* and *our*. I hated the way I was always *his* daughter, that nobody else could be *my* anything.)

"Adam, are you hungry?" asked his mom quietly.

"No, Mama, I am quite satisfied." His fork flattened the potato mound.

"I'll clear your plate then," I said half to myself and half to Adam. I stood up, leaning against the table. Then I lifted my chin and stared at him, full in the face.

Dad and Uncle Harry went over to the radio with their beers. My arms reached down to take Adam's plate. His hands held it. I waited until they found another place to sit.

"Who wants to play Ten Bible Questions?" bellowed Dad from the other room.

There was a chorus of "Me! Me!"

"Christine, what do you say?"

When I was little, Dad would test me on my Bible by making a game. He'd ask me a question. If I knew the answer, he'd give me a penny. I'd ask him a question. If he knew, I had to give him a penny. The one who had the most pennies in the end won. I didn't like to part with my own pennies, so Dad always used his. I got to keep my winnings. When I was little, I loved the game, but I didn't want to play that night, not on Thanksgiving—not with Dad and Adam.

"I'm not going to play," I said, standing between the kitchen and the living room.

"Then you'll ask the teams the questions," said Dad.

"I don't want to do that, either."

"I'll ask," said Mom. "Chris can finish clearing the table."

"No," said Dad. "She'll ask."

Something caught inside my throat. I swallowed hard and got out our family Bible from the living room drawer.

"Not that Bible," said Dad. "Get your own missal. You

remember, don't you? The one your grandmother Augustina gave you when you were confirmed."

I folded a napkin and closed the drawer. Dad waited. I straightened out my skirt, pulled back a few loose strands of hair and readjusted my barrette. It felt like the whole room was waiting—even Adam. I wanted to get away. I ran upstairs, nearly tripping over the top steps, and retrieved my missal from the bottom drawer of my bedroom bureau. It was hidden underneath all the other things I'd saved. My first pair of white gloves. The ticket stub to *National Velvet,* because it must've been something to be in a race that no girl had been in and then win. An invitation to my birthday party last year. My very first bra. (I like to remember changing.) Colorful candy wrappers (just because). And the missal Grandma gave me. Inside the jacket, on the front page, was my name. My grandmother wrote it. I could see her writing. Her hand sat on the book so her fingers wouldn't shake so much. And I *did* remember. I just didn't want Dad to know, because remembering for him had to do with things I was supposed to do and not do. None of that included Grandma and me and how we'd sat in her bedroom.

She'd asked me to get her the black beaded pocketbook she always carried when she took me to my yearly birthday meal at a fancy restaurant. Grandma had a black purse. I had a small white one she gave me one Christmas so we could be elegant ladies together. Inside her purse was a beautiful silver pen, which she used to write in the missal. We were on her bed together when she wrote out my whole name. "Christine Augustina Cook," Grandma said, pointing to thin, spindly letters, "this is your missal now." A month later she died.

Downstairs, the teams had formed. Adam was on one side. Dad was on another. I stood between the teams, flipping through pages. What should I ask? Inside were all these holy cards that I'd collected, some from swapping with friends. One card fell out, and she stared up at me from the rug. She was dressed in blue, and her eyes seemed so full of peace and love that I almost wanted to say something. *Oh, Mother of God, Blessed Virgin.* Then his hand was on the card that was held out toward me.

"Thank you," I whispered. My fingers touched Mary's hair. His held her dress.

"What is Lent?" I asked Adam while I tucked the card back inside my missal. I wanted to smile, laugh, touch the hand that had held all that blue.

"Too easy," yelled Ned. He was on Dad's side.

"Let her ask," said Dad.

Adam nodded curtly. He said something in what must have been Italian. The words sounded smooth and warm. I could see his tongue. I wanted to touch that, too. "That is the answer in the pope's language," he said.

"Hear, hear," yelled everyone on Adam's team.

"Do it in English," yelled my cousin Grace. She was also on Dad's team.

"And now I do so in Serbo-Croatian," said Adam.

I glanced at Dad. He's mad, I thought. He doesn't want to be beaten by a boy—and not this one. And Adam's showing off. "In English," I said. "In American English."

Adam clicked his heels together and bowed his head at me. Then he answered quickly and easily.

"What's the Eucharist?" I asked Dad, turning away from Adam.

"Too easy," yelled Beth. She was on Adam's side.

"Let her ask," said Adam. He seemed so sure of himself. He was enjoying the contest, too.

"No," said Dad. "Give me a hard question."

"What's . . . what's . . ." I searched around in my mind. I knew lots of hard questions, but I didn't want to ask any of them. "What's a mortal sin?"

"Disobeying your father," said Dad. All the uncles on both sides clapped.

"Venial," yelled the older kids on both sides. "That's a venial sin."

"Disobeying your mother is a venial sin," said Adam, winking at his mom. "Disobeying your father is a mortal sin."

"Hear, hear," yelled all the men. "Wrong!" yelled the women.

The older kids screamed, "Venial for both! Venial for both!" The little ones screamed, "Vengil! Vengil!" so many times that it started to sound like vaginal or virginal. I was sure that was what the boys heard, because Ned poked my cousin Brad several times—Brad has to be jabbed a whole lot before he gets anything—and a chain reaction started up: all the boys were poking each other, like they were looking up some female part in the dictionary.

"You're right," I said to Dad. I ignored Ned. My questions got harder and harder until only Adam and Dad were left.

"Dad," I said, "I want to stop. I'm tired and thirsty."

"Joan, get her a drink." Dad beckoned Mom.

I drank the water. I was still thirsty.

"I'm ready," said Dad.

"I, too," said Adam

Everyone watched, waiting for me to ask. "Nobody wants to play anymore," I said, staring hard at Adam.

"That is true," said Adam. "Therefore I am forfeiting. Mr. Cook wins."

Dad's face darkened. If he didn't forfeit, too, then he'd seem small, but forfeiting wouldn't be winning. I was mad at Dad. I was also mad at Adam.

"I forfeit, too." Dad shrugged, laughing like none of it meant anything.

"Somebody has to win," said Ned.

"No, they don't." I wanted to throw the missal at Ned. "Nobody has to be the winner and nobody has to be the loser."

"It's a tie," said Mom, standing next to me. "Adam and Bill both win."

Everyone clapped. "A tie! A tie!" the little ones screamed. They would have screamed anything by this time. If Mom had said, "It's a tonsillectomy," they still would have screamed.

"Shake hands," said Uncle Harry, slapping Dad on the back and nearly spilling his beer all over the rug. "Shake hands."

"Shake hands," all the cousins and aunts and uncles echoed. The little kids kept slapping Adam and Dad.

Adam stretched out his hand. It hung in the air.

"Shake hands, Bill," piped in the aunts. Slowly, Dad put out his. But it was the wrong hand. My cousin Grace held her hand over her mouth. Some boys laughed.

"Now, Bill—" said Mom.

I looked at Adam. I don't know what was on my face. Quickly he switched hands.

"Time for dessert," said Aunt Nell. Aunts and uncles and cousins clamored to the table. I sat on a chair away from everybody. The missal lay on my lap. I took out the card that had fallen, absent-mindedly turning it over and over. On one side was the Virgin. On the other was Grandma's name, the date when she was born, and the day when she died. I wanted her here with me. I wanted to be with her and Mom in her shiny black car. I didn't care how dangerous it was. We'd had fun then. Every Tuesday, when Mom was learning to drive, Grandma would take the car down to my school and pick me up. We'd stop for our special treats so I'd be fortified for the dangers ahead. I'd get my favorite: a hot fudge sundae. Grandma'd get a ginger-ale ice-cream soda that was full of bubbles, and we'd eat in the car. Grandma wasn't like Dad: she never worried if something dripped and stained her seat. Grandma's car was a wonderful moving kitchen. When we stopped at Mom's factory, I'd get in the back, where I liked to be when Mom was there. We'd wait until she ran out, her coat unbuttoned and flying.

Mom always headed to the passenger side. Grandma would point to the wheel, and Mom would walk over to the driver's side. I could see the fear in the way she moved away from the car hood, like if she didn't look at the mechanical beast, maybe it would go away or it would drive itself. All Mom had to do was hold the wheel.

"Today we'll learn parking," Grandma'd say. Or, "Today we'll practice left turns. Are you ready, Joan?"

Mom's face would tighten, but she wouldn't say no, because Grandma was Mom's last resort. Dad had tried teaching Mom, but he couldn't, so Grandma decided to take over. "You need your freedom, Joan," Grandma had said. "A car is the ticket to a woman's freedom." My grandma Augustina was a modern grandma. She knew how to drive when most women were passengers.

The three of us would sit in the car. I'd wish that Mom'd let me stay home alone, where I was much safer. Or I'd wish that she'd drop me off at Aunt Jenny's or Aunt Nell's or Aunt Mary's. But the driving was our secret. Nobody was to know until Mom passed her test. Then we'd tell everybody, including Dad.

Mom sped through the streets, making big wide turns that made me think she'd ram us into one of the parked cars. I slid to the middle of the backseat while Grandma softly moaned, "Jesus, Mary, and Joseph. Joan, don't pay any attention to me. Jesus, Mary, and Joseph, keep driving," until I wasn't sure exactly who Grandma was trying to teach, but I thought we'd all die with the trying.

At the table everyone chattered away. I sat alone in the corner. "Jesus, Mary, and Joseph," I whispered, holding the holy card. I wished I were in that car again, even with Mom speeding through the streets. I felt safer there with Grandma and Mom.

"Chris, have some pie." Mom broke into my thoughts.

I put the missal aside and pulled up a chair next to her and away from Adam and from Dad.

Later, the cousins laughed with the cousins while Mom washed dishes with the aunts, and Adam's mom helped them. All my uncles huddled around the radio. Right before it was time for Adam to go back to the camp, I slipped outside. For a change, nobody noticed. The porch light was on. Mrs. Dubchek's light was on, too, but the rocker was empty. She's probably at Joey's wife's house, I thought, with her grandson, Benny. For some odd reason, I wished she was on the porch, teaching me how to knit and reading me one of Joey's old letters for the millionth time. I wouldn't be bored and I'd learn the language needles and yarn speak when they're close to each other.

Behind me the door opened. "A penny for your thoughts," Adam said.

"Where did you learn that expression?" I asked, surprised.

"I learn many American sayings, such as 'A stitch in time saves nine,' and 'A penny saved is a penny earned.' There is also 'A bird in the hand is worth two in the brush.'"

"Bush," I said primly.

"A bird in the hand is worth two in the bush. The early bird catches the worm. Speak softly and—"

I put my hand over his mouth.

"I do not like that one, either," he said, speaking through the cracks in my fingers.

"I was thinking about our neighbor," I said. "Usually she sits on her rocker, even in the winter, except nobody's there tonight. She's probably visiting her family. Her son is fighting overseas—in Italy, I think. She hasn't heard from him." Pretty soon I'd be telling him how many letters Mrs. Dubchek got, what was in them, and how handsome Joey must have looked when he saw the pope.

"On our ship when we came over to America, I also see American soldiers who are hurt in Italy."

"Were they hurt bad?"

"Some, yes." He smiled in a forced, unhappy way. Snow fell on his hair and lashes, which were so large they could've swept you off your feet. I wasn't angry at him anymore. We stood near the front door, away from the wind. Suddenly it felt so public underneath the porch light. Our shoulders touched. We didn't move away.

"I showed very wrong behavior," he said. "I am used to being a polite person. I respect my elders. Tonight I do not know what came over me. I am sorry."

"You switched your hand," I answered. "My father put out the wrong hand, and you switched."

A snowflake hung on his lashes, whole and white. It disappeared. Maybe it melted. I wanted to be kissed so badly my stomach hurt.

Adam touched my head. I thought about how Father Walters would touch my head and how I felt blessed. This was different.

Kiss me. Please, kiss me!

"I like you, Chris Cook," he said. "I like you very much."

And he kissed me. Hard on the lips. I kissed back.

• • •

I have a globe in my bedroom that Mom got me way back in third grade, when I was just learning about cities and states and countries. Sometimes at night, I'd trace the land masses or lay my hand over the whole of the oceans and seas. Sometimes my fingers slid up and down the bumps that were supposed to be mountain ranges, or I'd memorize funny facts to tell Mom and Dad. The North American oceans have three syllables each. At-lan-tic. And Pa-cif-ic. But the Med-i-ter-ra-ne-an Sea goes on and on.

Before I went to bed, I'd twirl my globe hard so the blues blurred and continents ran into each other. I'd close my eyes and point, hoping that my finger would hit some strange-sounding place. Like Siam. Or Venezuela. What would it be like to be from these places? I loved imagining myself being all kinds of people, living everywhere at once. Experiencing everything. But how would I have felt if I'd been sitting in my bedroom in Germany or Hungary or Yugoslavia? What if Adam had knocked on my door?

Way back in third grade, I wanted to feel the whole entire world inside of me. But not that night when I'd been kissed. I was happy. Sort of. But what if I fell in love? I didn't want to. I wanted it to end right then with me thinking about being kissed. Because something was going to happen. Something bad. And nowhere felt safe. Nowhere at all.

How was I ever such an idiot? I wanted to impress and what did I do? What does an idiot do? He goes to the house of the girl he likes very much and he makes himself into a big puffed pastry in front of the girl's father. Then the idiot has the *chutzpah*, the absolute nerve, to kiss the girl. I will do fifty push-ups and fall exhausted into my bed, I thought—that is, after I consider her kiss.

For sure, she liked that kiss, but did she like me? I was such an idiot.

I decided that I would write a letter to her and apologize. The letter would sound as if it came from a boy who was only temporarily an idiot.

Dear Chris,
    Since I am unable to sleep, I am writing you to apologize. I am very sorry.

                            Adam

Dear Chris,
    Mama brews coffee on our little hot plate in the next room. She does not speak to me of this evening. No doubt, she thinks it best for me to be with a Jewish girl. No doubt, she wonders about a girl's father who plays Bible games on Thanksgiving. Or her own son who wants to play such a game and win.
    Mira sings "Don't Sit Under the Apple Tree." Over and over she sings it, but she never gets far before she stops. She does not know how to end the song.
        Neither do I.
        Will you forgive me?

Dear Chris Cook,

This is the third letter I write you. All the others sounded wrong. I am sorry. Please forgive me. Will you go to the movies with me on Tuesday night?

Sincerely,
Adam Bornstein

In response, I soon found two letters in my mailbox, one in English and one in Serbo-Croatian.

November 27

Dear Adam,

I can't go with you on Tuesday. Don't try to catch me in school, and don't put a letter in our mailbox. Dad is guarding it. I think he suspects something. He hasn't said anything, but he's making me come straight home after school every day this week. I am so mad at him! I can't go out for a week. I have to come home from school and do my homework and read. I will find a way to give this to you.

Chris

9 September 1944

My dearest Mama, Mira, and Adam,

I do not know if you will get this letter. I am well. Just of late I am learning that you are in the United States. What a miracle that is. How I am finding out is also a miracle. In our troops, one day someone is smuggling in a paper from Switzerland on which it is written the names of the refugees from Italy who are going to the United States. I find your names on the list.

I am still in Yugoslavia, but I have a Partisan friend who can

111

get this to England and then, I hope, to you. No doubt my address is also very confused, which you will have to correct me on if you ever get this, but I know that you are at Fort Ontario, which is in the state of New York in the United States. I will pray someone can find the right box.

How am I to tell you our whole history? There is a very long story here. And much of it is also having to do with miracles that cannot be explained. Every Jew alive from Europe has a miracle to speak of.

Papa and I made our way back to Grandmama's, but we were not able to find her. We did discover that Grandmama, by great fortune, missed the first roundup, when all the people in her building were taken. You remember Mrs. Radovic, Grandmama's very sweet Christian neighbor. She told us this. She also said that Grandmama, when she found her house in such a terrible way, directly went to her. You can imagine the scene. Grandmama was raging. How can anyone lock her house? Mrs. Radovic was shuffling about in those well-worn slippers of hers, no doubt feeling helpless. That is the way it is. One day you have a house and a family and a business. The next day it is all gone. "Go to the mountains and eat dirt, why don't you!"

Grandmama stayed with her dear neighbor over one night. That is all. Both were afraid of a second roundup. And there were Mrs. Radovic's children and grandchildren to consider. What if she should be found hiding a Jew? And Grandmama's name is on the Jew list to be checked off. So, too, are all our names, which is making even more difficulty for Grandmama.

After the one night, Mrs. Radovic said to Grandmama, "Go, disappear." As if disappearing is so easy. Every time you are moving, you must register with the police, who have everyone in their files. So the synagogues, too, have their membership lists, which are seized. And you know that there are many in this part of Croatia who consider Hitler their long lost brother.

112

"Go," said Mrs. Radovic. "Disappear." And that is what Grandmama has done. She has done such a good job of it that we can find her nowhere. As for Papa and me, when we heard this story, we, too, made ourselves into ghosts. We traveled nights until we reached the mountains. This is where we met up with the Partisans.

My dear family, I am fighting with Tito's army. You would not believe how many of us are fighting. Men and women and children alongside each other. Josip Tito, born in our own Croatian part of Yugoslavia, who even himself was fighting in the Russian Revolution, leads our liberation army. We have done much to make those Germans weak—so much that I think soon every last German will be out of this country. As for the future of Yugoslavia, when we have destroyed the Nazis and driven them out, then I will think of what it means to be a Communist country.

We are anxiously awaiting the end to all this blood spilling so that we can be together as a family again. With this letter I am also sending Papa's love. Traveling is hard on him. Thoughts of you safely in America will no doubt make him strong again. With God's will, we will be together soon.

Villi and Papa

If you have forgotten, I am eighteen today. So, Adam, yet again there is two years' difference. In May you will say how you are seventeen. Therefore, you and I are only a year apart. Nonetheless, every September I am again two years older. Adam, did you remember my birthday? I remember yours: 9 May.

My brother was alive! My father was alive! But would I ever see them again?

Part Two

THE BLUE LADY AND THE MAN OF MY DREAMS
December 1944 to February 1946

Chapter One
The Demented One

My friend's father and her brother were both killed, and she was in a concentration camp and raped. I heard a lot of horrible stories. I heard stories about their lives, too—not only the Holocaust. We'd walk around the fort socializing, getting together . . . It was the most marvelous experience that I had in my life when I think about it. I met people from all over. It was just something being there, something which made me feel good.

Geraldine Rossiter,
Oswegonian

CHRIS

I couldn't wait for Christmas! I only worried about Dick—the whole family did. Nobody had received a letter from him in a long time. "It's all right," we told Aunt Nell. "Everything gets delayed around Christmas." Aunt Nell would nod her head, then go back to making more brownies for her boys. She made so many batches that all of us got sick just looking at them, especially since sugar was rationed and so was butter. Aunt Nell did all kinds of substituting. Sometimes she and Mrs. Dubchek and Mom cooked together in the kitchen. Mrs. D. had heard from Joey just once in the last two months. I could recite that letter by heart, but I am *not* going to.

Wouldn't it be wonderful, I thought, to walk into a market without worrying about rations or to take a drive without calculating how much gas was used and if we'd have enough for the really important trips. I should've been happy that we had markets and a car then, even if I'd never be allowed to get behind the wheel of Dad's Ford. He was so possessive. He rarely let Mom drive it, so she had to use the black car Grandma Augustina left in her name. Mom liked to say how Grandma must've laughed her way through the will-writing, particularly when she gave Mom the car. She believed Grandma sat with us when she drove. I thought so, too. "Jesus, Mary, and Joseph," Grandma moaned, "keep driving!" At least Mom *was* driving. I figured I'd be twenty-five before I got to drive in anybody's car, because Dad would imagine all the accidents waiting to happen to me and prevent them by not letting me take over.

When it came time for our outdoor Christmas service, I went early, not waiting for Mom and Dad. We had a tree near the hospital full of beautiful ornaments, and kids from all the churches in Oswego sang together in the choir. The fort residents were invited, too, because Christmas isn't just about Christ: it's about peace and good will. I was singing "Noel" and looking at Adam, and the air resounded with all our church voices. I cogitated on all the ways you can sing that one word while I watched him, mouthing the words. *Noel, Noel, Noel, Noel, Noel, Noel, Noel. No-el-No-el. No-el-No-el. Noel-Noel. No-el! No-eh-el. No-oh-el.* In the middle of the twentieth *No-el* I almost burst out laughing.

Afterward, I found Mom and Dad milling in the crowd. "Can I go out for a little while with some friends?" I asked. (I didn't say *what* friends.)

Dad said all the usual Dad things: "Make sure you get home before it gets dark. I don't like you out in the dark. Don't run around without your coat. You'll catch a cold. Don't let any strange boy take you home." But he let me go.

Adam and I separated ourselves from the throng and slowly walked to First Street. Everywhere lights were on so that it felt full of Christmas spirit. We went to the pictures. *Gaslight* was playing. I decided that it was my favorite movie, and Ingrid Bergman was my favorite actress. She's wise and beautiful, and she looks like she needs to be loved, but it's not a helpless kind of look. It's as if love wouldn't be a complete thing if it didn't care for Ingrid Bergman. Adam treated me, even though I objected.

"You need your money," I said. His black boots were worn and had a buckle broken.

"Yes, I need my money." He grinned. "So I can spend it on you. Today I have a six-hour pass. I am a free man. We will celebrate together!"

Adam gave the woman at the ticket counter thirty cents. We went in and sat down. Suddenly, I felt shy: I didn't know how to be with him in this place, and soon it'd get dark. There'd be darkness all around us. I didn't know if I wanted that to happen. I tried to figure out where to put my hands—they felt so big. He was trying to figure out what to do with his hands, too. He placed them on his lap, but they seemed unhappy there.

When the mystery began, we made guesses on how it would be solved. We both agreed that it had to involve the gaslights. Then I stopped thinking about Adam and watched Paula, who was really Ingrid Bergman. "Your heart is not in your singing," her music coach said. "You're in love."

How beautiful she seemed, especially when Gregory (who was Charles Boyer) kissed her. Her lips appeared satisfied. Her whole being seemed full, like a meal you've eaten and you don't need a single thing more, not even a drink of water. Or like a Christmas present that doesn't make you think of better things you got or things you wish someone had remembered.

Adam figured out what to do with his hands. They held mine. That felt right for my hands, too.

"Yes, yes," Paula said. "It's something that's never happened before. I never expected it." (She was talking about her great love for Gregory, which made her not care about singing.)

Adam squeezed my hand. "She should be careful," he whispered. "He is a bad man."

"Do you think he'll try to kill her?" I whispered back.

A woman in front of us turned around. "Do you mind?" she said.

When she turned back, Adam silently mimicked the words, "Do you mind?" I covered my mouth to muffle my laughter. Then I didn't know what to do. If I put my hand down on my seat, Adam would hold it like he did before. But maybe he wouldn't.

My hand was stuck on my mouth. Adam's reached up. His fingers briefly touched my lips. Then our hands went down together. My palm held his. My fingers wedged themselves between his fingers so that almost all the inside places of our hands touched. I stopped, withdrew my hands, and leaned away from him.

"I betcha Gregory killed Paula's aunt," I said, because I wanted to still feel close. Adam nodded, drawing away, too, so that the space between us grew larger.

Then everything inside of me was lonely. I wrapped my pinkie around his while I listened to Gregory. How cruel he was, especially when Paula asked if he would put her away and how many doctors would come. "I believe two is the required number," he said. My body leaned into Adam's. Between us was the armrest. I couldn't decide if I was glad or sad that it was there. I'd never paid attention to it before.

He put his arm around mine. I had to go to the bathroom, get a drink, go outside where it was light. But I didn't want to disturb his arm. I made myself into a statue. Being a statue hurt.

"This knife," said Paula. "It's not a knife in my hand. I'm just imagining it." Gregory was tied up, waiting for Paula to loosen the rope. She could do it. She held the knife, but she pretended she was crazy, just as he had made her believe.

"She trapped him!" I said loudly.

"Don't you think he deserves it?" asked the woman in front of us.

Adam took his arm away. "Certainly."

Afterward Adam walked me to my house. We stopped at Bridge Street and stared down at the Oswego River, which was iced over. Above us was the gray sky; below, the river; and in between all that stillness were the sounds of street cars and traffic.

Everybody was shopping for things they could give to loved ones at home, because Christmas is Christmas. It seemed even more so with the war.

"I loved the movie," I said. "But I still feel sad, even with the happy ending."

"How is that so?" Adam seemed really interested.

"Because Paula had to realize that all of that love wasn't really love, you know? Gregory was just using her to get into the house. And she learned that he strangled her aunt. Not only that—the man that she loved tried convincing her that she was going mad. How can anybody be so cruel?"

"They can be much crueler," said Adam.

Then he told me two things: one very happy, the other sad. He told me about a letter that had come from his brother, which meant his dad and brother were still alive. He also told me the story of the demented one. When he talked, the sky filled with words that bubbled up and then burst into nothingness.

But I'm not the sky. I won't forget.

I put my hand inside his as if I were Paula and Adam were Gregory, the Gregory who was good and kind. We were a block from my house, and the lights on our tree sparkled. I liked seeing them from far away, knowing they were in front of our house.

"You have a beautiful tree," said Adam.

"I love Christmas trees. I love working with Mom and Dad and decorating ours."

"I like looking at the lights."

"Do you miss not having a tree?" We stood at the corner. I didn't want to go down the block. I would stand right there, with my house in sight but with me just far enough away that I could see other blocks.

"It would be nice to make lights, but we have our own holidays. The one I would never give up is Sukkoth."

"What's special about that?" My arm swung his up and down.

"You are sitting in a wooden hut—this is called a *sukkah*—with a roof above you that is made of pine branches. From the roof is hanging all sorts of fruits like apples and grapes and funny gourds that can knock you on the head if you are not careful. When I am in the hut, I feel that I am in the sky's house. I am a bird with wonderful fruit and wood smells all around me."

"I'd like to be part of the sky's house, too."

"I will invite you to my *sukkah* when we are in our own house again and we can make such a hut."

"Adam, do Jews accept presents from non-Jews?"

"Presents?"

"Christmas presents."

"Certainly."

"Even if they're *Christmas* presents?"

"You may consider it a Hanukkah present if you wish."

"I didn't say I was considering." My arm stopped swinging. Adam's other hand found mine so our hands were linked. I felt like I was six, and I wanted to play a baby game. *London Bridge is falling down. Falling down. Falling down.* My hands felt that way. My mouth and body wanted something else.

"I think it is good for a person to give gifts to somebody he likes." Adam's hands pulled mine so that my body moved closer to his.

"I like getting gifts better than giving." I jerked him forward.

"I thought that the giving was better than the receiving."

"I'll give you something," I whispered.

"What will you give me?"

"Close your eyes."

Adam closed one eye.

"Both of them."

He closed both.

"No peeking, either."

We stood there for a moment until our lips pressed against each other.

ADAM

The Demented One
(as told to Mira)

"Once, a long time ago, you, Mama, Papa, Villi, and I were in a small village in the mountains."

"The Julian Alps."

"Yes, those big mountains that reach up thousands of meters until they are kissing the forehead of the sky. In this village we hid ourselves. Papa had gotten us country clothes and crosses, and a kindly peasant took us in. We stayed in a room on the top floor of her house, far away from enemies."

"And we were very quiet. We know how to be very quiet."

"Yes, but one day, this woman, she hears that the Nazis are coming. They have been told that Jews are upstairs. 'Scatter! Scatter fast!' she warns us. 'Or we will all die.' So we run."

"We run fast, because we are good at running."

"We are very good."

"And Papa is the best runner and the smartest man."

"So it is. Villi, Mama, you, and I, we run into the forest, where we hide. But Papa somehow is separated from us. He, too, is in the forest, but in another part when the Germans come up to him. Instantly Papa makes of himself another man. He becomes the imbecile. The demented one."

"Show me. Show me like Papa shows me."

I waved my arms here and there, pretending I was Papa. "The German soldiers look at our papa in confusion. They speak in German. Papa understands everything. He knows German fluently, but still he plays the demented one. Maybe even he has some fun. He walks funny, almost walking up to the soldiers. He speaks gibberish."

"Speak gibberish!"

I flapped my arms and spoke gibberish. "Papa, he is making funny faces."

"Say 'I am making funny faces,' not 'He is making funny faces.'"

123

"Papa—I mean *I* am making funny faces. I am having a good funny time, though terror seizes my heart. Playing the fool, I will remember how I outwitted the real fools. The Germans watch Papa—the Germans watch *me!* One begins to aim."

"You must be the German, too."

"How can I be Papa and the German all at once?"

"You can! You can!"

"One begins to aim." I held out my arm as if it were a long gun. "The other lowers his friend's gun." I lowered one of my arms with another, then waved both arms around and around in every direction. I dropped them and was the Nazi again. "Why," I said to my comrade, "why waste a bullet on a fool?"

"And they go away."

"Yes, they go away." I, the German soldier, marched from the room. I, Papa, walked quietly back.

"And Papa is saved," said Mira. She did not want me to say "I" anymore. I was Adam, and Papa was Papa.

"Our papa has saved himself."

"Because he is very smart."

"Because he is very smart. Later this smart Papa of ours meets up with Villi and finds us. And much later he goes back for our Grandmama. Papa and Villi want us all together. That is the way it should be."

"Papa always called me *tutees*, didn't he?"

"Always he called you *tutees*."

"He never called you or Villi *tutees*. Only me. I am his special one."

"Only you he called his *tutees*."

CHRIS

I didn't care if I wasn't supposed to see Adam. Or that I wasn't supposed to be at the fort every evening. I didn't care if one day they'd leave. Yes, I did. But right then they were here in Oswego—so was I—and it was Christmas Day. Adam raced ahead of me inside the fort. I stuck my boots inside the boot prints he'd made on the banked snow mounds that were piled alongside the road, wishing that the snow would never melt, that I could come outside in June and see our boot prints— mine inside of his.

Then he slowed down. We walked together to the abandoned barracks while the air that escaped from our mouths formed thick white clouds around us. I tried catching Adam's cloud because there were so many ways we could be together, but my teeth and throat hurt from swallowing all that cold air. I held his hand instead.

We moved to the corner of an empty room. I don't know why we chose the corner—it seemed safer somehow and easier to fill. I sat cross-legged, and he lay on his back, his head inside the well that my legs had made.

"Someday," he said, staring up at the ceiling, "people will remember this camp and how they saved us. It might be they will wonder: How is it that the refugees left one fence behind in Europe only to be behind another in America? Yet we can go to school and learn. We can be regular people. A regular boy talks freely to a girl. He can put his head in her lap if she does not mind."

His earlobes were red. I pulled down his hat so that it covered his ears, and he smiled in a way that made me think he wasn't just seeing me. He was somewhere else, where I'd never been and maybe never could be. Then he took my wrist and drew his finger across my palm as if my hand were all of America. He made circles where camps would be. "There could be many of these places. Here. And here. And here." He pressed the skin inside my hand until it hurt. "That is why I am happy and sad. I am thinking that one day people will ask why there was just this one when there could have been so many. It is a tragedy."

"Our Lord was born today, Christmas Day," I answered. I didn't want to think of the camps. I didn't want to feel bad, because none of that was my fault. Besides, I loved him.

Later, I gave him my present, the one I almost didn't buy because I couldn't figure out what to get.

"How about aviator goggles?" Ann had suggested. "Boys adore looking like war pilots."

"No, I don't want to do that." How could I walk around with a boy who wore aviator goggles? I couldn't buy a wallet or a tie, either. That was something you'd buy your father. So I bought him gloves. Store-bought gloves that he'd look at and not think how somebody had given him something they'd out-grown—charity, because he was a refugee and they felt sorry for him. The gloves were wrapped in tissue paper and even smelled new.

Getting the card was more difficult. I'd never gotten a Christmas card for someone Jewish before. I didn't want one that said "Merry Christmas" or "Christmas Greetings" all over it. I wanted to find something that had Hanukkah in it, but there wasn't anything like that in our stores. I found a card that said "Season's Greetings." That's O.K., I thought. Everybody celebrates seasons. But the picture was wrong. On the front was a painting of Mary holding baby Jesus. That's not a Jewish pic-ture. Neither was the Three Wise Men card I saw. Nor Santa sliding down the chimney. After nearly an hour of searching, I decided to make my own card. I'm not an artist. I never could draw people. I draw stick figures. I've always drawn stick figures. When I was little, I drew them with green faces: I liked green. But I didn't draw them that way anymore.

I folded a piece of construction paper in half, and on the front I drew a globe that looked a little like a globe and a lot like a bubble. I put some places on it, such as New York and Zagreb and the Indian Ocean. I'd always wanted to see the Indian Ocean. Then I drew in the same stick people I'd always drawn, except this time I filled a whole sheet with them. There were stick figures with skirts, stick figures with pants, with brown faces, black faces, white faces, and red faces. One had very curly hair. Its eyes were green—it is hard to draw sometimes green and sometimes blue—and another had dark blond hair and blue eyes. There were stick babies with funny diapers on them, and stick mommies and daddies. All the stick people formed a chain, every stick hand holding another one. It was cute. Probably cute was stupid, but what can you do when your whole artistic talent lies in stick figures?

Peace, I wrote in large black letters. Just when I thought I was finished, I realized that I had to figure out another problem. How would I sign it? First I penciled in "Love, Chris." Then I erased that and wrote "Fondly, Chris." And "The best, Chris." And "Your friend, Chris." I got sick to death of the whole process until I almost wrote "Sincerely, Chris." The construction paper also looked ratty from all the erasing. I was afraid I'd end up with a hole between the stick Chris and the stick Adam. So I wrote my name "Christine Cook" with nothing else. I'm not sure why I wrote Christine and not Chris.

"I have something for you, too," he had said, "but it is not yet the right time for giving."

When is the right time? I almost asked. I wondered if I should have waited, too, so that our right times came together. But that might not have come until the summer, and how can you give gloves in June?

This was my right time for him. I'd have to wait and see about his for me.

• • •

It was just after Christmas when a thought struck me: nearly everything I'd wanted had come true. I'd fallen in love with a high-school boy. We'd kissed. I hadn't been to New York City, but I felt as if I'd been across the globe. Adam was teaching me about Yugoslavia. Every Tuesday and Thursday we'd meet outside the school and walk to the library. Adam had a special library pass from the camp. Sometimes, on the way there, he'd talk to me about books he'd read or things he enjoyed learning at school. He'd talk about the telephone system he and Ralph were creating to link their barracks, or he'd comment on some American mannerism that he couldn't quite understand; he wanted me to explain it, and, suddenly, I'd feel jealous because Adam didn't care what others thought when he asked questions. He wasn't afraid to show how smart he was, either. All that mattered was the learning. But I was always worried that I'd say something jerky, and I'd look dumb, so I kept quiet in class and didn't ask and didn't answer—unless a teacher called on me—and slowly I got to feeling like I didn't want to learn, except with Adam I started wanting again. I wanted to know all kinds of things, and I asked questions because I knew he didn't think I was dumb. Maybe facts didn't like to stick to me. Maybe I didn't have any sticky surfaces in my brain—Adam's brain was a regular lollipop for facts—but there were all kinds of ways in which I was smart, and Adam saw them all. Then I stopped being jealous and I saw them, too.

One Tuesday in January we didn't meet. The snow was too deep. From inside our house I could hear the wind howling. It was still vacation, so we didn't have a day off from school. What a waste! I thought as I wrapped myself up tightly in blankets until I looked like a mummy who'd escaped from her tomb and was shuffling distractedly through our house, mumbling to herself.

After lunch I took a bunch of cookies into my bedroom and finished *Johnny Tremain* for the third time. I didn't bawl my eyes out like I did the first time I read about Johnny gorging himself on all kinds of food because he'd been so hungry and felt so low. And I wasn't surprised by the mystery. I knew who Johnny's relations were. Still I felt the power, particularly when Otis made his speech about freedom and fighting for liberty. You have to sacrifice so much—your home and your money and even your life—just so a man can stand up. I thought about Joey—he was big then, but I still called him Joey—and Dick and Bob. They were standing up, too. Someday I wanted to be counted like that. I wanted to be somebody who people would look at and they'd know she's somebody. I knew I was somebody—I was even a smart somebody—but I wasn't enough of a somebody to be more than an anybody. One day I'd be a reporter or a war correspondent or a pilot. I didn't want to work in a match factory or with boilers, like some people I knew. I wanted to see the world.

When I wasn't reading *JT*, I was thinking about Adam and me. Wouldn't it be lovely if I were a Wac, and he were my patient, and I cured him? Too bad I hated nursing and hospitals. I could hardly stand reading about nurses. By the time I was in seventh grade, I was the only girl in the whole class who hadn't read one Cherry Ames book or volunteered to do a report on Clara Barton. I can't say how many repeat Clara Barton book reports I'd already heard. Sally Jenkins had read the exact same one so often (except for a few word changes that she looked up in some dictionary), I could've said it aloud for her. By heart! I never even wanted to be *like* Clara Barton.

"Gales of thirty to fifty miles an hour whipped new fallen snow into blinding clouds," Dad later read at the dinner table. He looked at Mom, quietly waiting.

"And you still went to work," Mom said, right on cue with her compliments. "For our boys."

Dad busily folded the paper and slapped it a few times on the table. He put his elbows up and sniffed his coffee. During the war Dad did a lot of sniffing and slow sipping. That made his one after-dinner cup last. In between sniffing, he sighed contentedly. Mom sighed, too, but she wasn't thinking about coffee. She had Dick on her mind. My Aunt Nell had gotten a letter from him. It was dated mid-December. He was in the midst of some battle. We didn't know exactly where, but it was somewhere in Europe. He'd gotten his Christmas presents, though. The box Aunt Nell mailed from our post office didn't go to France or Germany while he was in Tokyo, like I was afraid of. I wondered if Bob got his.

On Thursday, when the big snowstorm subsided into a miniature squall, Adam and I finally got together at the library. We sat in the corner and whispered while the librarian cleared her throat in that you-should-be-quiet way. I was studying for a test on the Civil War, which was making me really mad: our history teacher had assigned it right before Christmas vacation so we'd have time to study. Who'd want to open Christmas presents and then memorize Civil War dates? Christmas vacation should be a vacation, or teachers should give all the work before vacation and take their holidays to grade papers!

"During the Civil War," I told Adam, "more American men died than in any other war in our history. Brother fought against brother."

"You mean the United States was not united?" he asked.

The librarian went from throat-clearing to coughing. Adam and I moved toward the back window.

"No, the United States wasn't united at all. In fact, the South seceded from the Union. That means it dropped out and formed the Confederacy." I sounded like a history book. Old Christine Cook, the history book.

Adam stared outside at the swirling snow. "Is it all the time snowing in the North and the South?"

"No, it's very warm in the South." I opened up my geography book. "See, here's where we are."

"I know. In the north part of New York, which everyone is calling 'Upstate New York.'"

"And Florida's warm and rainy. That's way down here," I pointed to the southern tip of the United States. "And California's warm, too. It has dry weather and cactuses, or maybe it's cacti, that look very soft, but when you touch them, the prickles hurt terribly. That's what a friend told me. I've never been to California. I'd like to go. And it snows a lot where we are, and in Wyoming and Michigan and all along the north."

"In Yugoslavia, too, we have all kinds of weather." Adam walked over to the card catalogue. He came back with a book about Yugoslavia. "We have sunny weather near the Adriatic Sea, where we are swimming. Snow around Sarajevo. And rich plains over here in the basin. And here," he said, drawing his finger along a blue line that stretched all the way from Rumania through Yugoslavia, "is the Danube. That is a very big river that makes all kinds of small rivers like our Zagreb Sava. My uncle lives near its shores, here. That is, he was living there. Now I am unsure where. I am unsure if he *is* living." Adam put his hand over that part of the world so it disappeared and then reappeared.

"Here," he said, pointing to his uncle's place, "not far from Belgrade. Sometimes in the early fall Mama, Papa, Villi, and I made a trip from Croatia, where I am from, to Slovenia."

"What about Mira?"

"She was not born yet, so she does not have the same memories. She does not have as many good memories, although twice, when she was very little, she was taken along. We stayed with my uncle and his family. Always I missed a little school, which made this extra sweet. And we helped to pick my uncle's plums."

"I love plums," I stupidly blurted.

"The plums that my uncle was growing and we were picking were more reddish than your Oswego purple plums. When I was a young boy, Villi loved to tell Mama or Papa that I was eating too many plums so that certainly I would have diarrhea. 'Adam is eating more than he is picking,' Villi said. Villi always picked the most. His basket filled up very soon. This is because he did not consider if maybe one plum was not exactly ripe. I, on the other hand, gave a careful examination to each plum so that I could judge which were the proper picking plums. Those not quite proper but certainly satisfactory were best in my mouth and not in the basket. Some of our plums went into vats where they fermented. Some were put in special ovens where they were dried."

"You mean they became prunes?"

"Yes, my uncle made the sweet prunes that travel all the way from Yugoslavia to the United States."

"Maybe," I said, staring out at the white winter sky, "I ate one of those prunes that you made from your uncle's plums. It traveled all the way from your uncle's tree to your hand, into your basket, to the vat, and onto a boat that came to the market here in Oswego. I came that day with my list. Buy prunes, apples, cherries, and grapes. I stopped at a stall and found some dried prunes. On the way home I was so hungry that I ate one. Once it had been the plum that you picked."

"Then it was the very best piece of fruit you have ever tasted.

My uncle also made the best brandy from plums. On the Sabbath, I would have a sip. Yugoslavia is a country that makes the very best plum brandy. Only you have to taste a little, and your insides are full of a sweet warm fire. This brandy we are calling it *slijivovicu*."

"Do even children drink it?" I asked. "In France I heard they drink wine with meals. But here you have to be eighteen to drink."

"I sipped just a small bit from a paper cup on the Sabbath. And here," said Adam, his fingers seeming to want to feel everything on that map, "here on the west, this is the warm coast. On summer holidays, Mama and Papa and Villi and I took a train from Zagreb. Villi and I always fought for the seat near the window. He had a talent, my brother, Villi. He knew exactly when to hit me so that nobody saw him. I also had a talent. He hits me when nobody is seeing, and I cry when everyone is watching."

Adam's lips trembled. He stopped and closed his book. "I talk too much. Come. Let us go outside."

We pulled on our boots and our hats and our big coats. I put the gloves that I'd bought Adam on his hands—I liked doing that—and he put my green furry mittens on me. I stuck out my hands like I used to when I was in kindergarten and Mom helped me dress. When I pushed my hands in, I almost punched Adam's stomach.

We didn't walk on the sidewalk paths that were already made. We made our own path. Snow got inside my boots. It melted on the inside of my legs. My lips felt cold. I put my mittens up against them and tasted wool mixed with snow. Adam made a big snowball. He raised his hand.

"Don't hit me," I shouted. I made a snowball, too. Mine was bigger than Adam's.

Adam rolled his on the lawn outside the library. I rolled mine. He was a faster roller, but my ball looked much more solid.

"It's going to break," I said. The wind snatched up my words.

Adam patted his ball and lifted it. I lifted mine.

"I won't if you won't," I said. I really wanted to hit him.

"I won't if you won't," he mimicked, but he didn't sound like me. He sounded like a boy from someplace far away standing near me.

"You promise?" I started toward him.

Adam started toward me. "I promise if you promise."

Along the street, tire chains made their familiar winter clanging sound.

"You promise first," I said.

"You first."

We faced each other. Then we mushed our snowballs against each other's chest.

Chapter Two
Dogs in a Manger

⅋

And so today, in this year of war, 1945, we have learned lessons . . . We have learned that we must live as men, and not as ostriches, nor as dogs in the manger. We have learned to be citizens of the world, members of the human community.

> President Roosevelt,
> fourth inaugural address,
> January 20, 1945

CHRIS

On any other Saturday, I would've been running out to find my friends, but that morning, January 20, I ended up stewing in my room. It was the president's fault. If he hadn't won, we would never have gotten into this argument.

FDR (which is what everyone called President Franklin Delano Roosevelt) had won his fourth term in office. He'd been our leader almost as long as I'd been alive. At breakfast, we had a big discussion about that. We talked about Adam, too. Dad said we were talking. If you ask me, he was mainly lecturing us.

"Roosevelt," said Mom laying out boxes of cereal on the breakfast table, "has taken us through the Depression and now through the war. He will take us through to peace, too."

Dad poured out his corn flakes. Every morning Dad eats corn flakes. One bowl of corn flakes, two pieces of toast, and a cup of coffee. Before the war he drank two cups of coffee. That's the only change he has ever made in his routine.

"He's a good man," said Dad, blowing over his cup.

"It's not too hot," said Mom.

"Then it's too cold."

"No, today it's just right."

I sighed.

"Eat your cereal." Dad tapped a spoon near my bowl, just in case I didn't know where the cereal was located. "Your mother got the kind you like."

"I'm not hungry. I'm still tired."

"I'm tired, too, of your wasting. Now finish it."

Every Saturday we all sat together. Mom figured that since she and Dad were gone all week long, Saturday and Sunday should be eat-with-family days. I would've preferred to sleep in on Saturday. It was my only free day. Sunday I had to wake up early for church. I couldn't get Mom to change the Saturday routine. Rain or shine, sleet or hail, we were all at the breakfast table at 8:30 A.M. Then Mom would visit Aunt Nell or grocery shop while I straightened up my room (which looked neat for about a day) and Dad puttered around the garage. After lunch, I'd finally get to be with friends, but I had to be back home so Mom, Dad, and I could all go to 3:30 confession together. Eventually, they did let me go to an evening confession.

"And Eleanor is a fine first lady," said Mom, sitting down.

"There's only one problem with Roosevelt," continued Dad, ignoring Mom's comment. "He's not Irish Catholic."

"Neither is Eleanor." Mom smirked. I nearly choked on my Raisin Bran.

"One day," said Dad, "an Irish Catholic will be president."

"That'll be the day," answered Mom.

"One day," I said, picking out some milk-sodden raisins and popping them into my mouth, "a woman will be president."

"That'll be the day," both Mom and Dad answered.

"Yes, she will. She'll be large and impressive, and she'll care about all people just like Eleanor did when she came all the way up here to visit the refugees. Mrs. Roosevelt put children on her lap and shook hands with young boys. Nobody at the shelter will ever forget that."

Dad leveled his gaze on me. "Where did you hear that? Did that refugee kid who loves our Bible tell you?"

I searched for another raisin.

"Eat your cereal, too. It's wasteful to only eat the raisins."

"I told you I wasn't hungry," I mumbled.

"Bill," said Mom, "this refugee kid is named Adam, and I don't think he *loves* our Bible. He knows it. I would think that's impressive, wouldn't you? Besides, Thanksgiving is a time to give thanks and share. It's not a time for silly contests, even ones having to do with the Bible."

"Ten Bible Questions is *not* silly! Remember, Joan, you and I used that game to teach our daughter some fine lessons. As for this kid, I don't see why he doesn't stick to his own things, including his own Bible. And he didn't have to show off in front of everyone with all those languages."

"Bill, that was months ago. Let's drop it."

Let's drop it. That was just like Mom. Whenever we started an argument, she'd run for the nearest hole.

"That's fine with me." Dad sipped some more while he stared at the kitchen wall like he and the wall were buddies who had to put up with females. I counted slowly, listening to my heart. Before ten, he'd have to say something. Seven. *Beat-beat*. Eight. *Beat-beat*. Nine. *Beat-beat*.

"I simply wanted to know," he said on the last beat, "how Christine heard the story."

Mom peeped her head out of the hole and shot me a quick look. *Don't say anything. Finish your breakfast*. "From the newspaper, Bill. Where else?"

"I don't see why you should talk about showing off." I chose my own corner of the wall to talk to. "You were the one who wanted to play that silly game. I said I didn't want to. And Adam didn't mean to show off. He was even willing to shake hands. The right way. He was sorry for showing off, too. And I don't see why he shouldn't know the Bible, although it's not the Bible to him. It's the New Testament. He has the Old Testament, which is his Bible, except he doesn't call it the Old

Testament. He calls it the Bible. And we have the New Testament, which isn't part of his Bible." I breathed in deeply. After months of one-word sentences, it felt odd saying so much. Odd and scary.

"I see. May I ask where you got that piece of information from? Did that come from the newspaper, too?" He wasn't looking at the wall anymore. Neither was I.

"I didn't say I learned about Mrs. Roosevelt from the newspaper. Mom said that. I've . . ." My voice trailed off. "I've been reading. You learn things when you read." We looked at each other until my eyes slid away. "I like to learn new things," I mumbled.

"Not so long ago, I couldn't get you to pick up a book. You were too busy with your friend Ann."

"I've changed."

"Where is Ann, anyway? I haven't seen her around."

"I've changed in all kinds of ways, in case you haven't noticed." My voice rose like I was going to cry. I didn't want to cry.

"I *have* noticed." Dad's jawbone moved up and down under his face like it always did when he was mad.

Mom skirted around us both and busily cleared the table. "I have to get ready for work," she said.

"I have to get ready for school." I pushed back my chair.

"It's Saturday," said Dad. "And we're having a discussion. In my day this so-called 'speaking out' was showing off, plain and simple. Some punk kid who showed off to his elders was rude. Plain and simple. Rude!"

"Drink your coffee." Mom spoke to Dad like she did to me. "It'll get cold."

"It was cold to begin with."

Mom grabbed Dad's cup and slapped it into the sink.

"Joan, I have a right to ask things. 'I've changed,' she says. What do you suppose that means? And where *is* her friend Ann? I used to see her all the time, but I don't anymore. Why not? Ask yourself that! My guess is that your daughter is making new friends, and one of these so-called friends is giving her more than just Bible lessons."

I didn't say anything. If I did, I'd cry. I was *not* going to cry. I wasn't going to blurt out something I didn't want them to know, either.

Dad picked his coffee cup out of the sink. "We shouldn't waste coffee," he said to no one in particular.

"Can I be excused?" I asked.

"Finish your cereal," said Mom and Dad together.

I stared at the bran flakes. They were getting soggy. I hated soggy flakes.

"Mrs. Roosevelt is an impressive woman," said Mom after a while. She stood behind Dad, patting his back.

Dad sipped the cold, disgusting coffee. "There's only one problem with Eleanor. She's not Irish Catholic."

He was going to let it go. He didn't want all his questions answered. Not now. I felt relieved and angry at the same time. I didn't want him to think that something was going on. Something *was* going on, but it wasn't what he thought.

"Neither is Franklin," said Mom.

Both of them laughed like they had their own private joke going. Maybe they even had their own private world that made it all right. But it wasn't all right for me. I didn't want Mom to pat Dad on the back and make jokes with him.

"Adam is not 'this refugee kid,'" I said, talking into my bowl as if my dumb, soggy flakes would listen. "He's Adam Bornstein and he did feel bad about Thanksgiving. That's why he shook hands and even switched when somebody else put out the wrong hand and everybody was laughing."

Mom took my bowl away and slapped it into the sink, just like she did with Dad's cup. "Bill," she said, ignoring me altogether, "Nell is expecting me."

"Go later."

"I can't. She needs me, and I have to shop. We have no food here."

"We won't starve."

Mom sat down. She wanted to leave, but she wouldn't, because he'd asked her to stay. She always did what he asked in the end. She was different than he was, but she always gave in. Or she ran to the hole, which is almost the same.

"Are you seeing the refugee boy?" Dad punctuated the word 'boy' instead of 'kid,' like that really mattered. It didn't. What mattered was Jewish. That's the word he wasn't saying. Neither was I.

"He is not the refugee boy!"

"Then—what—is—he?"

"He has a name, just like I have a name."

"What is your name?"

"You know my name." I turned my head away from him. I wanted to turn my whole body. I didn't.

Dad leaned over and held my chin so that I had to look in his face. He needed a shave, but even though he was growing a stubble, he still looked handsome. Ruddy and strong and fresh, in a young kind of way. Only his hands felt used and hard. "Tell me your name," he said. "Maybe it's Pinsky or Abramovitch or Goldstein. Those are fine Catholic names."

I shut my eyes. It bothered me to think about my dad being handsome, especially when he was holding my chin and being so mean.

"Bill—" Mom detached herself from the little circle they'd made.

"I'm asking her to tell me her name, Joan. That's all."

"No, it isn't all, Bill. What you said isn't nice."

Nice. That was such a small word, but at least she said something.

"What do you mean 'not nice'?" Dad turned away from me. "Do you want her involved with this boy?"

I rubbed my fingers over my chin. It wasn't hurting—I just wanted to feel my own hand there.

"I think she should meet all kinds of people."

"I'm saying 'involved,' Joan. Don't pretend you don't know what that means."

"She's too young to be involved with anyone, and *she* knows what that means. She's not a child anymore." Mom's eyes swept over my face.

I looked down. A glob of sweat was forming under my rear end. A part of me wanted to ask how I could be *too young* and *not a child* at the same time. But I sat quietly and studied the table. At least it would remain silent.

"That's the point, Joan. She's not a child."

I was glad he admitted that, but it wasn't as if he wanted me grown up. If he'd had his way I would've been a child forever. A good child. A good Catholic child.

"Bill," said Mom, "she and I will talk. Later. Not now. Now I'm going to Nell's and then shopping so my family will have some lunch." Mom's slippers padded across the kitchen floor. I heard creaking. She was passing through the living room. If you stepped in one place, the floor underneath the living room rug creaked. I used to jump up and down on the spot to see how loud the creak could get. Eventually I began avoiding it. I didn't want anyone to hear me coming and going.

"So what's your name?" Dad asked softly, like his mind was a record needle stuck on this one place, and only I could move it.

The sweat on my rear must have dried: I felt glued to the spot. I pulled my chin away to where his hand couldn't find it again. But my hands were out on the table—I'd forgotten about those. Dad wrapped his fingers around my wrists. I could've slid my hands out if I'd wanted. There was enough room. I didn't. I shut my eyes.

"What's your name?" Dad's fingers tightened. There was no space left. I didn't care. I wasn't going to cry. My teeth clenched themselves together. He squeezed. Tighter. I wouldn't let him see me crying.

"Chris—tine." Still not crying.

"Chris—tine what?" Squeezing and pressing.

"Chris—tine." My teeth loosened their hold. "Cook." I opened my eyes. I couldn't stand the way he looked. All of this was just another game he played with me, another Ten Bible Questions, but this time he wasn't going to let me keep any pennies, like he did when I was little. He won, and I lost. "Stein," I added. "Cook—stein." My mouth spread apart. I couldn't help it. "Christine Augustina Cookstein." I laughed idiotically.

He loosened his grip. My hands lay on the table. I wanted to shake them out, but I didn't. I didn't move at all. His right hand went up. It was kind of funny, like the needle wasn't stuck anymore, but everything had been changed to another speed—slow and drawn out so you had to listen hard to understand the words. I knew if I said what he wanted, the hand would go back where it belonged, next to Dad's body or in his pocket. A part of me wanted to say it, too. But another part wanted to be Cookstein or Cooksky or a thousand other names that didn't sound like walls, because that was what Dad was doing. He was making walls with my name.

"Cookstein!" I repeated.

The palm of his hand found my cheek.

"That's my name." *Slap!* "Cookstein." I was choking and hiccuping, but I wasn't crying. "And he has a name, too. His name is—"

"I don't care about his name. I care about yours. Christine Augustina Cook. That means if a boy asks you out, you ask me first. And you don't go anywhere at night with a boy. You're too young. You hear me?"

My fingers touched my cheek. Everything inside me went flat, and I nodded, my eyes fixed on his hands. The palms were down. The nails on his fingers were clean. I knew he scrubbed them. Every day he came home from work and took a shower. He scrubbed his nails and cleaned his face. Sometimes he'd splash on men's cologne that smelled of forests and not of boilers. Every once in a while, when no one was around, I'd go into his bathroom—Mom and I used the upstairs one—and I'd pick up some of his things. The cup and brush he used for shaving. His shaving cream. His razor. I'd open his cologne bottle and smell the forest and him. Then I'd think how, when I was little, he'd take my hand in his. My hand would curl itself up inside the big flatness of his hand, but it wouldn't disappear. Before Adam, I wished I could find that old hand. I'd put mine inside of it, and he'd be the old Dad. I'd be the old Chris. But after, it didn't matter, because I didn't care where he was as long as it wasn't around me. It was just . . . I needed to know that, if I wanted it, the old hand would be there, and, if I wanted it, I could make my hand into the old one, too—just as long as I didn't have to disappear. I didn't want to make myself disappear. I didn't want anybody else making me disappear. And I didn't want to cry!

"And you don't go anywhere with this *refugee Jew* boy!" he said, nearly choking on his own words.

"Dad, he's not . . ." I forced my lips against each other, but hard, dry sobs pushed themselves out of my throat as if somebody was retching on an empty stomach. It hurt to cry like that. "He is not this refugee . . . this refugee boy. He has—"

"You don't see him during the day and you don't see him at night. He's what he is. And you're what you are. That's all you need to know."

My rear finally unglued itself. "He has a name," I said, standing. I shivered from all the wetness. I wasn't crying anymore. I swallowed hard.

"Go to your room. Now! And don't come out until I tell you to."

My eyes went to his. I guessed that in some funny way I'd won—I had his pennies and mine—but it didn't feel like winning. How can you win when you feel so bad?

He turned his back to me.

I turned away, too.

• • •

I didn't go to confession that day. I didn't go to communion on Sunday, either. I ate breakfast first so I didn't have to think about communion. I ate all my Raisin Bran, and Mom and

Dad didn't say a thing. I put the bowl in the sink and went back to my room.

Later they ate a big breakfast of pancakes and syrup. Mom didn't want to make pancakes and syrup, but she did it to pacify Dad. I guessed she loved him more than me.

I *am* going to see Adam, I decided. He *is* my boyfriend. I wondered if he thought I was his girlfriend.

Downstairs Dad talked loudly. He wanted me to hear him, even if he was pretending that he was only talking to Mom. "Joan," he said, nearly filling the whole house with his voice, "she better not do anything with that boy! If she does, as our dear Lord is my witness, I will take the strap to her. I will, Joan. My father gave me the strap plenty of times. When I needed a licking, he gave it to me, and I didn't love him the less for it. I've never done it. I haven't wanted to. Not on my daughter. But there's right and there's wrong. I can't have a daughter of mine doing wrong." He stopped.

"Adam Bornstein," said Mom. Her voice was softer than Dad's, but I could still hear it. "His name is Adam Bornstein."

"I don't care what the hell his name is. I won't have my daughter . . . Joan, listen to me. People will start to talk. Some people do that here. They say, 'Jew lover. Refugee lover.' I've heard them talking."

"Maybe you heard yourself and your friends!"

"Maybe. I admit that such words aren't . . . aren't nice."

"They're wrong, Bill." She said "wrong." I heard her say it.

"But people say them. In the shoe stores. In the butcher's."

"And just as many, if not more, say nice things. True things, Bill. Not rumors. They open their doors and invite the refugees to meals. They teach the children in school. Some are doing so well. They open doors and hearts! Because these people are human beings like you and me. Bill, if you heard some of the stories of what's happening in Europe, you just wouldn't say these things. And you'd be glad that someone's telling you the truth. We should make them feel welcome and pray that they can stay here in America where we believe in freedom and justice and mercy. We need to be good Christians."

"I do believe in freedom, Joan, and I *have* heard, but that doesn't mean I want this boy to be free with my daughter. You can't mix everybody freely with everybody else. The Negroes and the whites. The Jews and the Christians. The Buddha-lovers with who knows what else? You go mixing all over and you won't know who's who anymore. She's our daughter. Our young daughter. She has to know who she is. And she has to be careful. I have to make sure she's careful. I'm her father."

I strained my ears, listening, but Mom didn't answer. Still, she said his name.

For days after that I told my feet to go home or to Ann's. Not to the library. Not to the camp. My feet went straight where I told them to go. But finally, one day, they wouldn't listen. I couldn't stop them.

"Where have you been?" asked Adam when I entered his barracks. "I have been looking for you." Behind Adam, Ralph stood grinning. Tikvah was beside Ralph. They seemed so much like a group. Even without me, they were still a group.

"Around," I said. "Just around." I didn't want to explain.

"I, too, have been going around." Adam moved closer to his friends.

I touched his arm. "I missed you." I didn't want to be outside the circle they made with each other. I didn't want to hurt Adam, either, although a part of me wanted to hurt someone. Just a little.

"It is good somebody is missing somebody." Adam and Ralph punched each other. Tikvah laughed broadly.

He can hurt me, too, I thought. I hated Tikvah's laughter. I was mad at them all!

Adam grabbed my arms and kissed me, first on one cheek and then on the other. Ralph opened his mouth, but Tikvah covered it. "No teasing," she said. "Come! We go sledding." She wrapped her arm around mine so that I felt she and I were in one group, the boys in another. And I didn't back away like I did when Tikvah first put her arm around me. "Friends should be able to show affection," she'd said. "In my country, women put their arms around women. They hold hands in public. They are not ashamed. And the men, too, embrace. We wish to show what is in our hearts. We are not so afraid of touching as you Americans, who only touch when you play games that you are calling 'contact sports.'"

Inside the camp I didn't feel strange about strolling around arm in arm with Tikvah. I felt free. Inside the fence I felt free about a lot of things. I wasn't scared that something would happen—something bad. I was happy. But outside I'd get confused and make mistakes, like when I put my arm on Ann's shoulder just because she's my friend, and she stiffened up. Adam felt differently than I did. Outside was his free place. Walking with Tikvah, I wondered if there'd ever be a place where we both felt the same way. Or maybe my outside would always be his inside.

We improvised toboggans from planks of wood. Mira begged so hard to come that we squeezed her between us and slid down the slope toward the lake until the fence stopped us. "This is the job of the fence," said Adam. "Always to stop us."

I thought of the Robert Frost poem we'd just learned in English class about how fences make good neighbors. Sometimes they do. But there are all kinds of fences, and you can't keep people behind one.

"To many of you we are not people," Adam had said when we were talking about Robert Frost and all the fences there could be. "We are a problem that you have not solved. So we stay behind the fence. Later you will figure out what to do. Set us free or make us go back."

When Adam said that, he was making a fence, too, just like Dad did. Only the "ours" and "yours" had changed. I was the "you" to Adam. The American "you" who could never understand him. But I didn't say anything, because sometimes I just wanted to be with him: Chris and Adam making their own place.

I felt that way when we were done sledding. The five of us walked our planks of wood back to Adam's little apartment. His arm was around me, and his body made a curve that mine filled.

Inside, his mother offered us cookies she'd brought back from the mess. We sat on wooden chairs that Ralph's dad had built and on Adam's cot—it was pushed up against the wall and covered with a beautiful knit blanket that looked homemade—and we drank tea with our cookies. Mrs. Bornstein lit the Sabbath candles. On Friday night, right before the sun sets and the Jewish Sabbath begins, Jews all over the world light candles. That's what Adam's mom told me. She said her mother had taught her the blessing when she was just a young girl. She would stand next to her mother, and when the candles were lit, they'd watch the sun disappear. Mrs. Bornstein sounded so sad that I wondered where her mother was, but I didn't ask. People at the camp would tell you lots of things, but it was best to wait and let them tell. Then you were sharing—not prying. I thought about my mom and me. Evenings, sometimes, Mom and I would say the rosary together so we could be close to each other and to Mary. Those times with the rosary must be like lighting Sabbath candles.

Adam's family didn't want to go to the mess hall—it was freezing outside—so we had a light meal of this interesting cold fish that comes in a jar. Adam called it gefilte fish. I loved it with horseradish, but I didn't like the jelly around it, so I scraped that off. Outside it grew dark. The wind shook the windows; together they chanted some winter snow song I couldn't understand, but there must have been some snow words in it. Adam lay on his cot with Mira and told her a Yugoslav folk tale about a prince who went through all kinds of challenges until he was able to marry the princess who had been changed into a peafowl. It was a story with a lot of twists and turns and a prince who was not all that bright, particularly when he opened the door of the twelfth room, which the princess had specifically told him not to open. What I liked, though, was the part with the witch's stakes that held human skulls, except for one stake that was empty, because it was meant for the prince's head. And the empty stake kept saying, "I want my skull, Granny." That part scared Mira. Adam didn't make it any better. He cackled "I want my skull, Granny," over and over.

The rest of us played cards while Adam finished. It all ended happily. The prince got his princess. Lots of evil people died, including the horrible dragon who'd imprisoned the princess. When Mira fell asleep, we moved to the floor—even Adam's mom—and I taught everybody to play Hearts. I won the first game. "No fair. No fair," everybody yelled. But Adam's mom won the next game. Then Tikvah. Then me again. Then Ralph won.

"I am getting to be such an old man," he said, yawning. He stood up, stretched, and winked at me.

"Don't leave," said Adam. "I have not won yet."

"He's a slippery one," whispered Ralph. "Watch carefully or he will cheat."

Adam pushed Ralph to the door. Tikvah waved. "Thank you, Mrs. Bornstein," she said. She poked Ralph.

"Thank you, Mrs. Bornstein," Ralph mimicked.

When the two left, Adam's mom took Mira to the back room, where I could hear her coaxing Mira into putting on her pajamas. My feet told me to get up. Go home. Go to Ann's. The rest of my body said stay.

Mira padded back out. She wore p.j.'s with feet, just like I did when I was her age. It would be nice to have a younger sister, I thought. Mira jumped into my lap. "Story," she said to Adam. "Tell me another story."

"It is late," said Adam's mom.

I got up off the floor. "I have to go. Thank you, Mrs. Bornstein. It was wonderful."

"Adam, walk her to her house. It is late. Already I think her parents are worried. You have told them you are here, yes? I should have asked earlier. We have no phone. Perhaps they are worried."

"It's O.K." I made my face seem like everything was all right. "He doesn't need to take me home, either. There are lots of lights, and this is a safe town. Really." I didn't want Adam coming near my house.

"I will walk you to the fence," said Adam. His mom nodded in agreement.

147

Near the camp entrance, Adam held my coat sleeves. "Do not go yet."

"I have to. Your mother's waiting. Besides . . ." I was thinking about the strap and how Dad had never given me a licking. I didn't care about being hit. It was just I didn't want to think about what he wanted and I wanted. About what I should've been doing and why I was doing what I was doing. I wanted to be here. With Adam.

He held my cheeks in his gloved hands. "Maybe it is no good I am with you. Maybe I am causing for you trouble."

"No, you're not," I lied. "I like being with you."

Neither of us knew what to say next. Maybe we didn't want to say anything. The silence made me nervous. If I didn't fill up the space between us with words, we'd have to fill it up in another way. "Do you think folk tales can ever be true?" I stupidly asked.

"They are always true."

We leaned our backs against the fence. Adam's hand held mine. I wished it were warmer so I could feel his skin and not his glove. I wished my mittens weren't so big. They made holding hard. Then none of that mattered. Everything inside of me was silent—silent but not quiet—and my feet didn't tell me to go anywhere. Our backs bounced against the wire. Around us, the bare trees looked cold. My hands inside my mittens grew cold. Adam jumped up and caught a shriveled brown leaf that the wind had finally pulled off from a tree. He held it up. "Leaf, you are dead," he said, waving the curled thing in front of us, "but here inside this fence you are on neutral ground. You are not an American leaf. A pity. So I will make you fly away."

Adam shoved the leaf through the wire. "Now you are on American soil. A poor dead leaf. But free nonetheless."

I jumped up and caught another brown leaf. "Leaf," I said, "you may be on neutral ground, but you are the most American leaf I've ever met. Still, I will push you through the hole, too."

Adam's lips brushed against my cold cheeks. "I want my skull, Granny," he whispered. I laughed.

"Do my gloves keep your hands warm?" I asked.

"Amazingly so. Do you want to feel how warm?"

"I have to go. I really have to."

"Wait. How are you thinking of me?"

"You're a friend."

"A friend." Adam paused like he was thinking about the meaning of that word. I moved away. He pulled my jacket. I fell backward against him. He turned me around. "What kind of a friend?"

"A good friend!" I laughed. It wasn't like the laugh I made when he said "I want your skull." It was a funny, throaty sound that surprised me. "A very good friend," I added, laughing some more. "Now let me go."

"I cannot let you go until you are telling me what I want to hear." Adam brushed aside the hair that stuck out of my hat. "Tell me, Chris," he said, pulling it just enough so I could feel the pull, "what kind of a friend?"

"What kind of friend am I?" I looked down. I didn't want to see his eyes.

"A good friend!" Adam tugged my hair harder and laughed, too. I didn't like him laughing that way. "A good friend with beautiful blond hair."

"My hair is not beautiful. It's dirty blond."

"It is not dirty. It is appearing very clean."

"'Dirty blond' means it's dark blond. Not light."

"You have beautiful hair." He wasn't holding my hair anymore. He was touching my face with his gloved hand. Running his fingers down my cheek.

"Your hair is beautiful, not mine. It's black and curly and it's the first thing I noticed the day you came here."

"You were seeing me that first day?" A gloved finger traced around my lips. I tasted leather. Then air.

"Yes, you were holding your sister's hand."

"And you, I am remembering, you were standing on the shoulders of two boys and holding a bicycle. I see that and I say to myself, 'What American ingenuity.'"

149

"And your mother was beside you," I continued. "You had an old suitcase with a rope around it. And you wore an open shirt. I liked the shirt. I even dreamt about it."

"Was I in the shirt you dreamt about?"

"Yes, although it was torn."

"Was the suitcase there, too?"

"No."

"That is too bad. The rope was coming from Italy, you know. The suitcase, it was coming all the way from Yugoslavia." He sounded sad and distant.

Hold my hair, I thought. Touch my mouth. My gloved hand went to his hair. "You should wear a hat." I put my hat on his head. "Here."

"Now I am looking very handsome. My freckles, too. They are the most handsome."

"They are!"

Adam snorted. "This is your hat." He stuck it back on me. "It is looking best on your head."

"I have to go," I repeated for what must have been the millionth time.

"First tell me what I was doing in your dream."

"I don't remember."

"Nothing? Surely, you are picturing now in the dream that I am very handsome in my shirt. I have a sword." Adam swung his arm, slashing the air. "It is a sharp sword. Very long. And I am looking exactly like Errol Flynn, except I am the more handsome. And more smart."

"Smarter," I said.

"So I was smarter!"

"No, I'm correcting your English. It's *smarter*, not *more smart!*"

Adam bowed. "I thank you, teacher Miss Christine Cook. However, it is the dream I must know. I was in my shirt without the suitcase, and I was chasing someone. That is how it was."

"No, you were running away from someone."

"Aha, I was a coward. That is very bad."

"You weren't a coward."

"But I was running away. Who is this person that was chasing me?"

"Who was chasing me."

"Yes, who is this person that was chasing me?"

"It's 'Who was this person *who* was chasing me?'"

"Aren't I saying 'who'? How many times must I make like an owl? Whooh—whooh."

"My father—" I blurted.

The man in my dream wasn't Dad. He was someone strange. I hadn't known who he was, but when Adam asked, suddenly I knew. Even if his face wasn't handsome nor fresh and strong like Dad's, his hands were the same. They were hands that liked to pull things apart and put them back together again. Used and hard hands. Good hands if you're a toaster or a boiler. Or a flag that's not hanging right.

"Your father?"

"My father is expecting me home. I have to go. Now."

"A sad dream, I think," Adam said. He really did look sad.

"Yes," I said before I could even think, "it was sad, but not altogether sad, because in the end we kissed."

Adam turned up the collar on my coat. "That is much better. Then it was a good dream."

"It was long."

"The dream?"

"No." I don't know what got into me. "The kiss! It was very long!"

"You must show me the length. Exactly how long is this long?"

"Adam, am I a very good friend?"

He arranged my hair back on my coat. Everything inside me felt flat and squished. I started to cry. I didn't know why. I didn't know the reason for anything anymore.

"You are crying," said Adam, wiping the tear. "My girlfriend is crying. That is no good."

"I have to go," I repeated for the zillionth time. "Please."

"You are free. To come and to go, you are free."

"I know." Then I showed him just how long the kiss was. But this kiss was longer than the one in my dream. Much longer.

Chapter Three
Praying the Rosary

❧

CHRIS

My cousin Dick died. I didn't know what to do. Nobody did. We couldn't even have a real mass, because you need a body and we didn't know where Dick's body was. We didn't know so many things: if he died instantly or if he suffered; if anybody was beside him; if anybody prayed for him or buried him. Maybe he was in a mass graveyard with other boys. Maybe there wasn't a chaplain there to say the last rites.

We couldn't do anything in the proper order, either. No body, no coffin. Funerals are awful, but with a coffin at least you could have a real one. You could wheel the coffin into the center of the church, watch it, think of the body inside, pray, and imagine the soul moving out of purgatory toward heaven. You could concentrate on the six candles, three on each side of the coffin, and when the priest came down and sang his chant in

Latin, you could feel a little better because everything was in order. The holy water would be there to sprinkle over the coffin. There'd be incense. You'd have done what you should have for the soul of the deceased. A soul inside a body that'd find its way to heaven, because Dick was good and kind and generous.

"We will make an offering for a solemn mass," said Mom. Aunt Nell nodded. Then she gave Mom the telegram she'd been holding for so long it was wet with sweat. "We regret to inform you . . ." Mom stood over the garbage can. She didn't ask if she should throw it away. She stood and waited.

"Put it in the drawer," said Aunt Nell. Her shoulders sagged. "Then I'll know where it is."

We had a Solemn Requiem Mass. Everyone was there: relatives, Dick's old friends, even Mr. Santara, one of his math teachers who I'd had, too. I wanted to tell him that next year would be different. I wouldn't think about how I was solving problems that never could happen in real life. It's good to have problems you can solve: real life is so confusing. And Mrs. Dubchek was there. She sat next to Mr. Richards. I was not surprised—not after what happened. During the mass, one of the priests gave a sermon about Dick's bravery. We all went to communion. We had a special confession beforehand so everyone could attend. I had a lot to say. I didn't need all those brothers and sisters like I once thought.

I made my words find their way past the knots in my mouth. I bowed my head. "Bless me, Father, for I have sinned. My last confession was over a month ago. And since then I have . . ." I swallowed. "I have gone to the refugee camp against my father's orders. I snuck in many times. I met a boy there. He's not of our faith, Father. He's Jewish, but I still love him, even if I'm young. I feel older than I am and I know what love is. It's not what Dad thinks. I haven't done things, unless you count kissing, and Adam—that's my boyfriend's name—kissed me. I only let him, though I did kiss him back, too. But that's it. And going with Adam doesn't make me feel any less Christian. I feel very Christian, except in this dream I wasn't. I don't think. But,

Father, it doesn't matter, really, because the way I see it, you can be Jewish and be very Christian, too. I mean like when people say, 'He was a real Christian,' or 'He was being Christian about this,' they mean kind and charitable, and that's being human, isn't it? So Jewish and Christian is just part of being a good human being, except Adam doesn't believe in Christ, so he's not Christian, and if you don't believe in Christ . . .

"Oh, Father, I just love him, and if you love, you know, it's like . . . I don't know. I've been thinking about fences, Father, like which are right ones and which aren't, and I can't figure it out. My dad's got it all figured, and refugees are on one side of the fence. I'm supposed to be on the other. Jews, too, Father. And Buddha-lovers, which is what Dad calls people who believe in Buddha. Everything that's different for him is lesser, but it shouldn't be that way. All of that is just different, you know? And how do we know what's the right way to be? Just because I'm one way, it shouldn't mean that everybody's gotta be that way. Besides, I like difference because it makes you see differently. Like maybe we're all standing around a tree, and we all don't see the same things, but it's the same tree, so I don't see why I should feel that I'm sinning. But maybe I am. Maybe I do deserve everything Dad says I do, like a good licking, because maybe I'm not being a good Catholic. I'm not being a good daughter. I'm not listening to him. But he doesn't listen to me, either. He doesn't even talk to me. He won't say my name, because I won't be like he is, which means that I don't belong to him anymore. I'm not part of his family. But I am, even though I disobey him. I don't think I'm bad. I don't feel bad. I'm trying to figure things out. That's all."

"My child," said Father Walters, "be careful to keep the purity of focus of your faith."

I bowed my head. There was silence. "I won't . . . I won't see him," I said.

Father Walters absolved me.

Later, at home, I took out the holy card that Aunt Nell made for Dick. I had it tucked inside my special missal next to

Grandma Augustina's card. I kneeled down next to my bed and read.

O GENTLEST Heart of Jesus ever present in the Blessed Sacrament, ever consumed with burning love for the poor captive souls in Purgatory, have mercy on the soul of Thy departed servant. Be not severe in Thy judgment, but let some drops of Thy Precious Blood fall upon the devouring flames, and do Thou O merciful Saviour send Thy angels to conduct Thy departed servant, Richard Flannery, to a place of refreshment, light, and peace. Amen.

May the soul of the faithful departed, through the mercy of God, rest in peace. Amen.

Something was going to happen. I couldn't stop it.

ADAM

Why wouldn't she speak to me? What had I done? True, I had not given her my Christmas present. Still it was not the right time. But I did not think she was angry about that. Nearly two months had passed since Christmas. Why would she run away when I saw her at school? Why had she stopped meeting me at my locker? And when I went over to hers, why was she never there? When I sat in the cafeteria with my cold lunch that the women in the mess hall prepared for us high school students, why didn't she join me? She had seen the space I left at our table. Always she was running. Always the running was away from me.

I sat on my cot, wondering. In my mind I made a list of things I loved and hated.

I loved to be in school and learning, although I did not love having to run from class to class. In Europe the students stayed in their seats in one room; the teachers ran. Here the bell rang and I raced to another room.

I loved our Social Club and dancing. I did not love the way my feet moved when they danced. One foot warred against the other. They did not know the meaning of harmony.

I loved shop class, where I made an ashtray and a bookcase. When Papa comes, I decided, I would give him the ashtray. He would light his pipe and tap out an abundant amount of ashes.

I loved working to be an American. I knew the Constitution and the branches of government, the names of the presidents, all the states of the Union and their capitals. But what did it matter? We were in limbo.

I hated that word and what it meant. More so, I detested late Februaries in Oswego, New York, at the Emergency Refugee Shelter, where I had to take cold showers and hear everyone's pee splattering against the bathroom toilet bowls. The only good thing was that there were fewer days in this month than any other, or I would not have been able to bear it altogether.

I did not tell Mama any of this. Instead I lied, which I also hated.

"It is all right," I would say when Mama brought up Papa's name from someplace deep inside of her. "We will hear from him. We will leave this shelter, and we will officially immigrate into the United States. We will become American citizens."

Mama turned away from me. There was no mention of packing or of buying another suitcase for our belongings. Half the camp had already packed once. In Washington, we were told, they discussed the camp's closing. We heard they would allow us to immigrate. A great cheer went up. There was a stampede at a local store. Suitcases were bought. "Not so fast," said Mama. "Let us see."

We folded our clothes. We had something to fold then, although most of it was second-hand. Mira stacked all of her shirts neatly on top of each other. She counted, gripping a pencil in her hand, and wrote out a list called "My Belongings." A true American, I thought, already counting what she owns and not what she has lost.

When half the camp was packed and ready to leave, we heard

that this place was not closing down. It would remain open until arrangements were made to send us back to our homelands.

Mama busied herself brewing tea. Her back seemed smaller and thinner, as if February in the United States at the Emergency Refugee Shelter was more than she could bear, too. When she looked at me, I read the old message: We should have stayed in Italy. We should not have let them go. Of course, Mama said nothing. Always it was nothing with Mama.

I hated Mama's silence.

I hated not knowing why Chris would not speak to me. I wanted to speak to her.

I hated making lists, even in my own mind. I would never be good at it.

CHRIS

Maybe if I hadn't sat with Mrs. Dubchek I'd never have gone to confession, or I wouldn't have known what to say. I was glad I'd gone—I guess—even if I felt Adam was still my boyfriend. I wasn't going to see him. I wasn't even going to think about him. I'd pretend he didn't exist. He'd gone away, and he was never coming back. He actually would go soon, anyway.

After Aunt Nell read the telegram, I sat in the kitchen listening to Mom make calls. She said the same thing to Aunt Mary and Uncle Harry and all our other relatives until I couldn't stand hearing the same words that Mom hadn't wanted to say and nobody wanted to hear. I ran outside. At first I started toward the camp. I wanted to tell Adam. But then I couldn't do that, either. I tried picturing him with me in St. Mary's. He'd be sitting next to me. But every time I sat him down beside me, he'd disappear. There'd be Mom and Dad and Ned and Grace and nearly all my relatives and so many people from town, too, but I couldn't seem to make room for Adam. So I didn't go to the camp. I stood in front of my house, not knowing where to go. Everywhere was somewhere I didn't want to be. Then I heard that rocker. A short squeak going backward. A longer one forward. She's watching out for our block and talking to God, I thought. I needed to hear what she had to say.

I walked up the stairs and sat next to her. "Mrs. Dubchek," I said. She shook her head and patted my arm before I said a thing. I don't know how she'd found out, but she knew. She stared straight ahead of her. I looked out, too. Maybe I'd see something. She took out her rosary beads and prayed—fifty-nine rosary beads, and she was going through them all.

"Here," she said on number ten, "take this." She pressed a rosary into my hand and took another out. I tried to imagine how many she had stuffed in the recesses of her faded pink housedress.

"Hail Mary," she said.

"Hail Mary," I repeated. I thought of Mom and me and the way we sometimes prayed together. Of Mrs. Bornstein and her mother. Of Adam and Ralph and Tikvah and me. I missed circles.

Mr. Richards descended from his porch. He had his cane in one hand and dragged his metal chair with the other. The chair bumped down the stairs, nearly knocking him over while his dog howled up a storm.

"Hail Mary, full of grace; the Lord is with thee; blessed art thou among women," said Mrs. Dubchek. I said it, too, while I watched Mr. Richards inch his way past the blue rusted signs and step over the curb. The chair clanked and scraped along behind him. Once it hit a rock and twisted around, nearly toppling him, but he kept coming. We kept praying, "now and at the hour of our death." In the middle of the street, he sat down and caught his breath. One lone car passed, honking. The dog had a fit. Mr. R. lifted himself up and shuffled toward us. I thought about Jesus moving through the Stations of the Cross. Jesus and Mr. Richards.

I rose. I had to do something.

"No," she muttered, between "Amen" and what must have

been the fortieth "Hail Mary." "He's come this far. He wants to do it himself. Let him."

He reached the porch stairs, breathed deeply, held on to the railing, and lugged the chair up. His dog emitted a long, low howl that ascended in pitch until it sounded like some baby crying.

"Pipe down, Buster," shouted Mr. Richards, waving at the forlorn beast. "Come, Christine. Help me move the chair next to your neighbor."

Mrs. Dubchek nodded. Digging into a torn pocket, she brought out another spare rosary and dangled it in front of him. "The Lord is with thee," she muttered. I wasn't sure whether she was talking to Mr. Richards or reciting the rosary. Maybe she was doing both. Maybe she was carrying on one of those endless conversations about our block.

Later I went to the special confession. I said what I had to say about Adam and me.

• • •

John Sanders asked me out skiing. I almost said, "No, thank you, I can't ski" because that was another girl who'd danced with John. A long-time-ago person.

"I'll have to ask my parents," I said. I thought of me and John. We'd go skiing and see movies together. We'd eat a whole big box of popcorn and watch *Snow White and the Seven Dwarfs*. Under our breath, we'd sing, "Whistle While You Work," and everything would be happily ever after, because I'd be comfortable and safe with somebody just like me. I'd be John's happy girlfriend. Mom and Dad's daughter. And I'd feel right. I wouldn't want to do things. There was a girl in our class who had three-colored hair, and somewhere, she had a baby. Everybody knew. She'd done things. I couldn't.

"Can I go skiing with John Sanders and his family tomorrow?" I asked Dad, sitting beside him in the living room. "It's during the day."

"Who is this boy?" Dad looked at me over his paper.

"He's Catholic."

Dad carefully folded the paper, laying it on the floor near his feet. "First you'll have to eat with us. We all eat together on Saturday morning. After that, you're free. Remember, though, you're to come home before dark. I don't want you out with some boy after dark. And don't forget confession."

I nodded and thought, It's not good to be serious about anybody.

"And don't think because you go to confession you can do anything."

I nodded again. Dad went back to reading. "How's work?" I asked after a while. "Have you been working hard?"

Dad's face seemed tired and old. I'd never noticed that before. "I do whatever they ask of me."

"Dad, I'd like to work hard, too. Maybe I could find something, you know, to help out."

"You have schoolwork."

"Yeah, but maybe it's good for me to work, too, so I'd be busy all the time, and I wouldn't be thinking about things. I'd be busy."

Dad frowned, burying his face in the paper again.

"Well," I said to nobody in particular, "I guess I'll go."

If I fell a lot skiing, I wouldn't care, just as long as John didn't try to pick me up.

When I got home again, I took my special Wac bag out from its hiding place under my bed. I wiped the dust off the bottom and checked all the stuff I'd packed inside. Nothing had disappeared or gotten out of order. Everything was in place and folded. I don't know why that surprised me.

Slowly I unpacked. It felt good to take inventory and see it all there, ready and waiting. One pair of slacks. Check. A pair of warm socks. "If your feet are warm," Mom liked to say, "then you'll be warm." Check. An extra pair of shoes. A bra. A shirt. Check-check-cross out. The pants were short and a little tight, but they'd do. I was glad I'd remembered to replace the bra, too, but I'd forgotten about the shirt. It was much too tight in all the wrong places. A part of me felt glad. A part of me didn't.

I checked off the underwear department. Three pairs of panties. I sniffed. A little musty, but they passed the still-smell-clean test. With three pairs of underpants I could last nearly a week, if I wore each pair twice. Once the right way, once inside out. The unopened box of Kotex, just in case. Check. A toothbrush. Check. Toothpaste. A good hairbrush. Check-check. One big towel. Check. And, check, one washcloth.

Then the incidentals. My tattered copy of *Johnny Tremain*. O.K. A pack of water-resistant matches minus one match. I'd put one under running water and then struck it. It had actually lit up, even though it crackled a little. All in order. And a chocolate bar—a Long's chocolate bar. Very old but still good. I considered leaving that off but changed my mind. That old bar hadn't made me feel bad. I'd liked getting it.

I grabbed my bag and my diary and went to the train station, where I sat and waited. And read. And ate three hard, stale chocolate squares. They tasted old and good. I sat a long time, watching the clouds and feeling the wind. Everything was moving except me. I wrote:

Dear Diary,

I miss the camp and the stories and the plays. I miss hearing the globe spinning around and around in my head. I guess that's how a rock feels. Hard and still. I miss Mira and Mira's mom and Tikvah and Ralph. But mostly I miss him. Does he miss me?

~~Christine Augustina Cook~~

~~Chris Bornstein~~

~~Christine Bornstein~~

C. C.

When it got too cold, I stood up. "You have to do something," said my feet. "Do something!" And they repeated that all the way home.

Some nights I would take my model airplane set, which I had ordered in the mail, from out of a shopping bag that I had stored under my cot. Inside was a B-29 bomber that came with a knife and all the balsa parts. Then I would imagine myself a fighting man. A B-29 flight engineer. From my many dials I had to spot the first sign of trouble. Or I was a B-29 navigator. With my charts and instruments I had to guide the plane on a straight line to my target. I was tail-gunner Adam Bornstein, directing the heavy firepower. Side-gunner Bornstein, ready to meet attackers swooping from the clouds. Or the bombardier. The success of our mission depended upon my landing the bombs right on their targets. Of course, I was always accurate.

In consequence, everyone was proud, and they decorated me. They also wanted a parade, but I would not allow that. "Do not spend your money on such foolishness," I said. "Instead buy war bonds." My humility astounded even me. Then I walked many miles home. No matter. My plane was left sitting on the airstrip—no wasting gas for me. Finally I saw my post box. It said, "The Bornsteins."

"I am home," I announced, opening the door. My loyal dog, Jax, barked his greeting. He was a healthy-looking golden retriever. We went duck hunting together, the American man and his dog. I always bagged my limit, and Jax never lost a bird. And then there was my wife. Down the stairs she came, Chris Bornstein, wearing a light blue skirt that made her eyes seem even bluer. From the waist up there was nothing except her.

In a dream such as this, anything is possible.

"We have shattered the enemy completely," I said. "In Europe and in Japan, all have surrendered."

Before I went to bed that night I took out an old newspaper clipping I had kept in my drawer with all the other stuff I just couldn't throw away. I read it over and over: "At Goose Bay, Labrador, a Wac helps speed a B-24 on its way to Berlin . . . Behind the lines in Italy, a Wac flashes a message from General Clark to the storm center of battle."

I pictured myself in Normandy, tabulating vital front-line statistics. Or New Guinea, speeding mail for front-line foxholes. I was in England and North Africa and New Caledonia, helping our boys hasten the hour of victory. Or at Yalta with President Roosevelt. "You should sit," I'd tell FDR. "Nobody expects you to always support the full weight of your braces."

At the end of each long day, I'd go home to my barracks. I'd climb the stairs, two at a time, and open the bedroom door. He'd be there in his uniform, pressed and clean and full of decorations.

"I've been waiting for you," he'd say. He'd unlace a shoe that was so polished I could see the reflection of his face in it. I'd kneel down and unlace the other.

"I've been waiting, too," I'd say. "My whole life I've been waiting."

Chapter Four
When One Thing Leads to Another
♋

I have learned to love this country, its people and its customs, and my greatest wish is that one day I can speak of it as of my home.
  Steffi Steinberg Winters,
  former resident of ERS
  Oswego Palladium Times,
  March 15, 1945

A series of polls from 1938 to 1946 dealt with the images Americans had of Jews. The results indicated that over half the American population perceived Jews as greedy and dishonest and that about one-third considered them overly aggressive.
  David Wyman,
  The Abandonment of the Jews

CHRIS

I applied for a part-time job at the Swiss Chocolates Company in Fulton. I saw their ad in the paper and read it aloud at the breakfast table. (I'd gotten to be worse than Dad about newspaper-reading.) At first Dad objected, but I said how the Syracuse-Oswego bus would take me directly to the Fulton plant, so I wouldn't be out in the dark and I wouldn't be alone.

"'Chocolate is a Weapon, Too!'" I said, quoting the paper. "'A fighting food, chocolate is an essential part of many of the rations used to keep up the energy and vitality of our Armed Forces. Both men and women are needed at The Chocolate Works to help make this weapon for victory. You can help. No previous experience is necessary.'" I flashed the picture of the fighting man with his half-eaten chocolate bar in front of Mom and Dad.

"The paper says, 'men and women,' not girls," said Dad.

"I'm not a girl anymore."

Nobody commented on that statement.

"I'm not sure how making chocolate helps the war," said Mom. She paused. "Bill, do we have enough chocolate for our Easter baskets?"

"Can we talk about Easter later?" I pleaded. Mom didn't even collect herself before jumping from one subject to another. She didn't say, "On the subject of chocolates, do we have enough for Easter?" Instead she galloped down the field, hurtling herself over fences.

"You and I need to find hats, too." Mom scrutinized my hair like she was weighing all the pluses against the minuses. My hair quality had dipped down into the red zone.

"If I get a job," I said, "I won't think about things. I won't have ideas."

Dad snatched the newspaper article out of my hand and whacked the table. We ate in silence. It was the kind of silence that makes you think that the spoons and forks are too loud for their own good. I reopened the paper, smoothing out the page with the ad. That was noisy, too.

"Where do you think this scene is taking place?" I asked.

Dad gave a cursory glance. "It must be the Pacific. See, there's a palm tree behind him."

"That's right," said Mom. She was her old agreeable self.

"And he's smiling." Dad peered down, suddenly intent on examining every detail.

"That's because of the chocolate he's eating." I wasn't sure I liked the direction in which our conversation was moving. My eyes took in the half-eaten candy bar in one of the soldier's hands and the huge weapon in the other.

"He's smiling and eating chocolate while he's shooting." Dad snorted. "And they're shooting at him."

"I don't see any bullets coming his way." We were definitely going in the wrong direction. I telegraphed a couple shorthand bleeps to Mom: ENTERING ENEMY TERRITORY STOP LEAD US TO SAFE TERRITORY STOP.

No one said a thing, unless you count all the talking our silverware was doing. Finally Mom picked up the message. "It'll be good for her to work," she said. "Maybe her chocolate bars will go overseas like my matches. We all have to do our part, Bill."

"All right," said Dad. A spoon moved up and down between his fingers. "As long as she follows the rules." *Tap tap.* "No staying—" *tap* "—out late. No—" *tap tap* "—running around" *long tap*. He released his hold on the rebellious piece of metal. I imagined it sighing with relief. "And no spending on foolishness."

I would not call what Mom and I did the following week foolish spending, but we did go Easter shopping. We took the bus downtown and had lunch there, too. I ate a sardine sandwich with lettuce and mustard. Some people hate sardines, but I've always liked to eat them, particularly on special occasions like shopping trips with Mom. She had tuna fish, and we both drank Cokes.

After lunch we tried on hats for Easter Mass. We must have tried on a million of them. First there was the white straw one with a pink bow and yellow daisies that I liked, then a pink straw one with big roses on the brim, and a hat with a huge brim and black velvet ribbons dangling down the back that I made Mom try on, because I wouldn't let her get away with saying that she was just accompanying me and she didn't want a thing.

"In her Easter bonnet," I sang. I didn't think about Dad or Adam or Dick and my aunt Nell, nor about blue stars or gold stars or what it would be like to be a Wac. Instead, I stood behind Mom, looking at her image in the mirror. Some beautiful woman who was my mother was wearing the most elegant hat. It was a pink velvet brim with posies all around, which you placed sideways on your head.

"Buy it," I said.

"Look at that price, would you? Eighteen dollars and seventy-five cents is much too much." Mom studied the price tag as if she could change the numbers by staring at them.

"In her Easter bonnet," I repeated, "with posies right upon it. Look," I said, "the one I love with the big roses is twenty-two dollars and fifty cents. That's more than yours."

A saleslady was hovering around us like some spring kite. She swooped down, landing close to the discarded hats near our feet. When we didn't respond to her fluttering, she shrank into herself the way kites do when no one picks them up. Then she puffed herself back up, lifted herself off again, and landed somewhere else. She must have been disgusted. I couldn't blame her. Hats littered the floor under our table. We were behaving like regular "lookie loos" who, according to Mom, are customers who spend their lives looking and not buying.

"We'll buy the pink straw one for you, Chris," said Mom. "It's calling out your name."

I held the roses near my left ear. "I can't hear a thing. Absolutely silent." I held the velvet French-looking thing against my right ear. "Listen, this hat is saying, 'Joan Cook, buy me. I belong to you.'"

"Nonsense. Hats don't say anything, but pocketbooks do. We're buying yours."

The kite swooped down next to us again, crumpling. "Can I help you?" She looked from us to the mess underfoot. I had to give her credit; she smiled. I'd have probably screamed, *Ladies, what are you? Lookie loos or buyers?*

"We're thinking," I said. I could be heartless sometimes.

"You both look beautiful in your Easter hats."

Mom and I studied the tags. None of the numbers changed. "Can we really buy both?" I asked. I nearly stepped on the daisied hat beneath me.

"If we don't buy shoes," Mom slowly answered.

"Or new dresses," I added.

And so I had a lovely hat to wear to church on Easter Sunday. I'll concentrate on Jesus and how he was resurrected, on spring and flowers and the end of war, I told my mirror face the night before services. I will not think of Adam. I am not a lovesick idiot!

The person who stared back at me wore a pink straw hat, and she looked beautiful, even if she was sad.

I wondered if he was lovesick. I hoped so.

ADAM

Russia and America were in Germany. President Roosevelt returned from Yalta, where the Allies talked of peace. Belgrade had been liberated since October; Tito and the Soviets joined together. It was the spring of 1945, and the world was a very busy place. In the camp we argued over whether Yugoslavia would become a Communist country while we made a circle around the post office and waited like hungry wolves. Every so often a few of us trotted off to Building #188, where a list that had made its way from Switzerland was posted. On it were the names of people who had made it to the free world. Mama, Mira, and I were on the list. We searched for Papa's and Villi's and Grandmama's names. Perhaps they had gone to Israel or were in England.

We heard nothing.

But the world was busy, and so was I. I joined the Schools at War Committee. I collected bonds. I earned Boy Scout badges and became highly decorated. Ralph and I perfected our sound system between his barracks and mine and constructed a workable radio. I also earned extra money by volunteering for plumbing detail. Pipes burst all over the camp, so I rushed to fix them. When I was not so occupied, I helped with our camp's Passover program. On the Jewish holiday of freedom we would all celebrate our good fortune—we were safe in America. We would also sing a cowboy song that was being played over and over on the radio. "Don't fence me in!" crooned the American on his horse. We understood his feelings.

Passover eve we set festival tables and placed a Seder plate at each end. Mira and her friends were in charge of making the *haroseth*. She was not hungry when supper began. I suspected she and her friends had eaten half the nuts and apples that were supposed to go into the mixture.

"And what does *haroseth* stand for, Adam?" I went around the table, filling cups of wine and listening in my mind to Papa speak to me. His voice was as it used to be before the war.

"*Haroseth*, Papa, is thick and sticks together such as mortar does. It reminds Jews of when they were slaves building pyramids in Egypt."

"And what about the bitter herbs and salt water, Villi? What do they symbolize?"

Villi took up residence alongside Papa inside my mind. He, too, sounded like his old self. He was the older, wiser brother. "The bitter herbs are for the bitter times the Jews had in Egypt," said Villi, smiling knowingly at his inferior sibling. "And the water is for the huge tears that Adam sheds when I hit him."

"No drinking beforehand!" said Tikvah as I brought a cup to my lips.

Mira, Mama, and I sat at a long table with people from Poland, Germany, Austria, and our Yugoslavia. Once we had been strangers to each other. Now we were together inside this shelter—guests of the United States. Refugees. We chanted from the book that tells of the exodus of Jews from Egypt. And once we were slaves, I thought. And now we are free. We sipped soup with matzo balls, had turkey and salad, and broke the flat matzo. "This is the bread of affliction," we said together. "Let all who are hungry come in to eat." Later we sang songs of praise to God. *Dayehnu*. It would have been enough for us. If we were freed from bondage, it would have been enough. If we got the Ten Commandments, it would have been enough. If we were brought into Israel. I thought of Papa. And Villi. Of Chris. And me.

Was it enough? What would it take for us to be free? When would we eat freely together? When I woke one day and the fence was gone, what would happen then? Who would sit at my table?

Then, later, the letter we had been waiting for did come. I put it inside a black box and shoved it under my cot. There alone it would rest and not with all the other letters that Mama and I had written and never sent. Nothing could get into enemy territory. Nothing got out except bad news. And I wished that I was still waiting. In our tiny apartment in Rome. On the *Henry Gibbons*. On the train coming to Oswego. In this camp. I would wait forever, hoping.

"You must cry," said Tikvah. She looked at me with her real eyes—the wounded ones.

"I forget how," I said.

"Crying is not something one forgets. You need to cry."

Someone had to teach me how to remember.

15 March 1945

My dearest Mama, Adam, and Mira,

I did everything possible. There was no helping it. Papa had been ill for some time, and I could only give him what we Partisans had, which was very little of anything. What began as a cold turned into a worse cold. It sat heavily on Papa's chest, then turned into pneumonia. I told Papa that we should stop and rest, but there was nowhere to rest, and only with the Partisans did we feel at all safe. None of them said, "They are Jews." We were all fighting for our country's freedom.

Papa grew weaker. From here and from there I procured medicine, but the constant traveling and bad food were no good. And always he was too cold, however much I covered him. This past autumn, when the Russians were helping us drive these monster Nazis out, I thought, Now I can help Papa. But fall dragged into a cold winter. I did everything I could, but Papa died yesterday. Mama, he so wanted to see you. Every day he was telling me about you. How

you met. What places you visited together. Papa made me feel,
Mama, how it is to meet someone like you. Please forgive me.

There will be a plain, simple coffin for him, as is our custom. I
have made all the funeral arrangements. Nothing holds me here now.
I will work to get to England and then to America. I have friends,
and they will help. Mama, I beg of you, do not blame me. I did
everything in my power.

Villi

CHRIS

Finally one night something inside of me broke. I didn't have to
think anymore about how, any day, I wouldn't be able to stop
my feet from going where they wanted to. Then Dad'd do what
he'd said he was going to do, and it'd be a done thing. All the
clouds that had bunched themselves together would turn black,
and the rain would come down.

But before all the pouring, I was going through my Friday
routine. Wake up. Eat breakfast. Think about Adam. Count
how many days I haven't seen him. Think about what I
promised in confession. Be good. What's good? Don't ask.
Make breakfast conversation. Rush to finish homework. Think
more about Adam and how this is a weekend. I could go over
to Ann's. Don't want to. I could've agreed to go to the movies
with John. Wasn't interested. Go to school. Blah blah. At least
it's Friday. Think about how I was doing well last month and
now I'm not. So what! Want to see Adam. Don't. He's Jewish
and you're Catholic. He's leaving. You're too involved. Wasn't
that what Dad had said? So what! Have to get myself motivated
for my new job. Try something different, like working at the
newspaper. Really do want to be a reporter. Watch the clock.
Wait for school to end. Wait for Friday afternoon job to end.
Wait for weekend to end.

The black clouds tightened into thick, hard wads shoving
against all the hurting places.

172

After school, I walked to the bus stop and waited for the bus to Fulton. I thought about what a bad chocolate sorter I was and missed Adam even more. I boarded the bus, closed my eyes, and let my mind busy itself with dumb questions. Is this chocolate bad enough to throw out? Maybe it's a borderline, and if I throw it out, I'll be hurting sales. But maybe some kid would get it and say, "Yuck! What nasty looking chocolate!" That kid wouldn't buy our chocolate anymore, and that would hurt sales, too.

There were other questions that I thought about but couldn't answer because I couldn't figure them out. I didn't want to. Could somebody Catholic go with somebody Jewish? Should a person get involved with another person when that first person knows the second one is going away? And what if that first person is already involved? What does she do? And what does being involved mean anyway? Maybe one thing can lead to another. Everything leads to something, but that doesn't have to be a bad leading, and if I thought about how one thing leads to another and another and another, then I'd never do anything, and I can't do nothing. But what if he goes—what if this person goes—and this other person is stuck where she is forever and ever and she never even sees New York City because she's afraid? So what!

Then my head started hurting from all the thinking. When the bus got to Fulton, I decided to forget questions and challenge myself to be quick. I'd be like Ann. She worked part-time opening envelopes at a bank and she wasn't bored. She challenged herself in all kinds of innovative ways. "I time how long it takes me to open fifty envelopes and put the checks on the left and the envelopes on the right," she told me. "Then I time myself again by putting the checks on the right and the envelopes on the left. The second way shaves off five seconds every minute. Think of all the time I save." Big deal!

All the chocolate-sorting energy was sapping out of me. Outside the factory entrance a group of workers was standing, and nobody was moving. Nobody walked inside. How come? I sidled over.

On the door was a handwritten sign: "Factory closed due to the death of our president." I read it a couple of times, but it wasn't sinking in, even when I heard some other women saying it, like maybe if they read it out loud in front of other people it would make sense.

We were clumped together like a bunch of grapes, still not moving. None of us knew what might happen if we detached ourselves. Who knows where we might've rolled? Things could happen in an instant. Roosevelt was dead!

Nobody made any stupid remarks. Do you think we'll get paid for this day off? Will we have to make it up? It didn't feel like when we got a snow day off from school, a surprise holiday. A day to spend crunching around in the snow. Our president was dead.

One woman made the sign of the cross. When I saw her, I did, too. I don't know why. I was just doing something, I guess. Then we all rode another bus back to Oswego. A few older women formed little whispering groups. I stared out the window, taking in a whole lot of nothing.

"Sh!" said Dad when I walked into our house. "We're listening." He and Mom had made their own private circle. They were working through the horror together, so I had to make my own space—not that it mattered. Lately all the circles they drew that included me weren't my kind of roundness. I just flopped around on the edges.

"Take yourself some cereal," said Mom. She pushed her rocker closer to the radio, huddling over it as if it were a radiator. The house felt cold.

I ate my standard bran flakes with raisins quickly. Then I joined the silent pair. None of us looked at each other. We sat, Mom hunched forward with her elbows on her knees, me on the sofa near the window with my chin on my knees, Dad in his big chair.

"On the eve of his greatest military and diplomatic successes," said the voice from the radio, "he was stricken down."

Mom pressed her tongue against the inside of her mouth making "that's too bad" sounds. "He should have seen Berlin fall," she said to Dad.

Dad put his finger to his lips just like he did the previous summer when we'd sat around the radio praying for our boys in Normandy. Now the Germans were almost beaten, and Bob and Joey were safe. I'd lost count of how many times Mrs. Dubchek read her son's last letter. I made a blanket just listening—a dog blanket for Mr. Richards's dog. It was a little like a long snake but a little like a blanket, too. Ten months from June to April. Friday, April 13. A bad luck day. Dick was dead, and so was our president. And sometimes it was like I was dead, too. I couldn't feel anything moving.

"A massive cerebral hemorrhage," said the voice.

Dad tapped the back of his head. "At least there was no pain. He had a severe occipital headache." (Thank you, Dad, for showing us what occipital means!) "In seconds he lost consciousness. Swift and painless."

Mom pointed to my shoes on the couch. I kicked them off, stretched myself out, and held the back of my head with my hands.

"He was being sketched by an artist at the time," said Mom, drawing me into their circle.

How much had the artist sketched? Had he seen it in Roosevelt's eyes? Would I see it if I saw the sketch? Questions rose up in me in one great wave, then just as quickly fell away. I wouldn't ask them, wouldn't think about headaches and sudden death. Mom rocked backward. I wanted to sit on the floor next to her and be a part of the circle she and Dad made. They'd let me in. They wanted me in, but my body stuck to the edges, not budging.

"At 7:09 tonight Harry S. Truman will be sworn in as president. Mrs. Roosevelt will then leave for Warm Springs." I imagined the announcer talking into his microphone as though he were talking into the whole world, but he'd feel lonely, too. My head throbbed. Pictures bounced around inside my brain: our sitting here last year, me seeing Adam for the first time, dreaming, confessing but not confessing, venial sins, Adam kissing me, me kissing Adam. Mortal sins. Adam telling me how Mrs. Roosevelt visited the camp. She put children on her lap. They'll never forget. Telling me the story of the demented one. Christmas lights and Jesus and my presents. He hadn't given me his yet. Tikvah telling about being raped. Me wondering about people, how anybody could do such a thing. Mom and Dad joking about Eleanor and Franklin and how they weren't Irish Catholic. Dad grabbing my chin and my wrist, because he wanted to own me, but it wasn't me he really wanted—it was *his* daughter. Dick's death and his funeral. Nothing was in order. There wasn't a body. Me confessing, even though I didn't want to be a white shirt. The missal Grandma gave me. My holy cards. The Virgin Mary in a blue dress. Adam touched one side. I touched the other. Easter hats. The globe spinning. If I closed my eyes, I could point my finger to Yugoslavia. If I kept them closed, my feet would get to the camp all by themselves. And if I did nothing, I would disappear.

Mom and Dad huddled inside the fullness of their circle. I stood up.

Roosevelt had been the president of the United States almost as long as I'd lived on this earth. He said that we were citizens of the world. We couldn't be ostriches or dogs in a manger. We had to be responsible. We had to act responsibly. So I had to figure out what to do for myself.

The announcer went on about Truman and the San Francisco Conference that would set up a World Security Organization to make our world free from strife. Would Truman free the refugees? Would he send them back? Adam had to be asking those questions. I wanted to hear him asking. My hand wanted to hold his hand. My legs wanted to sit next to his legs. Not right on top of them, but close. My lips wanted to be near his.

"I have to go out," I said, talking into the center of the room.

Mom and Dad pulled their ears away from the radio. "Out where?" asked Dad.

I could have answered, "To Ann's" or even "To John's." Dad liked John Sanders. He was the boy of Dad's dreams. So they wouldn't have minded. They wouldn't have checked, either. They'd have talked about the war and Roosevelt and the war and Truman. Dad would have drunk an extra cup of coffee while they talked, and nobody would worry. But I couldn't make myself lie. I was tired of lying and pretending that nothing mattered. Things did matter. I mattered!

"I'm going to see Adam," I said. "Adam Bornstein." We all knew who Adam was, but I had to say his whole name.

"Joan," said Dad, rising and turning off the radio, "tell her to stay home."

"Please, Chris, stay home," pleaded Mom. "We'll talk."

"I have to go." I opened the closet and reached for my coat. Mom moved to the sofa and patted a space next to her. "Come on, honey."

I shook my head. Dad moved up behind me. Deliberately, he took off my coat like he was my date. It was that smooth and gentle. I didn't hunch my shoulders so that he'd have trouble. I let him take it off. Just as carefully, he took a hanger and hung the coat back up, then closed the closet door. Tight.

"Sit down, Chris," he said. He wasn't ordering me. He was asking me, because he didn't want to do the thing he had said he'd do. He didn't want to hurt me. He'd never wanted to hurt me, but he couldn't think of anything else to do. I couldn't either.

"I'm sorry," I whispered to nobody. "I have to go. He'll be so sad. Everybody was hoping Roosevelt would let them immigrate. Everybody was waiting. And now they'll have to deal with Truman. He'll be so sad. I just want to talk to him."

Dad's face closed around itself. "It's not just talking," he said.

I skirted past him toward the door. Dad blocked my way out.

"You'll get sick," said Mom, standing between us as if she was a referee. "At least take a sweater."

"I'm not cold and I won't get sick."

"It's not just talking, is it?" repeated Dad. "It's kissing, too."

"Bill—" said Mom.

"It's kissing, too, isn't it?"

He wasn't really asking me. He was telling me what it all was—what he saw in his own mind. Dirty pictures that had nothing to do with Adam and me.

"Bill, stop torturing her."

"Let her just answer my question. That's all she has to do. Either she is kissing this boy or she isn't."

"Are you kissing him?" asked Mom.

I didn't want to feel ashamed, but he was making me feel that way. "It's not like Dad thinks," I whispered.

"Are you kissing a lot?" Mom's eyes swept across my face like one big searchlight.

"You see, Joan, she doesn't know."

"I do know!" My voice cracked. I hated the way they were talking, like I was this *she* who didn't have a clue about anything.

"What do you know?" Mom's searchlight shone even brighter.

"Things. I know things!"

"What things?"

"Ask her if she knows how one thing can lead to another." Dad talked to me through Mom as though I needed Mom as my interpreter.

"Chrissy, you need to stay home tonight. We'll talk. We need to talk." Mom's hand stroked my back. The stroking felt good and warm.

"I have to go " My feet felt heavy and tired. "I have to." They pushed themselves forward until I almost stepped on Dad's feet. My hands reached for the door, but they couldn't get by him. He wouldn't move aside. I turned around and ran toward the back door before he could block that, too.

"You'll be punished for this," he said. It didn't sound like that, though. It sounded like "You'll be pun—ished f-for t-this." His voice was choking up in his throat.

Then I almost didn't go. But I couldn't go back. Not anymore.

ADAM

It was just after supper when she knocked at our door. Mama and I were seated near the radio. Mama held a teacup against her forehead, just as she used to do when Villi and I argued and her head hurt. Papa would suck his pipe. Mama would have her hot tea. When the energy to do is gone, habit remains.

"What should we do now?" Mama's eyes were closed.

"Answer the door," I said. I knew she was not asking about the door, but it was too soon. I did not want to be the one to speak. In the future I would tell her that we should stay in America and wait for Villi, but for the present I would say nothing and continue to be Papa and Mama's child, Villi's younger brother.

Mama lay down her cup and smoothed out the wrinkles in the black skirt she had worn that whole week. It was a useless kind of smoothing, like the kind of ironing an old woman does when she lays her hands across her face stretching out the skin. The knocking continued, faint now, as if the person on the other end grew shy. Soon that person would go away.

"There is someone at the door." I tried pushing her with my voice. All week long Mama had said, "Answer the door, Adam." So I got up and found outside the collection of men ready to say the Mourner's Prayer with me, or Mama's women friends carrying food from the mess hall, or Ralph and Tikvah pulling me away. Mama would not get up. She waited for me to let the world spill into our house. I did not want to do that anymore.

"Perhaps we should go back there." Mama stared into the inside of her cup. "The house may yet be standing. We will move in again, and then . . ."

And then what? I kicked my chair aside. "I'll answer it."

She must have been leaning against the door. When I opened it, she fell on my chest. I grabbed her. She pulled my arms away. Her face was not at all like the face of the girl I knew. She is sad, I thought. And cold, without even a coat.

"Chris?" The name felt strange to my tongue, like a language I had once known and forgotten. All that week I had forgotten about her, this American girl who lived outside the fence, who listened to my stories and corrected my English, who gave me gloves to wear so my hands would be warm. She came to me once in a dream and she was wearing a skirt, nothing else. All week long I could feel nothing for this girl of my dreams. Now everything ached, wanting.

"Come in," I said, sucking in air. Her fingertips touched mine. We were together beneath the roof of our hands. We shivered.

"Shut the door, Adam," said Mama harshly. For sure she was thinking, What is she doing here? You are too young to be attached, Adam. And why not with someone from inside here? From where we come from. Who believes in what we believe.

"I should go," said Chris. "I'm sorry I disturbed you."

I stood helpless, while our fingers pulled against each other. Her lips were purple from the cold. "No, you must make yourself warm," I said. Please Mama, I thought. Let her in.

"Does she need a sweater?" asked Mama. She was not letting her in, but she was not shutting her out, either.

"No, I'm fine," Chris answered. Her hands held her shoulders as if to convince them of warmth.

"She is cold," I said.

"Mira, get her a sweater," said Mama.

"Does she need a black sweater, too?" Mira crawled out from under the table, where she had retreated. After I told her about Papa, she spent days sitting beneath the table as she used to do in Rome. Early that morning I had sat with her. We had closed our eyes and dreamt a winter dream. Then the knocking commenced.

"No, Mira," Mama's voice softened, "you and I wear black, but she can have colors. You find her a nice colorful sweater."

Mama is letting her in, I thought. I stood away from the door, opening it wider. Chris hesitated.

"Adam," said Mama. "Close the door before the cold is inside as well as outside."

I led Chris to the center of the room. Mira brought out Mama's sweater with the small painted buttons on it, the one that made you think it possible to wear bits of the sky. "Here," she said, holding it up.

"That's O.K.," said Chris. She looked at Mama.

"Take it." Mama rose slowly from her chair, dismissing the matter. Perhaps she was dismissing us, too. "Mira," she said, taking hold of Mira's hand, "you and I will go in the other room. It is late. We will get ready for bed."

"I shouldn't have come," said Chris. She looked at Mama's retreating back.

Then, together, we watched them shut the bedroom door. Together we smiled.

"Let me help you with the sweater," I said. This is how Mira dresses her dolls, I thought. But she likes the dressing. I prefer the undressing.

Chris's right arm slid into the sleeve. She blushed and looked away from me, but she stood still. Her left arm struggled to find the hole. Such serious business. Her lips wanted to part, but she held them in place. I began buttoning, though the buttons were too small; she was not built like Mama. There was so much more of her. My fingers fumbled, trying to shove one button into its hole. I was entirely awake. So was she.

181

"You don't have to," she said. "I can do it myself." She moved back.

My hands touched her neck. Her heart beat under my fingers. It was frightening to be so close. My hands went to the back of her head and pulled back her hair. I do not know why I loved to do that. It might be because of her large ears—not at all what you'd expect. They were hidden under a mass of hair, and when I would pull it back, there they were. I smoothed her hair behind the ears. Her chin quivered. Inside of me there was a dissolving. I held her shoulders.

"Adam," she said. "I heard about the president. President Roosevelt . . . I wanted to talk to you about him." Her shoulders were moving up and down, my hands moving with them.

"I have to tell you," I began. I grabbed her still-heaving shoulders. We were holding on to each other while beneath us the floor swayed. I was going to be sick. Worse yet, I would cry. We sank into the sofa. I leaned on my side and put my head inside her lap, breathing deeply and trying to calm my stomach.

"Why did Mira ask if I had to wear black?" she asked.

From the other room came Mama's and Mira's voices. Mira did not want to put on her pajamas. She wanted to stay in her clothes and sleep under the table. "People do not sleep under tables," said Mama.

Chris ran her fingers through my hair, untangling the knots, "Why are you all wearing black? Is it because of the president? Franklin Delano Roosevelt was the president nearly all my life."

My right hand touched her knee, silently slipping under her high socks.

"Please tell me, Adam. Did somebody die in your family?"

I pulled down one sock and felt her bare leg. Her skin was warm. Behind the knee was soft and fleshy, and there were soft blond hairs you could hardly see lying against the bulge of her calf muscle. For a moment I wished I could be like those hairs always close to her skin, moving with it as she walked down the street.

"Adam, is it your brother or . . . your dad? Is it your dad?"

I pulled down another sock. I must have scratched her leg,

because she jumped. My hands kept going. Taking the shoes off. Taking the socks off. I held her ankle, my hand wrapping around its hard sharpness. Please, I thought, don't ask me. Her lips were on my neck. Someone was trembling. It had to be me. I turned around, and her lips touched my nose, brushed over my cheeks. My mouth shook. The legs would not stop shaking, and I felt that I was there again, on that ship, staring at the basket, the man inside who looked back at me and wondered why I had legs when he did not. But my feet, they had followed their own destiny, even as the two suns shone in the sky, the feet kept moving, so that now I could not go back, because the only thing that remained the same was my name. My fingers tightened on her shoulders. I lifted myself up. It was not my fault that Nissim was selected. It was not my fault that the American soldier lost his legs and arms. No one should blame me for Papa, and if Grandmama would never be found, that was not my fault, either. I was alive. I deserved to be alive.

"Papa," I said, almost choking, "he is . . . Villi wrote us, and he said that my father . . . Papa . . ."

She did not say useless idiotic things such as one says when one does not know what to say. "Do you want to go outside with me?" she asked. Or maybe I asked it. I cannot be sure. I nodded. It was quiet in the other room. Too quiet. I did not trust the door. I trusted myself even less. She bent down and put on one sock. Her hair fell over her ears and cheeks, and I sat beneath the hair, slowly working the second sock up her foot and over her ankle. Her hands moved to get her shoes.

"No," I said. "I want to." I wanted to take everything off of her and start over.

She lifted one foot while I pushed back the tongue of her shoe, held her ankle, and slipped her foot inside. "It is a beautiful shoe," I said stupidly. "Good leather."

My hands held her knees. "Let's go outside," one of us said.

"Yes," responded the other.

Chris took off Mama's sweater. "It's too small," she said, laying it over the chair.

"I noticed." I pulled off my own sweater and gave it to her.

I had no black sweater. Only green, which I wore over my black shirt. "It will keep you warm," I said. "It is not too dirty." We laughed. "Sh," I pointed to the back room. "Let us go."

It was quiet outside, too. No one was running to an English class or to a lecture on American politics or to a meeting of musicians. No one was taking out garbage or heading toward the laundry. All were in their apartments, waiting for news. Only the moon kept us company, sitting quietly as it always sits, saying nothing. There was so much I wanted to tell Chris, but where would I start?

"We saw a moon such as this," I said, pointing up, "when we first came into New York. Mira called the moon a giant peach. You know why?" I put my arm around her shoulder. "Because on the ship she is falling in love with anything from cans, most especially canned milk and peaches. We were so hungry. You cannot believe how hungry, and there was so much food—all of it fresh. We ate cold cereal from funny boxes that you cut open with a knife, and you can throw them away. Everything in America you can throw away, even food." The words gushed out of me. "You should see all the food they were dumping overboard. It would make me sick, watching, but you cannot believe, when I saw the Statue of Liberty, I wanted to be here already so much that I could hardly sleep on the train ride. Besides, Mira and Mama were on another train, and I was worried. What if I don't see them again? What if they disappear? You think I am childish. Yes?" I searched her face. No, she did not think that. She did not pity me, either. "You are so fortunate," I said. "You do not wake and wonder from day to day, 'Will I be alive? Why are all these people hating me? They do not even know who I am.' And then always to pretend I am someone else. Sometimes I forget who I am."

She drew closer to me. My arm slid around her shoulder. I squeezed it. "Then I come to school here. That, too, is a miracle. I want to study hard. I am not trying to impress anyone. Only now I *can* study. I want to do such things. Everyone in America will say, 'There he is, Adam Bornstein.' Sometimes, though, I do foolish things. This past month I did not need anything, but

I wrote a request slip for pencils. Not one, but two pencils. And I got two pencils! Do you know how that felt?"

We walked around the camp. Suddenly it felt strange to speak and it felt strange to be quiet. I did not know what to do. My arm held her waist. We bumped against each other, walking. Past the Teen Club building, where we refugees learned new American dances. We made believe that we were Frank Sinatra or Bing Crosby. Holding the microphone, we crooned, imagining girls crying, "Frankie, Frankie" as they swooned at our feet. We passed the Infirmary where babies were born. They were American babies. Then the building that held our theater. The field where we played soccer. The old graveyard, where American soldiers were buried. I thought of Villi. He had buried Papa—I had not. Did he choose a good place? Papa did not like the sun. He needed shade and coolness. Then I heard a sound such as I had not heard in some time. Some sad person was sobbing in such a way as one might believe all of the world had fallen apart inside of him. My face felt wet while the person kept sobbing, uncontrollably. She was holding that person. I felt her arms around me, and we slid down on the damp ground near the gravestones.

"It's all right," she said, blotting my tears out with her thumbs. She brought my hands up to her cheeks. Everything around us waited.

"Come," I said, pulling her forward. "Sit on my lap. Then only one of us gets wet."

"That's O.K. I don't mind getting wet."

The damp seeped into my pants. Soon I would be soaked, but I did not mind, either. I leaned into her, and she sat up, leaning into me. We kissed while my hands slipped under her blouse and felt her back. It was warm.

"Adam," she asked, "you don't think it's wrong to do this, do you?"

I kissed her.

She pulled back. "You don't think I'm wrong, do you?" she continued.

"I love you," I whispered. I laughed, surprised by what I

had said. Yes, it was true. My hand felt for the clasp of her bra. Undid it. Felt the bones of her spine. The curve of her sides. The flesh that gave way when I pressed it. The hands stopped. They were surprised, too. She was bigger than I had thought. She shivered underneath me. My hands moved ahead, suddenly frantic with need. With excitement. Between her breasts was dampness like on the ground, but warm and moist.

"Adam," she said, "we shouldn't." Her body lay against mine. There was no space between us, so it seemed as if her breathing was mine. Mine was hers.

"All right." My hands continued. It was like we were learning how to breathe underwater. I felt lightheaded. Dizzy. But I could stay down forever. I pushed against her. She held my back. Then she jerked away, nearly falling backward.

"I can't," she said. Her voice trembled.

"Why not?" My mouth sought hers.

"I just can't."

I gulped in the coldness around us. We were outside again, not underwater, and the air stung. I coughed. So did she. "O.K.," I said. My voice sounded small and defeated. I wished to disown it.

We leaned against the stones, facing each other.

"Adam," she said, "you aren't mad at me. Are you?"

"No, I am not mad." I was not mad—only sorry.

She wrapped her hands around my wrists. "Are you sure?"

"If I were mad, would you let me?" Still hopeful.

"No." She was quiet. "No, I wouldn't."

"I did not think so." I sighed. She did, too.

"It's better to wait, don't you think?" she said. She sounded sad and relieved at the same time.

"Oh, yes. It is better," I said, sad and relieved, too. We both laughed.

"Adam, what will you do now?"

"What do you want me to do?" I played with her ear, thinking that there was always a slight chance.

"I'm serious. Will you stay in Oswego?"

I clasped my arms around my knees to guard them from

crossing over to her side. "If they let us. My brother Villi will come, and we will stay."

"But not in Oswego. You'll go somewhere else, right?"

"Who knows what we will do." I stood up and wiped my pants. They were hopelessly wet and wrinkled. I did not want to answer questions or think about the future. Or the past. What good would that do? Still the thought nagged at me. I did not want to go away. I had friends. I had a girlfriend. But Mama was right: a refugee camp is not a home.

"Your mother doesn't want to stay, does she?"

And then I was mad at her, at Chris. What did she know about homes, about waking up one morning and not having a home anymore? "No," I said gruffly, "Mama does not know what she wants. Her friends are going to New York. Mama has learned the beauty-school trade here. She thinks she will start a business if we save money. But it is possible we will return to Yugoslavia. Everyone is waiting for us there." I laughed ruefully.

"Will you really go back there?"

"No, I do not think so." She knew so little, even with all she had learned. There are some things she should never have to know, I thought.

"Will you write me from wherever you go? I like to get letters."

"Would you like me to be gone already so you can have my letters to show around instead of me. That would be much easier. A piece of paper instead of me." She *did* want me gone. I was giving her too many problems. I was too different—not someone she could marry. Only an experience for her. *The refugee!* She could talk of me to her children. "Once I went with this boy . . ."

I was making myself angry, but nothing made sense. I did not want to be outside with her. Not inside with Mama, either. And I wondered, Why did she look so sad when she came? Why does she sound so desperate? What does she want? Who is she afraid of? Maybe I do not know, either, and I do not want to know.

"I don't want you gone." Her voice cracked. "I love you."

She held my face as if I was the moon and anything was possible. I could be brought down from the sky to sit forever inside the cradle of her hands, never missing the stars or the clouds.

"I will not go," I said foolishly. I would kiss her, would begin again on the journey of hands and lips, and this time we would not stop. I wrapped my arms around her. "You had better go home," I said abruptly. "I had better go home." Nobody was listening to me—not even my own body.

"Adam, let's go to New York. Tomorrow! You and me! I've been to Syracuse and Newark, but I've never been to New York City. Let's go together."

"I do not know—" I faltered.

"Please!"

She seemed like a small child. All I had to do was say yes, and she would be so pleased. I held her hand, playing with her fingers.

"Let's go early and come home before dark. Ever since I was little, I've wanted to see New York. It'll be like a dream coming true. Going with you will be like all my dreams coming true. We'll see everything. The Empire State Building. Times Square. We'll go everywhere. Do you have money? I have some at home. I can give you some. Let's go. It'll be so much fun." She rushed over the words, stumbling.

"Chris," I held her close so I could see her eyes in the moonlight, "why do you want to go now?"

"Because. I don't know. I want to be with you. Alone. Don't you want to be with me?"

"What about your father? You cannot run off. We must ask. I do not want to worry your family."

"I don't care about my father!"

I held her chin. "You will get in trouble. You are already in trouble."

Her eyes slid away from mine. "I'm fine. Adam, do you need money? I've got extra. Really!"

"I have money, too."

She was lying. She was not fine. She was in trouble, and I was causing it.

"So you'll come to New York? Please, say yes."

I shook my head. I would go back to the apartment and not see her again.

"Say, 'Yes, Chris, I will come to New York with you.'"

Tomorrow was time enough to think of her father, of Mama. When the mourning was over, she would ask me why I was out so late with Chris. "This is not the new life, Adam. We are waiting. That means you leave her alone. She is not for you. She has her own kind. We have ours. She will hurt you. You will make sorrow for her."

"Yes, Chris," I said, "I will come to New York with you."

CHRIS ·

The front door was locked when I got home. So was the back one. I'll go to Ann's, I thought. No, I won't. I wanted to be done with it already. I rang the bell. Dad answered it. I figured he would.

"Is that Chris, Bill?" asked Mom from upstairs. She didn't come down. I wasn't surprised about that, either.

"It's your daughter," Dad called up.

Tears sprang into my eyes. I'm your daughter, too, I almost said. I nailed the lids shut, my mouth, too.

"What do you think I should do?" Dad asked like he was continuing a conversation he'd had with himself.

I shrugged.

"Is that *his* sweater?"

More shrugging.

"Did he let you walk home alone this late? It's almost midnight."

"He walked me up to the corner."

"How did he get out of that place? Aren't there guards? I didn't think those people could wander around this late at night."

"We snuck out. We do that. There's a hole. And the guards know us. They don't care." I didn't have to say all that, but I wanted to hurt him.

"They don't care about you kissing, either, do they?"

"I don't know. I never asked them." I wanted to hurt him a lot.

Everything in his face grew still and hard except his jawbones, which moved up and down the way they did when he clenched his teeth and held in his anger. When they stop moving, I thought, he'll say something. My stomach hurt. I put my hand against it so I'd feel better.

"Your knees are filthy. So are your socks," he said disgustedly.

I brushed my knees, then stopped. I didn't care what I looked like or what he saw. It wasn't the truth.

"Take off his sweater and wait for me in the garage."

I folded Adam's sweater. The shoulders wouldn't line up, and it fell out of my hands. I sat down on the sofa and tried to lay one sleeve over the other, but my hands wouldn't work right. For a second I wanted to run outside and sit on Mrs. Dubchek's porch. We'd knit together—big blankets that could warm the whole world—and we wouldn't talk. We wouldn't need to talk.

"Tell me that you won't see him again," he said. "Then we can both go to bed and forget about this whole thing."

I didn't look at him. If I did, I'd see how hard it was, because he didn't want to go through with it, not really, but I wasn't leaving him any choice. I folded the top of the sweater to the bottom. Everything looked rumpled and crooked. I couldn't get anything straight.

Dad grabbed the sweater and threw it on his chair "Tell me!" he shouted.

"I was trying to fold it," I muttered, reaching over. He was quicker.

"Leave the damn sweater alone!" He balled it up in his hands and tossed it in the corner.

"I was just trying . . ." Get up, I thought. Go upstairs. Don't look at him. He'll let you go if you don't look.

I stared at the grass that was caught in my high socks. I wanted to be with Adam again in the graveyard. I'd tell him he was the best thing ever to happen to me, even if he was going to leave. I would always love him.

"Chris, I'm asking you to say it. 'Dad, I won't see him again. I promise.' That can't be so hard." He was pleading with me, like all I had to do was repeat his words and everything would be all right, at least for a while. "'Dad, I won't see him,'" he repeated slowly.

Behind him were the stairs and my room. I could go up, lock the door, sit on the bed and think all night. Then, early in the morning, I'd slip out of the house, and Adam and I would go to New York together.

"Dad, I won't . . ." My throat tightened. "I won't lie," I stammered. "Please, don't make me lie."

His voice flapped back and forth inside his mouth. "Go, wait in the garage," he said, throwing the key on top of Adam's sweater. I picked up both of them and went outside.

Chapter Five
Bringing Down the Moon

&

It was the nightingale, and not the lark,
That pierced the fearful hollow of thine ear.
Shakespeare,
Romeo and Juliet, III.v.2-3.

ADAM

The sun had not come up yet when she knocked on the door—softly, so as only one who was waiting would hear. "One minute," I whispered. I did not need to dress. I had been ready for hours. I held the door open and quickly wrote a note. "Mama, do not worry. I will be home this evening."

We walked to the bus station. I wanted to say a hundred things, but all of them seemed foolish, so I concentrated on the street signs and the curbs and the sound of our feet. Midway there, I grabbed her hand, and we ran.

"Two tickets to New York," I said when we arrived at the station. I had the money ready. I had it all planned. She tugged at my jacket sleeve. "I will pay the fares," I said. "You can pay for what we do there."

On a bus, in the dark, you can be anywhere, and everyone is a stranger except the girl who sits beside you. I touched her neck, still warm under her hair. She was wearing my green sweater—that surprised me—and her clothes were rumpled. She, too, must have been up most of the night. She curled her knees into her chest, sighed deeply, and leaned into me. Relax, Adam, I told myself. On a bus, in the dark, no one would notice or care where my hands went. I made myself still them. She shifted positions while the bus rocked. Seven hours from Oswego to New York. Seven going and seven coming home. I closed my eyes and drifted off.

When we awoke, the sun was high. Tall buildings rose into the air, while below, our bus crawled forward, surrounded by other buses, cars, and taxi cabs.

"Yellow taxis," I said, poking Chris's arm. "In Zagreb they are all black, but these are bright yellow!" I was like a schoolboy. I could barely stand myself. We shook our legs and got off the bus. All around us people were shoving, yelling, calling out to each other. I nearly collided with another person. "Hold my hand!" I yelled, too, as my fingers gripped Chris's.

"It's so crowded!" She craned her neck. "You have to search to find the sky."

"Zagreb, too, is a big city," I said as if I had to remind myself that once upon a time I had lived in a large city. I had gotten used to seeing wooden houses with large porches and wide streets, to looking out onto the quiet of the lake and being surrounded by spaces that filled as I entered them.

We stood near a billboard in the middle of Times Square. On it was a large picture of Frank Sinatra's face. Around me girls jumped up and tried to touch his chin.

"You're handsomer than Frank Sinatra," said Chris. "But not as handsome as Gene Kelly. Kelly is Irish and charming, and he can really dance." She threw her arms around me.

"More handsome," I said.

She looked at me and laughed. "All right, more handsome."

"No, I was not saying that I am more handsome. I was correcting you. It is not *handsomer*. It is *more* handsome, and I can dance, too!" I twirled her around and around until we both wobbled down the street as if we had drunk too much. Maybe we are drunk, I thought. There was no fence here. No guards watched us. Nobody cared what we did. Everybody moved fast, as if they had to get somewhere soon. I have to get somewhere, too, my body said. I was not sure where, but I ran. Chris dashed in front of me, weaving in and out of people.

"It takes practice not to bump anyone." I stopped to catch my breath. "How do they accomplish such a task?" The spaces between bodies seemed like vertical slots—only large enough to accommodate the thickness of a coin.

"The dogs don't even bump each other," said Chris. "And they don't bark and chase one another."

Dogs appeared like magic, spilling out of brownstone buildings. Big dogs. Little dogs. All colors, shapes, sizes. All on leashes. Clattering down the stone stairs as preoccupied as their owners. We have something important to do, everyone said. The air was charged with the importance of doing. And the faces surprised me. So many people with different faces. The colors of the world converged upon Chris and me. We entered into the mix.

Around noon, we stopped in a big cafeteria with vending machines all over. Neatly wrapped sandwiches waited behind sliding glass compartments. Chris bought a tuna fish sandwich—she told me that her favorite sandwich was made with sardines, but there was nothing like that in the machine—and I got peanut butter and jelly, which has been my favorite since I came to the States. We deposited more money into slots. Milk cartons disappeared, falling into the bottom tray. Then we, too, fell into seats at a long table.

"I will like to live here," I said. Outside was a free fashion show. I thought of my three pairs of pants and the two hangers that held them. When I had gotten that third pair, I had felt like a million bucks. In New York, though, I was sure it would be easy to feel poor and to want. Already I wished for things I could not name.

"Won't you miss anything back home?" she asked, watching me.

Her eyes seemed needy, too. I wished I could buy her something lovely that would always remind her of New York and of me. I reached for her hands.

"Adam, will you miss Oswego?" She poked a straw into her milk.

"All the time we are in Oswego, you talk of New York, and now that we are here, you talk of Oswego. How is that?" I clapped her hands together as if I was teaching her some baby game.

She pulled away and sipped her milk. I knew she wanted to ask if I would miss her. I busied myself with the sandwich, bending it in half. She watched. I grinned and straightened it out again. Eat as she does, in small bites, Adam. And don't fold!

Her shoulders rounded over her carton. "I guess I'm not hungry." She pushed her sandwich away.

We pretended to listen to conversations around us. One elderly woman talked about her medication. Another about a play. A younger man in a rounded hat went on and on about Japan. "They will be reduced to being a silk-weaving country," he said. "Exporting silk will be all they can do."

"Adam." She leaned on her elbows and stared directly into my face. "You'll miss something. Won't you?"

I knew what she wanted, but for some reason I could not say it—not now with the camp so far away. And a part of me wanted to hurt her; she was an American, and I was not; she believed there were always choices, but we are not always free to choose. President Roosevelt decided to make this camp. President Truman would decide, too, and I would have nothing to do with it. A letter would come. Send them home. Keep them here. Them, the stateless. The refugees. But me, Adam Bornstein, what did I matter? Who thought of me? And if I said I missed her, what of it? My entire childhood was missing. Why linger over places where even the ashes have been swept away?

"Certainly," I said, "if we are to go, I will miss so many things. There is our little apartment and our two rooms and certainly the mess halls, where we all eat together. And let us not forget the showers or the toilets, which are lined up in a row. I will miss not hearing my neighbor relieving himself. As for the fence, I do not know how I will survive without that." I opened my carton and gulped down the entire contents in one shot. Then I slammed my fist over it, crushing the cardboard.

She jumped, startled. There was a look on her face that reminded me of a dog that a friend of mine once owned. He had been found abandoned. We did not know his history, but there was a scar across his nose. One day my friend's grandmother walked into his house with her cane. The dog cringed and backed away.

"Chris," I said as if I was speaking to one of Mira's friends and I had to go slowly, "I am sorry. I will remember Oswego. I have so many friends here. I will miss the school and our fine principal and the teachers who make it their business to help us. I feel safe here. Everything is provided for us. When we leave, we will have to start over again. We will need to find a house. Earn money. We will not be surrounded by people we know. I will speak Serbo-Croatian, and nobody will understand me. I will have to explain and explain."

She flattened out her sandwich and tore the inside into little pieces. "Is that what you've been doing with me?"

"No, no, with you—"

"With me, what?"

"Come! We will not talk about what is inside the camp and what is outside. We are here in New York. Let us have fun!" I stood behind her and pulled back her chair. She pushed it in again.

"I don't want to go out." She stripped the crusts away from what remained of her bread and made the outline of a lopsided circle with them. "You can go alone."

"Chris, if we are freed, and Mama and Mira and Villi and I move to New York, then you will come to visit us. It is not like I am going to another country. It is only here. You will get on the bus and see me as often as you like. Every weekend if you want." I leaned over her. I would miss her. I was missing her already just thinking of it. See me every day, I thought. Every weekend is not enough.

"May—be." She sucked noisily on her straw.

I grabbed the milk away. "What do you mean by may—be?"

"I'd like to come and see plays and museums, and I'd like to watch all these people and shop and visit a few of my friends who have moved here."

"A few of your friends?"

She gathered up the pieces of uneaten sandwich and the cartons and sauntered over to the garbage can. I tore the paper off an unopened straw and blew. It hit her back.

"That's not funny!" she said.

I took another straw. She took one, too, and we sat across from each other armed with straws. Paper hit our faces. I shielded myself with my hands. "You win!" I shouted. She kept blowing. I ran around to her seat, but she escaped me. Soon I was chasing her down the block, and we were laughing wildly.

"I love you, Chris Cook!" I screamed. She held her hands over her ears. "I love you, Chris Cook!" I screamed even louder.

"Be quiet! You're embarrassing me. I don't know you."

"If you do not stop, I will shout it out in five languages."

She laid her palm over my mouth, then her mouth replaced her hand, and our tongues spoke, silently, as tongues do that have no need for words until we, too, felt rushed. There was so much to do.

"I want to see the Statue of Liberty," she said.

"There is not enough time." When I am free, I thought, she and I will go together. "I wish to see the Empire State Building," I answered. In America I would fly from building to building, just as Errol Flynn sailed through the hall over the heads of the prince and his guards.

High above the rushing people and cars and colors of the world, Chris and I stood. I lifted her arms up. They were heavy somehow, and her body stiffened.

"Chris—" I started to say. I was confused.

"Oh, it's so beautiful," she interrupted, spreading her arms up. "Like being a bird."

Mine lay beneath hers while the air moved under us. And we were flying, free together.

• • •

Back on the bus, she fell asleep, her head against the window. I was afraid she would bang it, so I placed my jacket under her head, careful not to wake her. She moved, still asleep. A truck zoomed by, its sides lit up. That is when I saw the skin on her back, and the red marks.

No, I thought and turned away. It can't be. Yes, it can, but I had to be sure. My fingers felt beneath the sweater, tracing a line up her back. It was raised and swollen, and there were other, smaller lines. My eyes smarted. Someone had beaten her. Recently. My teeth held onto each other. I shook my head and said such things as I never said. I did not care if someone heard. Someone should hear.

"Chris?" I spoke into her neck. "Wake up, Chris."

She stirred. My mouth buried itself in her neck. Her hair smelled sweet and sweaty at the same time. How could anybody? How could he? "Chris, tell me who did this to you." I knew who it was, but I had to ask.

She pressed herself against the window, away from me.

"Chris, you are not fooling me. You are awake, so tell me." My hand felt under her sweater. She shuddered. She would not tell me, but she would let me find out for myself. That way she did not have to admit anything. "He is evil," I muttered. My finger traced a line down the length of her back. "He is an evil man."

"No, he's not evil. He told me . . . I could have stopped it."

"How could you have stopped it?" As soon as I asked, I knew. It was in her face even though she tried to hide it. If she agreed not to see me . . . I drew my hand away, held my chin inside the pocket that my palm made, and covered my nose with my fingers. It was such an old habit from who knows where, and yet my nose felt safe that way, secure inside the hood of my hand. "Oh," I whispered disconsolately. "Oh."

"Adam, no, it's not . . ." She grabbed my wrist.

I moved to the edge of my seat, nearly falling into the aisle.

"Adam, please, I could have lied. Really. I could have said things."

I bit my lips with my teeth. If I touched her, I would yell, call him all kinds of names, and she would be unhappy because she did not see it. She would not see it. He was her father, but he was evil. "What things?" I said.

"I don't know. Adam, I'm tired. I want to sleep. O.K.?"

Only seven hours from New York to Oswego, and we were moving closer and closer. To home. To the camp. To him. To the fence. "I cannot allow this to happen," I said. I was like some dog who digs around in the bush, poking his nose in the snow when he is sniffing after someone's old pee and needing to make his new pee over it.

Her finger touched my cheek. "He won't do it again," she said.

"Because you will lie?"

"Yes."

"No! You will have to stop seeing me."

"Then I won't lie." She smoothed my cheeks with her hands and forced my lips into a smile.

"That is right. You will not lie because you will not see me." I grabbed the armrest. I wanted to hit something. Someone. Him.

"I will not lie," she said slowly and carefully, as if she was teaching me English for the first time, "because he is not going to do it again."

"Because I will not let him." I spoke slowly and carefully, too, except I faced the empty aisle, refusing to look at her.

"Because he never wanted to. Even when he was doing it, he kept missing and hitting the car." Her fingers touched the back of my hair and played with the curls, pulling them.

"He was not always missing." I jerked away. Soon I would

hit her. No, I would never do that, but I was not some child to be toyed with. I could not stand by and just let him do this to her.

"Adam," she pleaded, "my dad never wanted to hurt me. He kept giving me chances, you know, like if I said I was sorry or if I promised him like he asked me to. He thinks I'm looking for trouble, that I'm being bad."

I turned to face her again. She seemed so unhappy—unhappy and uncertain, as if she thought what he said might really be true: she *was* bad. But that was not true. She was good—even more than that. There was something inside of her that stayed shiny and bright no matter how much one rubbed away at it. I could see that, and it made me even angrier. He was making her think she was being bad, but it was him, not her.

"Do you think you are being bad?" I asked. In front of us, a light went on. Newspaper rustled. Someone was trying to read without disturbing the sleeping passengers. Someone else opened a bag. The smell of American French fries made my stomach roll.

"No, it's just . . . He thinks there's a right way to be and a wrong way."

"And the wrong way is being with me?" I had answered my own question. So had she. She looked down. I lifted her chin. "Being with me is wrong, because I am a refugee. A filthy, dirty refugee."

"Don't say that, Adam." Her lips trembled.

"'My daughter, with a boy who stepped off the boat.' He says that. Right? 'Filthy. Dirty.'" Tears flooded her eyes—I was making her cry—but I could not stop myself. It was not only him that I was speaking about. It was all of them. It was everything I wanted to say and did not, because always there were rules, and if I said those words to myself, the enemy would read them in my eyes, and I would be lost. So I kept them hidden. But here in America . . . I thought I would come and the world would open its arms like the Statue of Liberty. Welcome you homeless, you people from all over the world of many colors and many races and religions. Welcome Jews and Adam Bornstein, welcome, welcome. But everybody was not that way, so I had to say something. Here in America I could speak freely. My hands balled themselves into fists. "'A filthy, dirty Jew!' He says that, too."

She was shaking her head. Trying to convince herself. "Adam, no, it's not that. He talks about everybody who's not like him. That's just the way he is."

"And what about the way I am? You know, he is not like me, either. Did you ever stop to think about that? Everybody in this entire country is not like me, including you!"

"Then why did you choose me?" She stared into my face, her lips parted.

"Because . . ."

I sat on my knees, facing her, holding her head in the cradle my hands made. And now she was the moon. She would never miss the clouds or the stars. Neither would I. I would be the sky, and the heavens would be what we had created together. My hands molded themselves around her jawbones. When she was gone, they would shape her form again. I was not going to drown inside the depths of all my missing.

"When I saw you that day lifting the bicycle," I said, "do you remember? You were so sure of yourself. You stood on top of these boys' shoulders and you were the Statue of Liberty. I looked up, and there you were. And you looked at me and Mira. Welcome, you were saying. And there was the fence and all these people watching us. All these Americans. And you above me, handing me the bicycle. You were glad I came. Happy to see me. So I fell in love with you."

She kissed my eyelashes. My cheeks. Her lips against mine. I did not want her kissing. At the same time I did want it.

"Move in with me," I said. "You can stay in our apartment. We have room. We will get another mattress. I will explain to Mama." My voice grew more and more uncertain.

"That's O.K. I'll be all right. Nothing will happen, really."

"I will stay away from you."

"No, you'll be going soon. You can't stay away."

"While we wait to go, I will not see you." I wanted to end the talk, but before I stopped seeing her, she had to know. "He is a bad man," I said. "Your father is a bad man."

"No, he's my father. He wants to protect me. That's all."

"And I am your boyfriend. I will protect you. I know the right thing. He knows nothing!"

We sat in the growing dark. "After tonight you will not see me," I said again.

She said nothing. I hated this nothing.

"Do you want me to leave?" I hated myself more.

She began to cry. It was hard seeing her cry. She was so simple and quiet about that, too, as if it was all right for her to cry, as if it was all right for me to hurt her. I won't see her, I told myself. I made up my mind. Then I unmade it just as quickly.

Close to midnight, we got off together. My legs unfolded themselves. "Come to the shelter," I said. "I must give you something." It was the right time. Now.

"I have to go home."

"To say hello to the strap again and your loving father?"

"At least I have a father."

She sped up in front of me, her hair flying. I grabbed her shoulders. She cried out. "Don't make me say anything," she said. "Don't make me answer questions. I can't answer questions. Not yours. Or his. And I *am* sorry. I shouldn't have said that about having a father."

I stood behind her. "Please, I must give you something." Christmas had been too soon. I had needed to be sure. Now I was.

We walked to the shelter. There was no moon this time. It might be that we had brought it down. Together. There were only the stars, thousands of them. We slid through the hole to our barracks, and already I was counting everything I would miss. Here in this camp I got to be a boy. I did not have to think and imagine and hope. I could look everywhere. I looked at her, and she looked back.

"Wait here," I said, stopping her outside our barracks. If Chris came in, Mama would say nothing. She would sit like a stone until I, too, felt myself become immobile.

"I am sorry, Mama." I skirted around her crumpled black dress. How long had she sat waiting for me? "I will not do it again. I promise. But I have to go out one more time. I will return in a minute."

I went into her bedroom, where the old suitcase lay under her bed. I pulled it out. Mira turned in her sleep and moaned. "Dream of honey and berries," I whispered in her ear. She smacked her lips. In the dark my hands searched inside the pocket where Papa once kept his socks when he made trips to get new printing orders. Yes, it was there. Right where I had put it. I had outgrown the peasant shirt, and it was torn so badly Mama had turned it into a rag. But this was the same. As good as always.

My hand closed over it. Was this made for a man and not a woman? How did one determine those things? I had never asked myself that question before, though I had imagined there was a girl. But perhaps it was too big for Chris. And did she wear things like this? I had never seen one on her. Was I the wrong person to give such a thing as this to her? I nearly put it back in the case, but I had to give it to her. She had to know what I felt.

CHRIS

He came out. Under the lamplight his face was bright. His freckles stood out. I was sure that in the summer there would be more of them. Maybe I'd see them. I'd make him sit still while I counted the freckles. Then, when he left, I'd think of the sun kissing his face all summer long, and I'd pretend I was the sun.

"Come," he said, "I will take you back. It is too dark for you alone."

"That's O.K. You don't have to."

"I want to."

203

We hurried along the streets. "What did you have to get in there?" I asked.

"You will see."

I picked up my step. At the corner we stopped.

"I am to leave you here," he said. "Yes? Always at the corner."

"I can see my house. It's not dangerous."

"If it were not for your father, I would go up to your porch."

"And kiss me at the front door?" I laughed.

"And kiss you at the front door."

"You can kiss me here, too." There were no cars around. The light in Mrs. Dubchek's bedroom was on. I didn't mind. It was all right for her to watch out for our block. Mr. Richards's dog barked. "Quiet, Buster!" I warned. "Or I'll take away your blanket." He wagged his tail.

"Close your eyes," said Adam, "and open your hands."

I held my palm out flat. He dropped something cold and hard inside of it and cupped my hand around the object. "Can I open my eyes now?" I felt it with my fingers.

"Yes."

I kept feeling, my eyes looking into his. "It's a cross, isn't it?" I'll always love his eyes.

"See for yourself."

It was so beautiful and different—not at all like the ones I was used to. This was a deep red so that it made you think of Jesus' blood. It was bumpy, not smooth, and it hung from a thick chain like a man would wear. But a woman could wear it, too, outside her sweater or blouse. Or underneath a nightgown. "Where'd you get it?"

"When we were escaping, Papa had each of us wear one. This was mine."

"Where did he get it?"

"I do not know. One day he enters the house with crosses and peasant shirts and pants. 'Wear these,' he says. We do not ask where he got them. We do whatever is necessary to save ourselves."

"Why are you giving me the cross? To save me?" I felt giddy with laughter. "You could, you know."

"No, I cannot save anyone."

"Don't say that. Please!" I couldn't bear his sorrow.

"I was thinking," he said, taking the cross and opening the clasp, "that it would find a home with you. On my chest it was always feeling that it was on foreign soil. So it sat as a lonely thing inside Papa's suitcase. You will make a friend of it."

"It's beautiful. Adam, would you rather I wear a star? I could, if you wanted. I dreamt that once. In my dream I was wearing a star."

"Would you want that?" He studied my face.

I said nothing.

"Would you?" He persisted.

"No, I want the cross."

"That is what I thought."

He stood behind me and put his Christmas present around my neck. He closed the clasp and kissed my neck beneath the chain. "Go home." He pushed me gently away from him. He seemed so sad. Not angry or disappointed. Just sad.

"You can walk me all the way, if you want."

"No, I leave you here." Again he nudged me away.

I hurried down the block. "Quiet, Buster. Quiet," I said, climbing up our stoop. I wished Mr. Richards had brought him in, but it was getting warmer. Soon summer would be here. I'd be sixteen. Sixteen going on sixty. I walked around to the back. In the open ashcan outside the garage entrance was the strap. Dad had thrown it away. It didn't matter. Not really. One thing had led to another. I couldn't lie. Not to Dad. Nor to Adam. And not to myself.

Chapter Six
Outside the Fence

&

*They left, and it was sad, I mean for me, it was
very sad. I was so upset in a way over them all
going. It was going to be a whole new life for me.*
                                        Geraldine Rossiter,
                                        Oswegonian

ADAM

In April I gave her my present. I did not see her all the rest
of that month nor in May or June. Sometimes I told
myself that it was because of all that was happening. I had
to study for exams and pass a test so that, when I left
Oswego, I could go on. I would advance to senior status and be
given credit for all the languages I knew. I could even go to col-
lege when I passed the New York State exams. I did not want to
be a pilot anymore. I would be a lawyer and study constitutional
law. I would help people like me. If they let me stay. If I became
an American. Nobody was sure. One day we thought we would
be allowed to stay here, that the government would change its
mind and make us citizens. The next we were certain they
would send us back. Amid all this, the lists continued to surface.
Who was alive and who was dead? We swarmed around pieces of
paper like flies about to be glued to our fate.

In June, right after a general Boy Scout meeting, our scout-
master gathered us refugees together. We were Troop 23, and

we always said the Boy Scout oath loudly and clearly: *I will do my best to do my duty to God and to my country.* "There will be hearings," he said, "to determine whether you stay in America or not."

We listened. There was a committee in the United States Congress devoted to us. Subcommittee VI of the House Committee on Immigration and Naturalization. I thought of Rome and the apartment, of the clerk who typed Mama's name on an official paper. Again, somewhere, we were in some file. It would be marked "Oswego" or "Emergency Refugee Shelter." Again there would be a choosing. I tried not to think.

"Congressman Dickstein heads the committee," said our leader. "He is sympathetic. Refugees will speak, and citizens of Oswego. The special assistant to the Secretary of the Interior, Dr. Gruber, who has helped you come and get settled, she will be one of your advocates. There are many here who want you to stay, and they will work to convince those who need convincing. You, too, must work. You will come in your Boy Scout uniforms. You'll carry the American flag, and you will speak about becoming American. You can do that, can't you?"

We all nodded.

I put on my Boy Scout pants and shirt. Badges decorated my chest. I had made knots. Created fire from flint and steel. Marched miles. Pitched a tent. Had a blind boxing match with another scout. Read before an audience an essay called "How Scouting Began in the United States." I had seen a motion picture, *The Trail to Citizenship.* Passed Tenderfoot requirements. Survived. It was 25 June 1945. School was over, yet I still had to pass the greatest test. I tried to feel strong. I would carry the flag in.

We all marched into a room where the men of the subcommittee sat. We said our oath and were asked questions. First one boy, then the next. Sometimes, when I heard others, I felt like laughing. Do you play baseball? Yes. Do you like it? Yes. Do you like basketball? I played it a few times here; I played it lots of times in Italy.

Sometimes when the others spoke, I felt like crying. How

old are you? Fourteen. Where were you born? Belgrade, Yugoslavia. Were you there when the Germans were there? Yes. What happened, do you remember? I don't know—my father was there, and they put the men all up in a line and they took every fifth person. Where did they take them? No one knows. My father was the fourth man. So they didn't take your father? No. Where is your father now? I don't know. When did you hear from him? We don't.

And would you stay here with the idea of trying to become a real American? Yes.

Would you be willing to defend your new country if they allowed you to stay here? Yes.

We all said yes. We meant it.

That was in June. Soon afterward, Chris was sent away to Girl Scout camp. We both knew why. We did not see each other until school began again. It was my last year of high school. Eighteen going on eighty. And still asking myself, When will the new life begin? How could I think of her? I did.

CHRIS

When I got home from New York City, Dad didn't say anything. For a whole long time neither of us talked to each other. I'd say something to Mom, she'd repeat it to Dad. Dad would say something back to Mom, who'd then transmit it to me. We were a regular Western Union office, and Mom was getting sick and tired of standing at the window. Nobody said anything about my cross. I kept it underneath my shirt so nobody'd ask. I wanted it close to me, too, but mostly I didn't want people looking at it every day. I liked the secrecy of it, just me knowing.

I didn't talk to Adam, either. If I made like he was away already, it'd be easier when he did leave, so I avoided all those places where I knew he'd be—where we'd been together. I was afraid of what I'd do if I did see him, and I was afraid of what I'd do if I didn't. I was afraid a lot, so I stopped going to the library. I stopped going to the fort. I never saw him much at school, and when I did, he was in the distance with Ralph or Tikvah or some of his other friends. I still loved him. I wanted him to still love me.

Before school ended, I started going to confession again. I also got out this pamphlet called "Everything a Catholic Girl Needs to Know." I thought it'd tell me something. It didn't do anything except give me a word for something I'd begun wondering about. The pamphlet called it "self-pollution." According to Ann, millions of people all over the world were self-polluting, so I shouldn't think it was bad or anything. When Ann started describing in detail the difference between male and female self-pollution, which "Everything a Catholic Girl Needs to Know" said nothing about, I suggested that she write the next guide and walked away. I didn't like Dad's pictures, but I wasn't ready for Ann's either. I had time.

Besides all that and my not telling Father Walters anything he hadn't read in the pamphlet, I got very busy. Late in May I began working at our town newspaper. I wrote a few short pieces where I ran around talking to other kids about topics like: "How do you feel now that Germany has surrendered?" and "What has the war meant to you?" What they said made me think. They made me want to write more, too—not about big, important people, but about regular people you see every day. Sometimes I even got to thinking that there were a whole lot of stories in Oswego, so I didn't need to run off to New York City or Paris—at least not yet. I liked where I lived and I wasn't bored. I just hated getting dressed in the morning. I'd look at my face in the mirror and I'd feel like something was missing. He was.

In June I had finals again. I did O.K. Not great, but O.K. Another birthday came and went. I wasn't all that excited and I didn't have a party. That all seemed so childish. I didn't even

want a cake, but Mom insisted. We went downtown together—
I bought shoes—and then we sat in the kitchen with my cake.
Dad, Mom, and me. I stuck the candles inside the icing between
the pink roses. I hate ruining roses.

"Close your eyes and make a wish," said Mom.

"Go ahead, Chrissy," said Dad. He'd started calling me that.
I didn't correct him, because I knew my name. Let him say what
he wants, I thought. It doesn't change a thing.

I closed my eyes. I couldn't summon up any wishes—all the
old ones were gone. Like getting kissed. Wanting to run away
and become a Wac. Meeting the man of my dreams and going
to New York with him. And my new wish didn't feel like something I wanted to come true.

I wished I could stop loving him. I wished he would go
away already. He'd forget about me. I'd forget about him.

So I wished for nothing and blew out the candles.

When I got to feeling like I had to see him again, Dad and
Mom shipped me off to Girl Scout camp. We all knew why. I
guessed Adam did, too. Then school began again, and Adam
really was getting ready to leave. In his mind, I thought, I'm
somebody who's going to visit him in New York.

In my mind I was nothing.

ADAM

When it was finally official and President Truman granted us
permission to immigrate, I said to Mama, "I am Adam
Bornstein, an American."

"A cold-water flat," she answered. "We will be very poor,
without all our friends here."

"Mama," I reminded her, "we are starting our new life. We
have much to pack." I remembered Rome. "It is packing we
must be doing," Mama had said. That was a long time ago, the

summer of 1944. Now it was January of 1946, and we had lived for five years without a home of our own.

"We must buy another suitcase," Mama said, thinking aloud.

We had come to the shelter with only one suitcase. Now we had all of Mira's clothes. Mama's equipment for the hairdressing business, which she was buying a little at a time. My few pairs of pants. Some dishes and cups and silverware. The hot plate. An extra lamp. We had become property owners again. The Bornsteins. We did not speak of Grandmama. Someone in the camp told us she was last seen in Auschwitz. "Which line?" we asked. The woman could not remember. So we hoped and prayed, silently. We did not speak of Papa, either. Only Mama said, "We will take the old suitcase, too. We will not get rid of that. It was your Papa's." Her mouth trembled, but she held her face in place. I held mine in place, too.

In the meanwhile we prepared ourselves. The Americans, once they make up their minds, do things quickly. Men came and told us of this-and-this Jewish community and this-and-this city where we would be helped by an agency. People sat with maps of the United States on their laps. Some went to places where their relatives lived. Ralph's family went to Kansas.

"My father always wanted to be a cowboy," Ralph told me. "That is his dream, so he chose Kansas. He heard cowboys live there."

Tikvah decided to stay in Oswego. She would finish school and look for a job.

My family would go to New York City. Ralph, Tikvah, and I pictured ourselves scattering all over this country. We put our arms around each other. We would never be together like this again. Never safe like this again. But a camp is a camp, and a fence is a fence.

In a building the Americans set up immigration quarters. Some of my friends—including Tikvah—typed out papers. I asked her if she had come to our name yet.

"No," she said. "I type from G to L. Someone else types up to G."

It was not my fate to know this typist, either.

Mama sat at the table reading the camp directions for departure just as she had once done in Rome. And Mira left off from hiding under the table. Spring was nearly here.

CHRIS

I knew he was leaving. I even knew when he would leave—he showed me his departure slip—and I watched the leaving. All that week I went to the shelter after school. Dad didn't say no. It wasn't that he had changed, but he realized that they were going and he couldn't do anything to stop me from seeing them. At first I thought he'd argue or lock me in the house. He didn't do either, and I was right. He didn't hit me. That was over.

"It's your life," he said.

"I know," I answered.

"It can be your funeral, too."

It won't be, I thought.

We stood against the fence. Across the street were the same houses that were there the day he'd come. But now he was wearing my gloves. I was wearing the cross he'd given me. "Adam," I said, "remember how we stood here and shoved leaves through the holes?"

"'Leaf,' I was saying, 'now you are not on neutral territory. You are free.'"

I touched his eyes and his cheeks. I never did get to count all his freckles. "And now you are free."

"Yes," he said, like he was saying it to me and freedom at the same time.

"Remember Christmas, too, when you told me how there should be more camps like this?"

"You gave me my own pair of gloves. Also you made a beautiful card. I have kept it."

"It was an awful card. I can't draw, except for stick figures. Adam, you told me how there should be more camps, and I said, 'Jesus was born today.' But I wasn't thinking that."

"What were you thinking?"

"That there should have been more camps like this. Without fences. We should have had so many."

And we didn't say that we'd miss each other. We didn't say when we'd see each other or if we'd see each other. No one said, "I love you." I guess that would have felt too much like finishing. Nothing was finished.

Instead, we walked outside that neutral territory. Outside the fence. And our lips came together.

EMERGENCY REFUGEE SHELTER
Oswego, N.Y.

Bornstein, Manya Rut and family   Bldg. 17

You are scheduled to leave on Feb. 2-1946 at 6:00 A.M. in Bus No. 3, Seat Nos. 25, 26, 27. The tag on your baggage must bear the number of your bus. You will travel to Buffalo and from there to Niagara Falls at which point you will cross the Rainbow Bridge to the town of Niagara Falls in Ontario, Canada. There you will descend and be greeted by the American Consul, who will give each of you a visa and a red seal and ribbon. Welcome to America!

Author's Note

On December 22, 1945, President Truman made an announcement indicating that everything would be done to "facilitate the entrance of some of these displaced persons and refugees in the United States." On January 17, 1946, the first three busloads, carrying ninety-five refugees, left the Emergency Refugee Shelter at Fort Ontario, Oswego, New York. To enter into the United States legally, they first had to exit. In the weeks to follow, the camp was slowly emptied until its closure in early February 1946. Eventually the barracks were torn down. None of the center remains, except for some administration buildings. Fort Ontario, the interior fortification around which the exterior Emergency Refugee Shelter was set up, remains, as does the graveyard. Visitors can tour buildings and watch period garrison life demonstrations. On the banks of Lake Ontario, Fort Ontario is a New York State historic site, but in all the grassy spaces outside this garrison there is little to remind one of the former refugees and their place in American history. There is a plaque dedicated to the refugees. Several years ago it was defaced. The members of Safe Haven, Inc., are working valiantly to set up a museum at the fort. Many of the pictures that they have collected are housed in a building on the premises, and the Oswego branch of State University of New York has kept material in acid-free boxes in their special collections library. There is also material at the Columbia University Library. However, there is a great need for money so that material can be microfilmed. As I sat in the research library, wearing my white gloves and poring over the camp's newspaper, I grew afraid that some of this valuable material would indeed disappear. Already it was crumbling. A re-creation of a barracks room is in a museum in Albany. Occasionally a course is taught on the refugees' experience in Oswego. Many people in town know of this event and want their children to learn its history, and yet, through no fault of their own, even within Oswego, there are still people who know nothing of the Emergency Refugee Shelter. It is not highly publicized, and there are no official tours to that area outside the fort. Children play baseball there—I saw them running—and they live and thrive, just as the children and the teenagers inside the camp did. I suspect little is known of this period in history either inside or outside Oswego, because it was a difficult time, and there are no easy answers as to why there was only one safe haven, but the questions are there for the asking, and the people who lived at the center need to be heard. Many are still alive. Many made taped recordings at the Fiftieth Reunion for Safe Haven residents. Copies of the tapes can be purchased from Safe Haven, Inc., which also has a Web site (www.syracuse.com/features/safehaven/) documenting events and some personal histories. This book was my way of beginning to make my own contribution. In part it answered some of my questions. I hope it will do so for my readers.

I learned that these former refugees are people with faces and histories, many of whom shared their lives with me so that I could better understand part of America's life and history. As for the former refugees and their attitudes about the camp, it has seemed to me that older people had much more difficulty, expectedly so. Many left careers, money, their property, their sense of well-being and self in community. They came knowing no English and filled with anguish over relatives and friends who had mysteriously disappeared. Some had themselves been in concentration camps and knew all too well what had happened there. Most of the younger people fared much better. They could live as children and teenagers. They could go to school and have normal lives. They also weren't as imprisoned, because they went outside the fence every day to school. Several had no compunction about sneaking under the well-known hole. The older people didn't do this. And, in typical fashion, mothers and fathers worried more about what would happen when they left the camp. How would they live? Beyond this, the camp did offer many a chance to heal.

As for Oswego, I heard countless stories of good deeds that came from the heart: from the Girl Scout leader, from grade-school and high-school teachers, from families who invited refugees over for holidays and meals. I also heard some stories of anti-Semitism and read some articles about how Oswego ignored the refugee problem. By and large, though, it has appeared that the city proved a model for what could be done. That so many appreciated the city, the camp's director, Joseph Smart, teachers, principal Ralph Faust, etc., was evident in the reunion. So many people attended. So many voiced their feelings of love. Many, too, could not forget the fence nor their bitterness at being kept behind it: they had ideas about America; had ideals; their anger could not be ignored. One wants to be free. Given all this, though, the camp allowed countless people to make new lives, and these people contributed invaluably to America. They became the most American of Americans—as is so often the case with immigrants. They did not take democracy and freedom for granted. They knew, too, that democracy is like a novel that never gets finished. It is always a work-in-progress. The author must be vigilant if the work is to become better

As for the hole, it is still there, if you look closely. There are segments of the fence and the hole. When I was last in Oswego, I was struck by this picture: around a portion of the fence, a tree had managed to wrap itself. Part of the trunk was growing around iron. I thought that this was like the lives of those people whose stories I'd heard. A former refugee put it aptly when she said, "We were a hardy bunch."

I remember this and what our late president Franklin Delano Roosevelt stated:

> We have learned that we cannot live alone, at peace; that our own well-being is dependent upon the well-being of other nations far away. We have learned that we must live as men [and women], and not as ostriches nor as dogs in the manger. We have learned to be citizens of the world, members of the human community.

ACKNOWLEDGMENTS

I'd like to thank those who wrote books that aided my understanding. Of particular importance is Dr. Ruth Gruber's *Haven*. Dr. Gruber, a well-known author, former foreign correspondent, and special assistant to Harold Ickes, Secretary of the Interior during the Roosevelt administration, went over to Naples, boarded the ship that brought the refugees to America, documented their stories, and, during the eighteen months of their stay at the Emergency Refugee Shelter, worked for their betterment in Washington. I'd like to thank her for granting me a personal interview. Also of great value was Dr. Sharon Lowenstein's scholarly work *Token Refuge;* the lengthy report by Julius A. Krug, Secretary of the U.S. Department of the Interior from 1946 to 1949 entitled *Token Shipment: The Story of America's War Refugee Shelter,* and Lawrence Baron's "Haven from the Holocaust: Oswego, New York, 1944–1946."

I'd like to thank Scott Scanlon, president of Safe Haven, a nonprofit organization devoted to making the public aware of this important event through the collection of primary source materials and the building of a museum at Fort Ontario. From him I was able to view pictures and primary-source material, and to purchase tapes already mentioned. I'd like to thank those who agreed to be taped for willingly making public both painful and joyous reminiscences. My thanks to Dr. William Schum, former president and dean of the State University of New York at Oswego, for seeing me and sharing World War II memories of his boyhood. Thanks to the staff of the Special Collections Room at the Pennfield Library, State University of New York at Oswego, for sitting with me while I donned white gloves and read a year's worth of *The Ontario Chronicle*, the weekly paper published by the refugees at the shelter, and pored over personal letters and paraphernalia that former refugees had donated to Safe Haven for the museum. Thank you, Ed Vermue and Dr. Nancy Osborne. Thanks to Terry Prior, director of the Oswego County Historical Society, for sharing his historical knowledge of Oswego with me, giving me my own personal tour, and allowing me to check out information he had. And to Naomi Wilensky, board member of Safe Haven, who taught a summer high-school class on the shelter and continues to share her enthusiasm for this important historical period with her high-school students.

I thank Mrs. Dorothy Faust, former teacher at Oswego High and wife of Ralph Faust, former principal of Oswego High, for her tea and cookies and warm stories about her husband's deep connection to his students and former refugees. I thank her for sharing invaluable World War II memories with me and for showing me what care and responsibility means. I thank Geraldine Rossiter, the girl after whom I patterned Chris Cook. While Gerry did not fall in love with a boy inside the camp, she did pass her bike over the fence; she snuck in daily, she made good and fast friends, and when I spoke to her, I understood community and the deep value of shared experiences. She made me want to create a girl with an open heart. Fortunately, too, she did not have to do battle with a father such as I created—hers was a loving family. Gerry, my deepest gratitude.

To the following former refugees, who either spoke to me by phone or agreed to personal interviews, I give thanks. To Walter Greenberg for calling me, even after he had just had open-heart surgery, and telling me the most concrete stories of coming to America. To Hedy Gaon for giving me a glimpse of what it was like for a very young girl to be at the fort. I cannot personally thank Dr. Ivo Lederer, and that grieves me, for he recently passed away. But in respect, I wish to say that he answered my letters, communicated with me via the phone, and managed to take time out of his amazingly busy schedule as director of A.T. Kearney to answer innumerable questions about his life in Rome, his passage over, his teenage years in Oswego, etc. He cared about my project because he cared about transmitting information on Safe Haven to our teenagers. My thanks to Kostia Zabotin, who brought me into his house and shared his experiences at Ferramonti, his feelings about the fence, and his boyhood escapades at Oswego. In a very short time I learned much about living and learning and responsibility from you. To David Hendell, I give thanks for allowing me to see more of the boy in Adam. From you I learned about the abandoned barracks—although what occurred in them was left for me to imagine and fictionalize. From you I heard about plumbing jobs and radio construction. From you I learned more of the pragmatic of living. I wish to thank Edith Klein for also welcoming me into her house and for so thoroughly describing her escape and her family situation as to make me tremble. And to Steffi Steinberg Winters, who literally spent a day with me at her Teaneck, New Jersey, home, missing an appointment with a friend to continue giving me coffee and lunch and snacks as she delved into her past. If anyone else should write a story of this time, it is Steffi. Her words moved me beyond telling. When she showed me her correspondence with people around the world, I understood what global communication on a truly personal level means. I also was very moved when she shared her high-school year book with me and showed me her commencement program. I knew how she and the rest of the former refugees valued education. I tried to show that in this book. Thank you, Steffi.

None of this could have been done without the support of my university and academic affiliations, the love of my family, and the encouragement of my friends. Thanks to the Children's Literature Association for giving me a Research Grant to travel to Oswego. My deepest thanks to Western Michigan University for granting me a sabbatical during the 1995–1996 year for this project and continuing assistance with the Faculty Research and Creative Arts Stipend and release time. To my former department head, Shirley Scott, and to my present department head, Arnold Johnston, your commitment will not be forgotten. Also thanks to the staff at the Kalamazoo Public Library and Western's Waldo Library for clarifying dates, names, etc. And to my critique group who spent so much time listening to my manuscript, correcting my errors, and giving me encouragement, thank you so much Bob Weir, Lynn Pattison, Jane Vanderweyden, Jacqueline DeHaan, and Karen Bjork. Also thank you Joe Novara of my critique group, for answering many questions regarding religious practices. Thank you, Ellen Howard, for reading an early draft and saying I could write this story—and Carol Fenner for hearing an early chapter and supporting me. You are wonderful friends, critics, and writers.

And to John Allen, my editor—you believed. You also worked exceedingly hard and, after many reads, continued to encourage me by your support and commitment to the book. As I saw your numerous edits, too, I had to think of Adam. You are a regular lollipop for facts. That you are sensitive, too, and have directed me to move ever closer to a realized work will not be forgotten. I hope we can continue to work together.

Finally, to my husband and my children, my complete gratitude for encouraging me, allowing me to be distracted, putting up with my frustration, listening to tapes and learning with me,

222

and loving me. I love you, and I promise you free time. We need that time to be together and enjoy this wonderful country of ours.

As for this book, while I have depended upon true stories, newspaper articles, and books, this is a work of fiction. In particular, Chris's father is totally fictional and is patterned after nobody in real life. So, too, are all the other characters who, at times, may voice opinions stated by real people, but who are, in themselves, creations of my imagination.

Miriam Bat-Ami is the author of several picture books and novels. She is an associate professor of English at Western Michigan University and lives in Mattawan, Michigan, with her husband and their two sons.